Stand Naked in the Wind

Stand Naked in the Wind

A NOVEL

LORRAINE MAGNANI

265 W 37th Street
New York, New York
10018

ISBN -10-0-615-30338-2
ISBN -13-978-0-615-30338-3

Printed in the United States of America

For Lou…my raison d'être

Acknowledgements

I'm grateful to the nurses, doctors, patients, students, ancillary personnel and friends who have touched my life, thereby contributing to this book.

I'd like to express my appreciation to:
> ...my muse, author Phyllis Robinson,
>> who served as my reader.
> ...the multi-published Ray Robinson,
>> for his encouragement.
> ...my editor, Lawrence Dukore,
>> who slashed and burned.
> ...my final readers, Diane Magnani and
>> David Strichartz for their patience
>> and perseverance.
> ...my children, Barbara-Jean and Michael,
>> for their love and support.
> ...and finally, to my husband Lou,
>> the Dashiell Hammett of my life.

"For what is it to die
but to stand naked in the wind…"

Kahlil Gibran

Stand Naked in the Wind

Prologue

The harsh sound of the telephone pierced my sleep. I groped for it without opening my eyes. As I shifted my body, I felt a stabbing vaginal pain. The horror returned. I died last night.

My first attempt to say hello didn't materialize, so I cleared my throat and tried again.

"Hello." Oh God, another stabbing pain. I held my breath.

"Kate? Are you alright?"

"Frank?" Oh God, Frank. Oh God, God, God. Pull yourself together. Clear your head. Nothing has happened. It was all a bad dream. "Hi honey, I'm fine. I was asleep. You woke me up, that's all."

"Asleep? At noon?"

"Oh, I worked last night until midnight for Marie Louise. I guess I was really tired." I clenched my teeth.

"You sound strange. Are you sure you're okay?"

"Aside from working a thirteen-hour shift, I'm just fine." But I'm not fine. I feel sick. I hurt inside and out. I wanted to cry. I wanted to crawl into Frank's arms. Instead I said, "How did everything go in London? When are you coming home?"

"Not until tomorrow night."

"Oh?" I guess I should be grateful. It will give me time to recuperate. "Okay, honey, I'll see you then."

"Bye."

"Frank, wait don't hang up. Talk to me."

"What do you want me to say?"

"I don't know. 'I love you,' I guess."

"Come on, Kate, you know I love you." His voice was impatient, then it softened, "I'll see you tomorrow…we'll talk then."

I did know that he loved me. I wondered if he would still love me if he knew. I sank back into the pillows and pulled the eiderdown up to my nose.

I hurt with the horror of the night before. The minute I had entered the apartment, I'd put my underwear and pantyhose into a paper bag and thrown it in with the trash. I spent the next hour and a half doing a full body pre-op scrub in the shower, hoping that some of me and all of him would eventually spiral down the drain. It didn't make me feel the least bit better. Nothing would make me feel better ever again.

I couldn't believe what had happened. How could he? Of all people not him. I was vulnerable and stupid, but he betrayed me. He raped me. He was supposed to "do no harm" and he brutally raped me.

I was dead. I was cold–so cold that my teeth began to chatter. It was as if I were standing naked in the wind.

If only I had the power to make my life go backwards. Now all I can do is pull the bedcovers over my head and try to shut out the reality of one yesterday and all the tomorrows.

Chapter One

"…life goes not backwards
nor tarries with yesterday."
Kahlil Gibran

1

My flight to New York was leaving in less than two hours. I planned to meet Frank at Zavantem airport and I was behind schedule. I raced around the apartment, stuffing my immediate needs into a large Dior tote bag while trying to avoid getting in the way of the Belgian moving men. I quickly glanced around to make sure that I hadn't missed anything.

"Oh God, I almost forgot."

I ran into the bathroom to check the results of my home-pregnancy test. The darkly formed circle in the urine didn't upset me in the least. I assumed that the cleaning woman must have somehow disturbed the contents of the cup. I knew that even the slightest vibration, or movement of any kind, could result in a false positive and I desperately needed to believe that test was negative. I realized that a woman having unprotected sex with five different men had a good chance of

becoming pregnant and in order for a diaphragm to prevent
conception, it had to be put in place more than most of the
time. I refused to consider these obvious factors, so I blamed
the cleaning woman and pushed them to the back of my mind.
I tended to repress anything that was unacceptable. I was good
at it. It was my primary defense mechanism.

I thought aloud, "I'm forty-five. I can't be pregnant. I just
can't." I grabbed the cup, threw its contents into the toilet and
tossed the cup into the trash basket.

Satisfied that I had done all that I had to do, I looked into
the bathroom mirror and hastily ran some pale gloss over my
lips. The face that looked back could have easily passed for
thirty-five.

2

The Sabena jet surged forth, pushing me back against the
seat. I looked out of the window. Nothing but gray mist. I was
going home to my world, my kids, my mother, my friends.
I'd be able to work in a familiar environment. I thought of the
joy of hearing English spoken, all day, every day. Then why do
I have this free-floating anxiety? Is it too late for me to start
again?

These past months had been the worst of my entire life.
I'd tried hard to "repress" but I couldn't hold on much longer.
I had sworn that I wouldn't behave like a victim, but that's
what I was—a victim. It was hard enough to pretend that the
rape had never occurred, but now the possibility of a
pregnancy. Oh God, what will I do? Frank and I hadn't spent
much time in bed since it happened and when we did it was
tense—stiff, with forced responses. So I avoided my husband
with excuses—too tired, too busy, too anything. Frank realized
that something was wrong. He didn't say anything but he grew
more distant sexually and flew to London more frequently.
London—I wondered what the attraction might be? I looked at

my watch. I had about six hours before we landed at JFK and I had to make some life-changing decisions.

I remembered when I first moved to Brussels. It was 1973. Like many American travelers, my suitcase was packed with all of the American things I thought I couldn't do without, and that Europeans couldn't possibly provide. I guess I stayed too long. Now my suitcase was filled with all of the European things that I was really sure I couldn't live without. But it wasn't only the contents of my suitcase that had changed. I had, too.

In five short years, I'd gone from being the closest thing to a nun that a married woman could possibly be, to a sexually liberated, over-achiever. I'd not only cheated on my husband, I had cheated on my lover and even on myself. And I'd probably go to my grave believing that I was an accessory to murder.

Had anyone told me that my life would have evolved the way it had, I would not have believed them. I had moved from Kathleen Mary Mullin, the obedient perfect child, to Kathleen deMeo, the obedient faithful wife, to Kate deMeo, whom I was still trying to explain—at least to myself.

What caused the change? Maybe I'd rebelled against my typical American Irish-Catholic upbringing. A lifetime of "Thou Shall Not" rules. The rules, which I thought were gender-biased, were clear-cut and demanded perfection. Breaking a big rule could send you straight to hell. Breaking a small rule called for doing time in purgatory. I didn't think that I had been really all that concerned with heaven and hell, but I'd been concerned (if not consumed) with being perfect. The smallest mistake seemed intolerable. I needed to live in a place where there were no shadows—only sunlight in every corner.

As children, every Saturday, we had the chance to cleanse away our sins and purify our souls and become perfect once again. It was called Confession. Our parents sent us to Catholic School to give us a moral base, never realizing how terrifying some aspects of religion can be to children. Mortal sins would lead to eternal damnation–burning in hell's fire forever. The sad part was that the worst mortal sin my best friend Sheila McCarthy and I had ever committed was in telling our parents that we were going to the Church Confraternity dance, when in truth we went to the Knights of Columbus dance. Both were on the same street, had the same music, but the appeal was that the K of C drew an older group of teens and they weren't limited just to our parish.

The K of C was where I met Frank. The moment Frankie deMeo walked through that door I knew what I wanted. Although I was only thirteen, I knew he was the only boy for me. He called me "kid" the entire night. He probably didn't remember my name, but it was a beginning. I had plenty of time. It took four years, but when I turned seventeen, he was mine.

Frank was always an upwardly mobile dynamo, entering the unknown, a new job, a new way of life and in his world the stakes were a lot higher than they were in mine. He never shared his innermost feelings with me, or with anyone else for that matter. Well–that is except for politics and religion–his two most favorite topics for discussion. He never seemed to be afraid. He'd just walk right in and take over. He was always "in charge"–at work–at home–socially. He was in fact a social animal. He loved having people around, dinner parties, cocktail parties. He'd strike up conversations with people in restaurants and then invite them to our apartment for after dinner drinks. I was never all that comfortable, but I managed to play the part. I could be charming and functional, but I was never really relaxed.

I looked out the plane window. Still nothing but gray mist. Living in Europe had been good for us. It probably saved our marriage—up until now anyway. On balance, it had been a wonderful, rewarding five years—almost no regrets. I worried over the possibility that Frank and I would revert to the life we left back in the States. Separate interests, disconnected ways. Kathleen Mary Mullin could have easily gone back. Kathleen deMeo would sincerely try, but Kate deMeo would never go back.

The pregnancy test pushed its way back into my mind. I saw the perfectly formed circle. But now, I had a far more serious worry. I didn't know who the father was.

Chapter Two

"...children of space restless in rest,
you shall not be trapped or tamed."
Kahlil Gibran

1

The sixties were a turbulent time: the Viet Nam War, the Civil Rights Movement, the Sexual Revolution, and Mick Jagger and the Rolling Stones. Everyone was being tossed about by rapid change. I had my share of turbulence too. I was about to be twenty-nine. I had a successful, good-looking, fun-to-be-with husband, two terrific, happy kids, a supportive mother, all of whom loved me—all this and a large comfortable home in Oyster Bay. Good God, I thought, I'm living the American Dream. And yet, I couldn't shake the sense of incompleteness—of an ever-increasing restlessness. It wasn't an unusual syndrome for a woman who was losing her youthful twenties—pushing thirty. I felt like an expensive car idling, consuming gas and not going anywhere. I needed to accomplish something. I wasn't really living the American Dream—I was existing within it. Frank and I were the grown-up versions of Ken and Barbie living in our plastic world.

In the sixties, women over thirty had traditional roles, which many clung to and followed like Dorothy's "yellow brick road." Women under thirty were caught up in the sexual revolution. They were out there making up their own rules, living life as they saw it. At twenty-nine, I felt neither young enough nor old enough for the climate of the times. The question was, "Which side of thirty are you on?" Most women didn't know where they belonged. Physiological and chronological age had to be entered into the equation. Women eventually aligned themselves with one side or the other. I looked for a pragmatic, unifying solution.

It came, and it was a silent protest. No marches, vigils or sit-ins. Women of all ages were returning to school. While returning was not in itself unique, it was the ages, and the number of women who were doing so. Unlike some of their younger predecessors, they weren't there to "turn on" or "drop out," but they did "tune in." Women were beginning to realize that their potential could be developed through education. They were embarking on new careers, new lives. I wanted some of that newness too. I needed to be counted. I applied and was accepted into The University of New York's Baccalaureate Program in Nursing.

I worried the entire day about talking to Frank. I couldn't even begin to think about telling him. Not that he'd ever denied me anything. It was just that he had some rather Old World ideas concerning women. But he was in tune and even ahead of the times in many other respects. I counted strongly on that. I had to.

I needed to discuss my plans with my friend Fiona Jones. She was always objective and helped to clarify my thinking. She was extraordinarily tall and lean, with a tanned face and arms. She was my fifty-eight year old mentor and I loved her. Fiona enjoyed playing Devil's Advocate while I prepared and rehearsed answers for Frank and eventually for my mother, Mary Ellen. I thought if I could convince Frank, Mary Ellen just might roll over. Having Fiona on my side gave me the courage of my convictions and automatic absolution.

Finally at two in the morning, Frank and I were showering together after returning from a neighborhood dinner party. I was warm inside from drinking wine, and the tepid water running on my body made me feel good. I brushed suggestively against him. He began soaping my body. I looked at his penis. It was hard and erect. I smiled self-consciously. It was always hard and erect. I grabbed the soap from Frank and my face flushed with embarrassment even before I started lathering him.

We began rubbing our soapy bodies together and kissing with the water streaming on our closed eyelids. Holding me tightly, Frank pushed the shower door open with his shoulder and we went sprawling on to the white-carpeted bathroom floor. In an instant he was inside me.

"Frank. Oh Frank," I whispered.

" Mmm."

Our sliding bodies made slapping and sucking noises as white foamy lather gently flew about us, coming to a momentary halt before disappearing into the carpet. I wanted to tell him how good it was–how much I loved how he made me feel, but my throat tightened. Then all my thoughts dissolved into nothingness as the complete possession of orgasm began taking over both mind and body. We came to a noisy, convulsing climax.

Frank rolled over on his back. God, I felt good. He was good. I had no one to compare him with, but I couldn't imagine sex with anyone else being better. I wished that I could tell him how I felt.

"Anyone ever tell you that you're a good lay, Kathleen?" he teased while playfully biting my arm.

"If I am, it's because I've had the best teacher."

I felt the discomfort of our spoken words and the soap beginning to draw on my skin. I got up and went back under the cleansing water of the still-running shower. We toweled off. Frank walked naked towards the bed and threw himself on it. I followed with my robe pulled tightly around me, shedding it at the last moment before slipping between the sheets. I stretched full length and casually mentioned that I would like to go to school and finish my education. He looked surprised. He couldn't understand why I needed anything more than I had. I reminded him that I had promised my grandmother, Margaret Mary Mullin, to one day finish my education. It was only then that she given us her blessing to marry. I carefully worded my answers, masking some of my feelings. In reality, I was asking his permission, seeking his approval.

"How will you manage the house, the kids...?"

I jumped on his words and assured him that I could and would. Ten-year-old Gina and nine-year-old Mark would be in school full-time, plus after-school programs.

"I can arrange my classes so that I will be home before them and still remain available as the 'Little League Mom,' and the 'Brownie Mom.'" And anything else you can throw my way, I thought.

The more I talked, the more I felt as if I could handle anything. Then all at once he seemed pleased with the idea of my going to school. Although he didn't ask, I reasoned that I could do my school assignments after the children were in bed. "Frank, just one more thing...my major will be in Nursing."

He shook his head. He was not at all happy with this bit of news. This wasn't how he pictured his wife. I didn't dare breathe, much less say a word. There was a long, brittle silence before he spoke again.

"Kathleen, as long as you've decided to go through all of the trouble of going back to school, why don't you become a doctor? You're certainly bright enough. You're the one with the IQ."

His question disturbed me. I told him that I didn't want to be a doctor. I wanted to be a nurse. I didn't realize it then, but so many people would put that same question to me over and over again throughout the years. Nursing and medicine are totally separate disciplines. One is not an extension of the other. Each has a vital role in caring for patients.

"Anyhow," his voice softened, "I'm really pleased that you will be doing something that will make you happy, honey." Turning out the light he continued, "You can go to school as long as you like, be whatever you want to be, just as long as you don't get the idea into your head that you're ever going to work."

Work. Work? Why would I want to become a nurse and not work? Jesus, Mary and Joseph, he means that I can play, but I can't work. Frank had just categorized my going to school with taking an adult education class at the high school or tennis lessons at the Country Club. Oh God. He was absolutely serious, and his tone of voice signaled the end of the discussion.

Frank was the slayer of dragons, keeping me safe and protected in his castle. I tried to think of a working wife among our friends and acquaintances. There were none. No sense in talking to him now, I'd lose. I'd just shelve that problem until a later date. I drifted off to sleep feeling that I had made a very small opening in the door that would lead to my future.

Chapter Three

"...tell us all that has been shown you
of that which is between birth and death."
                        Kahlil Gibran

1

The University of New York's campus was a short drive
from Oyster Bay. It wasn't the most beautiful campus I'd
ever seen, but the nursing program was all that I had hoped it
would be. Nurses were no longer being trained, they were
being educated and their clinical experiences took place in
many different health-care agencies, rather than in just one
hospital. I was so excited, I could hardly wait for my freshman
semester to begin.

    I learned a lot more on campus than nursing and liberal
arts. This was where Kate began to emerge. There were sit-
ins and rallies. I held my place in the peace vigils–candles and
all. I witnessed Black Panther parades. I listened to the
divergent political views of the Republican Vice President
Spiro Agnew, and the black activist, Stokley Carmichael. I
listened to the returning Nam vets in my core curriculum

classes. I concluded that women's rights seemed a logical culmination of the anti-war and civil rights movements. I was caught up in changing times–in a permissive free society. I began to move from my strict Catholic background–from obeying authority to questioning authority. And although somewhat pretentious, many students carried a copy of Gibran's "The Prophet" and quoted him to each other. I was transforming. I wanted to help to improve the human condition, and I was becoming a vehement dove. The only jewelry I wore now was the medallion around my neck openly declaring "War is not healthy for children and other living things." I was "Another Mother for Peace."

One day all hell broke loose on the campus. A huge banner had been draped from the windows of the Administration Building. Its large red painted letters read "Visit Sunny Cambodia." Rumor had it that the Students for a Democratic Society had taken over. Administrators and faculty were behind locked doors. There were no classes. As students arrived on campus, they gathered on the quadrangle. Some were singing, "Give Peace a Chance." They looked like a flock of sheep without a herding dog. Hardhats jeered at them and the police made threatening gestures with billy clubs. I finally got off my ambivalent ass and joined the students, not in violence but in peaceful protest.

2

During my fourth semester I was one of ten students assigned to obstetrics-gynecology for the first time. The rotation took place in a large medical center that had about 600 beds and was chronically understaffed. The situation made some of the nurses quite cranky and therefore they were never as nice to the students as they should or could have been. I had just completed my assigned patients' a.m. care when I heard moans and cries coming from Room 2024.

There was no one else in the hall, so I went in. The young girl in the bed couldn't have been more than fifteen years old. Her eyes were swollen with tears and she looked terrified. I picked up the sheet and noted blood oozing between her legs from her perineum. "Hang on," I said in a calm voice, "I'll be right back."

I tracked down the nurse who was in charge of the rooms on the even-numbered side of the hall. Unfortunately, this was the same nurse who intimidated students by making them kneel on the floor before her in order to check the length of their uniforms. If the hem didn't reach the floor, she deemed it inappropriate. I had refused to kneel.

I briefly told her of my observations in Room 2024. "Oh her," she shrugged, "she's had a salting, that's all. Let her suffer the consequences. You students will soon learn that a nurse's job is to save lives, not take them."

"Yes, but, but, she..."

"I haven't the time to discuss this with you, young lady." She started down the hall on her spindly legs. "If you're so concerned," she called over her shoulder, "take care of her yourself."

She left me standing there, rapidly absorbing every word, every intonation. Salting was hospital slang for Saline Infusion, in which some of the amniotic fluid is replaced with a twenty-percent solution of sodium chloride. It was a procedure used to interrupt a pregnancy.

I could still hear the cries echoing through the hall. I ran back to the nurses' station and pulled the chart for 2024. The summary sheet told me her name was Rosemary Moran and she was only fourteen years old. I quickly flipped to the medical history and found that she had been the victim of multiple rape, a high school gang-bang. My insecure instructor, Mrs. White, was nowhere in sight. I had the feeling that she hid from students in general and me in particular, so I latched on to an intern heading for his coffee break. I queried him on the procedure for post-salinization.

I ran into Rosemary's room with something that resembled a room-service cardboard ice bucket, clean linen, sterile gloves and fierce determination. She was wet with perspiration. I slid a sheet beneath her and draped another over her. Her wristband validated that she was indeed Rosemary Moran. I turned her pillow and wiped her brow with a cool wet washcloth. Not much, but it was all that I could do.

"Please Nurse, please don't leave me alone," she sobbed, "I'm so scared. I don't want to die."

"You're going to be just fine."

I stayed with Rosemary, listening to her periodic screams, trying to reassure her and giving her my hands to hold. Before I knew what was happening, her body went rigid and something squeezed out of her vagina. I picked it up, placed it into the cardboard bucket and put the cover on it. She was quiet now. She looked exhausted, less frightened. Her vital signs and bleeding were within textbook normal limits. I picked up the bucket, sent the returning intern to her and escaped into the utility room. It was empty. I closed the door and leaned against it. Then I removed the lid slowly and looked into the bucket. A tiny fetus lay there, no longer than my thumb. It had an unreal transparent look about it, but I was convinced that I could clearly see the face, arms and legs with fingers and toes.

Oh my God, what have I done?

I walked over to the sink where the large bottle of preservative stood. I had to cover the fetus with the liquid before sending it down to the lab. My hands shook as I started to pour. I heard my own voice sounding hollow and distant, "I baptize thee, in the name of the Father, the Son, and the Holy Ghost." I was embarrassed and angry to think that some hidden part of me believed that a vengeful deity would lock the gates of heaven on an innocent. I put the lid on the bucket and labeled it for the lab.

During lunch in the cafeteria, I spotted the Catholic Chaplain at a nearby table. I grabbed my tray, hurried over and asked if I might join him. We chatted about the hospital and our work. I told him that I thought my business had more volume than his. He countered by saying that his was picking up. "You know hospitals, like foxholes, don't have a lot of atheists."

I had no answer to that so I posed my burning question. "Just as a matter of curiosity, Father, since there have been so many changes in the church recently, does one still baptize by saying 'I baptize thee in the name of the Father, the Son and the Holy Ghost?'"

"Yes, that's basically correct, but we've been using Holy Spirit and not Holy Ghost for quite a while now."

"Oops?"

"But don't worry, the baptism is valid." He smiled, adding, "The words just show your age and that you've been away from the Church for a long time."

After lunch, all the nurses and nursing students were assembled in the conference room. Hospital administration announced that we would be given twenty-four hours to review our feelings about abortion and no one who had moral convictions to the contrary would be obliged to work in that area. Then they announced that anyone who had questions, needed clarification, was to call the Assistant Director of Nursing.

As soon as the hospital personnel left the room, the students put eleven chairs in a circle for the usual post-conference discussion. We began by sharing our patient experiences with each other. Mrs. White, our rather tense instructor, served as the facilitator and I was the last student to be called on. My "salting" experience prompted Mrs. White to ask what we thought of the administrative announcement. I looked around the circle at my fellow students. This particular group was made up of the young and inarticulate. They were either staring straight ahead or at their shoes. The room was perfectly still. The silence bothered me so I said, "I don't need twenty-four hours to think it over. I'll work there. An abortion is not my decision in the first place so it holds no moral brief for me as a nursing student. My primary concern is the patient. Isn't that what we're taught?"

Mrs. White nodded, "Patient-centered care, yes."

I couldn't let it alone. "Isn't it true that abortion is primarily a legal issue?"

Mrs. White nodded again but didn't appear to be committed to her nod. She looked uncomfortable as she turned her gaze to the other students. It was obvious that they were not about to share their views—if indeed they had any.

As we filed out of the open door, the spindly-legged nurse I'd met earlier that morning tossed me a contemptuous look. "You're disgusting," she said in a stage whisper.

It was easy to shrug off her disdain. I had learned that abortions continued, whether legally or illegally, so they might as well be kept in a hospital where there was a chance of saving one life instead of losing two. There was also a good chance that the legalization might put an end to quacks who dealt in the butchery of women, and to the self-administering coat hanger and knitting needle brigade.

But most of all, I had learned that Frank had indeed kept me safe and protected in his castle. Living in the real world wasn't anything like reading about it in the New York Times.

3

After four years of hard but fulfilling work, I earned a Bachelor of Science in Nursing and easily passed the Registered Professional Nurse licensing examination. The top ten percent of my class was heavily seeded with women over thirty, women from all walks-of-life. We were an extremely motivated group primarily because we chose to be there. Many of us graduated cum laude or higher. The commencement exercises were pure pageantry. I wanted so much for Frank to share my happy experience. Unhappily, he was in Brazil on business, but my mother Mary Ellen and my teenage children, Gina and Mark, were there. As I stepped onto the stage, I saw my kids jumping up and down, shouting "Mom, Mom, that's my Mom." Their enthusiasm meant a great deal to me. Mary Ellen beamed, sitting straight-backed, head held high as she watched me receive my baccalaureate. She was proud of me.

4

Before graduation, I got a full-time job as a staff nurse in a progressive 350-bed hospital. It was the result of a four-year campaign to convince Frank that I was surely in the noblest of professions and it would have been such a waste of talent for me not to work. I was the same age as Florence Nightingale had been when she began working. Of course, it helped that some of the women in our social group had begun to enroll in classes and were already talking about working.

I was convinced that the basic nursing degree should be at a baccalaureate level, but I wanted more. I enrolled in St. Joseph's University for the Master of Science Program in Nursing.

I discovered that I was articulate and grasped concepts quickly. At school and at work people listened to my ideas and my opinions. I began to feel a sense of accomplishment.   As much as I had complained about being Frank's "satellite," I had always been involved in something of my own. I had been involved in local school board politics, the PTA and various fund raising events. I guess some people had listened to my opinions; but I was a volunteer, and volunteers were never taken too seriously.

Now I had a job that was socially redeeming and they paid me for doing it. As soon as I finished my Master's, I began my doctoral studies. I was thirty-six years old and I felt the power of independence and worth. I remembered that Marilyn Monroe was dead at thirty-six and I was lucky enough to have my whole life ahead of me.

But there was a negative side. Now that I had begun to find my independence, I was less concerned with Frank's life. It no longer mattered to me if he came home at seven p.m. or six a.m. without calling. It wasn't that I didn't care. I was just too tired to stay up and worry. I could remember the time when it was a shattering experience for me. Even when the wives of men who worked for Frank would call me up at two in the morning concerned about their husbands, I'd cheerfully assure them that everything was okay. "They're either too absorbed to answer the phone or they've gone out for a drink and lost all track of time." Unconvinced by my own rhetoric, I'd naively call hospital after hospital hoping that he wasn't a Long Island Expressway accident victim, his 240Z draped grotesquely across the divider.

Frank was spending more time in the city at his job and with his friends. My time was splintered between the hospital, school and two teenagers. Frank and I were amicably drifting apart and neither of us realized it. The times we did spend together were mostly at weekend parties or in bed. It was more like dating than being married. Our mutually satisfying arrangement lasted until one humid Friday in August 1972.

I had just finished an exhausting summer semester in my doctoral program and it was my first day off in six weeks. The kitchen was being wallpapered. The phone rang. Frank's voice was so enthusiastic and happy that I suppressed the urge to say "oh shit" when he told me that his European transfer had come through earlier than expected. Instead I responded like the good Boy Scout that I was, obedient, loyal, brave... "Sounds terrific, Frank. Yes, I know how anxious you are to start. Umm...just how early is earlier?" I asked, trying to keep my voice light.

"October first," he answered.

"October first," I dumbly repeated, "that's less than two months away." I couldn't believe it. Originally his transfer had been set for June of next year. Now this. Frank was explaining to me how the wheels of business functioned. As far as I was concerned, October first was the spoke that made my wheel go backwards.

As I replaced the receiver, I wanted to scream and rip off every last shred of the new wallpaper. I'd never have the opportunity to enjoy it. It was perfect, exactly what I wanted. I could live here for the next hundred years without changing a thing. I meant it. Why not? I had a good job and I was working on my dissertation. For the first time in my life, I felt as if I were a complete person and not just an inconstant moon revolving around Frank's earth. I wondered if he knew how I felt?

I glanced around at the newly decorated kitchen. I focused on the pale yellow flowers in the wallpaper. It gave the room a warm and inviting presence. Frank thought the pattern too busy. I bought it anyway. "Oh shit," I said aloud, "What the hell am I going to do?" Here I was within nine months of earning my Ph.D. and my pink balloon was about to burst. I'd been killing myself for a degree I'd never get. I was about to lose my job, degree, home, family, friends, and most of all, my kids—and all at the same time.

I couldn't very well complain to Frank. It wasn't his fault. We had discussed his European transfer and I had agreed to it. Of course I agreed. It sounded like a great adventure. As long as I could work, I didn't care where. I suppose it never did seem real to me. Now I was faced with reality. I had to make a decision.

I needed someone to talk to. I couldn't call Fiona. She was dying from pancreatic cancer. A silent killer. Pain was the first symptom, making an early diagnosis all but impossible. Few people outside of her family knew her situation because she tried to continue her life as close to normal as possible. I'd seen hospitalized patients dying of pancreatic cancer, and they needed to be heavily dosed with narcotic analgesics. I shuddered as I thought about Fiona's suffering—the severe pain and the inevitable ending. Fiona believed that the chemotherapy would buy her time, and in that time a cure might be found. She was one of the strongest women I'd ever known. I was so sure that if anyone could beat death, she would. I was so sure. Please God…

My problems as compared to Fiona's were ridiculously infinitesimal. I felt guilty as I pushed her to the back of my mind. I had to think, decide on a plan of action and discuss it with Frank. Our discussions were rarely favorable to me. I kept telling myself that as a Gemini, I had great communicative powers, but in twenty-two years I rarely came out on top in a discussion or won an argument. Was I intimidated because he was a successful advertising Vice President, a Leo, smarter—and older?

I married Frank at the tender age of seventeen, moving directly from my parents' home to his home. The year was 1950, a long-ago age of innocence. I was still innocent—still the obedient child. Frank was the adult in the family and he approached everything from an adult point of view. He lived in the real world. But now, so did I.

I reviewed my options. Okay, I had passed all of the courses and the candidacy exam. I was ABD (All But Dissertation). I knew that it wasn't humanly possible for anyone to write a dissertation and pass the orals in less than two months. Many students never wrote a dissertation and were content to be ABD for the rest of their lives. They believed that they'd done the most arduous part of the doctorate anyway. Could that possibly work for me?

Never!

I had to tell Frank that I couldn't go with him. Getting my

doctorate was now the single most important thing in my life and I wasn't about to back down. I watched the little cuckoo clock bird, that Gina named Sigmund, as he announced four o'clock. The kids would be home soon.

Gina (born Regina Mary) was in pre-veterinary medicine at a nearby university, unlike Mark, who elected to do his studies in California. They were both home on summer holiday and both had part-time jobs. They were as different as silk and wool.

Gina worked in the University's Vivarium, responsible for the care and feeding of its inhabitants, among whom were wooly monkeys, alligators and vultures. Her favorite was a ninety-five-pound capybara she called Harold. These South American rodents were herbivores and grew to be between seventy-five and one hundred forty pounds. Gina would exercise Harold by walking him on a leash. He wasn't exactly obedience trained. She considered it a good day if Harold didn't playfully knock her over while being put back in his cage.

Mark liked working outdoors, so he started his own business trimming the dead limbs of stately oak trees. Using his mountain climbing techniques, he'd pull himself and his chainsaw upward. Once near the top, he could swing from limb to limb, from tree to tree, sixty feet above the ground. He believed that all trees were different, even those of the same species. He liked tulip trees the least of all. It was soft wood, all trunk and no limbs. He would have to wrap his arms and legs around the tree and shinny up. His friend was his chainsaw, but it could also be his enemy. If the tip were to hit a branch, the saw would jump right back at him. He was careful. He never used spikes. The tree owners loved Mark and paid him well.

I heard his car drive up. It had a different sound than Gina's. He came through the squeaky door from the garage entry, said "Hi Mom," went into the living room and collapsed on the couch.

Half an hour later, Gina came through that same squeaky door and went directly into the kitchen.

"Hi Mom. I love the wallpaper. How was your day off?"

"Terrific. How about you, have a good day? Mark is home. He's sacked out on the couch. I gather trimming trees is exhausting." I really hadn't given that much thought as to what his job was really like. My own life had gotten so complicated, pieces of it had slipped through the cracks.

"Are you going out tonight?" I asked. Without waiting for an answer, I turned on the oven, containing a waiting casserole.

Gina sat at the table, smiling at me.

"Yes and no." She laughed melodically. "I had a good day. I'm not going out tonight, but Alex may come over later."

She was so young, so pretty, so bright. She had the Irish fair skin and eyes. Her long straight dark hair was caught up in a knot on the top of her head against the summer's heat and held in place with a pencil. She went on talking about her job, and her professor friend, Alex Rothman. I asked some questions about the Vivarium and teased her about Alex.

"Mom, I'd like to talk to you before Dad gets home," she said, a little too seriously.

"How about right now? I'll make a pot of tea and we can go into the den. It's cooler in there."

She disappeared into the den with the tea tray.

"We're having Formosa Oolong," I announced as I pushed the door open, joining her. "Okay," I said as I poured, "What did you want to talk about?" I held my breath.

"I'd like to move in with Alex."

Well, this is 1972, I thought. She is of legal age. Why does she look twelve years old to me? I'd always enjoyed intellectualizing with fellow students and friends about the practical application of young people living together. Now it was no longer an academic exercise. It was my own daughter.

I said, "He seems like a nice boy." I was trying to gain thinking time.

"Mom…he's twenty-eight, hardly a boy…but you're right. He is nice."

"Gina, you must realize that I love you and I want you to be happy. Uhm, you see, you've only known Alex a short time and I feel that all this is a little precipitous…"

Her face clouded over and she drew her teeth together. I quickly said, "Come on, Gina, you're not giving me a chance. You can't hit me like that and expect an immediate yes or no. Jesus, I'm assuming that you took time to think it over…discussed it with Alex. Please allow me the same courtesy. It's because I do love you and care so much that…"

There I go again, sounding like a mother. Well, I was a mother–her mother. But what could I possibly tell her? I'd been married to the same guy for twenty-two years. I had no experiences to draw on. I hadn't had an extra-marital relationship, much less a pre-marital one. She was an adult. She didn't need my permission. She had to make her own decisions and live her own life.

I put my hand on hers. "Honey, if you have thought this over and I assume you have–if you feel that it's right for you, then it's okay with me."

"Oh, Mom," she said, hugging me, "I know it's right."

"I just want you to be happy, Gina," I whispered, kissing the top of her head.

"I am, Mom, I am," she said reassuring me.

I picked up the tea tray and moved towards the kitchen. "Don't tell your father yet. Give me a little time to talk to him."

She was Daddy's little girl. He loved and protected her, as a good father should. I just couldn't be sure how Francis Charles deMeo would feel about Alexander Rothman, Jr. taking his daughter's hand in marriage, much less their living together. As I put the tray on the kitchen counter, I realized what had been bothering me. It had nothing to do with Catholicism, conscience or morals. She had not once mentioned the word love.

Had I known six years ago what I knew now, I would have handled it differently. If Gina and I were to have had that conversation today, I would have told her that she had time. She should have more than one relationship, and not settle so fast for one guy. I'd have warned her not to put herself in a position where one day she'd wonder what it would be like with someone else—where she'd ask herself, "Is it all the same or is it different with every partner? Will I go to my grave only knowing one man?" Women who marry young and have only one relationship set themselves up for infidelity later on.

By the time Frank came home, I was so preoccupied with Gina's announcement that I'd all but forgotten my own problem. I even forgot to let him know that he was late again. He talked all through dinner about the challenge of his new assignment. Mark was equally enthusiastic. He was truly his father's son. There was an undeniable bond of maleness between them. Mark had the same dark curly hair as Frank, only much longer. He had it pulled back into a ponytail and secured with a navy blue grosgrain ribbon. He had the same Italian good looks and the same blue eyes. Mark had the easygoing nature of a second child.

Mark excused himself, mumbling something about a date. He whispered into Gina's ear. They both laughed. Before he left the table, he cleared off his and Frank's dishes and kissed me good night. Gina cleared off the rest of the table and I loaded the dishwasher. Frank went into the den to watch television. I turned off the kitchen lights and headed straight upstairs for the shower.

It's amazing how good water feels on your body. Even infants recognize that. It's the pleasant sensation of a hot tub bath in the cold of winter or a tepid shower in the heat of summer. It's more than revitalizing, it can sometimes be a complete renewal. I toweled off, climbed into bed, and waited for Frank.

Most people I knew did their serious talking over the

dinner table, over coffee, some at cocktail hour. Frank and I had always done our serious talking in bed. We spent more time in bed than any other couple I knew. Of course, everyone exaggerated some, but even taking that into account, I always supposed that Frank was more sexually active than others because of his Italian heritage. Mary Ellen never liked Italians. She had once told me confidentially that Italian men wanted to do "it" all the time. Sometimes I think one of the reasons I married Frank was because I thought I'd enjoy doing "it" all the time. Of course I never revealed those thoughts, or she would have sent me for an exorcism by no one less than his holiness the Pope. I wondered if it ever occurred to her that he was Italian, too.

One of the deals I made with Frank when I returned to school was that it would in no way intrude into our lifestyle. It was fine with him if I elected to change my life, but he had no intention of changing his. He still expected a well-run house and a hostess who looked liked Miss America, memorized the Sunday Times and acted like a whore in bed. That was a tall order even without working and going to school. I didn't think it fair to impose any more responsibility on Gina than she'd have if she lived on campus, so here I was, literally and figuratively running my ass off. And I wouldn't give in. I'd be damned if I was going to be the one to suggest that we leave a party early because I had to be at the hospital the next morning before seven. Thank God that I'd inherited my mother's energy.

"Sleeping, Hon?" Frank's voice broke through.

"Huh, oh no, I must have nodded off for a minute." I watched Frank getting undressed. He really was beautiful. He had a great body. It was hard and tight. I guess regular exercise pays off. Push-ups, tennis–whatever.

"Frank," I said louder than I intended. He looked startled. Jesus, I had certainly gotten his attention. Okay, now say something, Kate. You aced that course. You're practically an expert in verbal, non-verbal and therapeutic communication. Say what's on your mind. You have the floor.

"Frank, I've been doing a lot of thinking today and I...well, you know that I do love you and..."

He came over and sat on the bed looking right at me. No fair, no fair. Oh God, at best I'm going to melt. At worst I'm going to be intimidated. Last chance, I thought.

"Kathleen? What's wrong?" He looked so concerned as he took my hand. "What's bothering you?"

"Well...when I said that I wanted to go with you to Europe, I really meant it. Believe me, I'm not trying to renege, but your transfer has come through ahead of schedule. What I'm really trying to say is that I'm staying here until I finish school. If I don't, I lose all that I've worked for. It's important to me. It's my single gratifying accomplishment. Try to understand. We can visit back and forth. I'll visit you during Easter break..."

I went on talking, not knowing whether or not I was doing the right thing. Was I throwing away over twenty years with someone I loved just to do something trendy? A whim? I remembered when my girlfriend Jenny and I burned our bras at a feminist rally. Then we'd gone to Janet's barbecue wearing bell-bottomed hip-huggers, leather headbands, with our full breasts and nipples straining against skimpy white T-shirts. All of our husbands hooted and cheered. Frank commented, "This women's lib stuff is great...girls, hurt us some more." He knew I hated it when he used "girls" to describe us, but the men all nodded in agreement and one of them said, "I'll drink to that," and they all did.

Libby, who was twenty pounds overweight, told us to go home and change because we looked like those disgusting hippies. Janet was disappointed and said that she would have gone with us had we told her about it. She didn't mind burning her bra; she rarely wore one anyway. Moira hadn't said anything at all. But then Moira still wore full slips.

No, God damn it, this was no whim. It is not a protest of any kind. For the first time in my life I was sticking my neck out for something that was important to me, something I wanted. I wanted that Ph.D.

Frank smiled. "Funny, five years ago you would have asked, not told me. You've changed, but I do understand how you feel. We'll work something out. It won't be too bad. Maybe I'll start by calling you Kate. Everyone calls you Kate now, even our kids." He put his arms around me and said, "I'll visit you too and the time will fly. Besides, it will give me a jump on organizing the job before you get there." He smiled and added, "you can have the 240Z. That should make you feel less lonely, and I know how you love that car."

I couldn't believe it was all that simple. I couldn't believe he was taking it like this. I really thought that he'd insist on my leaving with him. Was he really being considerate of my needs or did this work out better for business? I'd rather believe that I wasn't the only one who'd changed. I put my arms around his neck and pulled him down on me.

"Want to fuck, deMeo?" I asked, sticking my tongue in his ear. "That's something I wouldn't have said five years ago either."

"Why not, you smooth talker, you."

5

August was drawing to a close, and I decided to prepare a barbecue for the family that evening. I had some lamb and beef marinating in the fridge. On my way home from the hospital I stopped for corn at the farm stand on Route 25A. It was an old Indian Trail. I liked the idea that I was taking the same path as the Native Americans did to get corn for my family. It was never very good at the end of the season. Too yellow and chewy, but Frank and Mark liked it that way. I was just trying to hold on to what was left of the summer. I didn't want to think about the fall.

I got home about a quarter of five, put the bag of corn on the kitchen counter, and went into the laundry room. I pulled off my uniform after carefully removing my gold nursing pin and tossed the uniform into the hamper. I pulled on a pair of faded jeans and a T-shirt, went onto the back patio and started wire brushing the grill. I heard a car pull up on the gravel drive and then Gina's voice greeting the dogs.

"I'm on the patio, honey," I called.

"Hi, Mom. What's happening?"

"I thought we'd cook out tonight–take advantage of what's left of the summer." We put a bright red-checkered tablecloth on the redwood table, and set out the citronella lamps.

"Mark can start the fire and fill the torches when he wakes up. There's no hurry."

"Someone call me?" Mark stretched and yawned loudly as he passed through the patio doors.

"Well, hi there, Tarzan. Tired from all that swinging?" Gina asked.

"Yeah, but at least I don't have to wrestle a ninety pound rat."

"Harold is not a rat. He's a Capybara."

Gina and I went into the kitchen and worked together threading the meat and vegetables onto skewers.

"By the way, have you spoken to Dad about my moving in with Alex?"

"No. No, I haven't. I will though. One shock at a time," I smiled.

"Don't."

"Don't what?"

"Don't tell him."

"I can't do that, Gina. He'll have to know. He's your father. He has a right…"

"You don't understand, Mom. I'm not moving in with Alex. I've changed my mind."

I put down the skewer and wiped my hands on a paper towel. "You're right. I don't understand. What's happened?"

"I'm staying here with you. I don't want you to live alone."

"So that's it. Well, I appreciate your concern but it's not necessary. I'm thirty-nine years old and quite capable, and I won't have you changing your plans because of me. That wouldn't be fair to either of us. Besides, I'm rather looking forward to living alone. I've never before had the opportunity."

"Please, Mom, I've already made up my mind. This is what I want to do."

I couldn't be sure of her reason, and I hoped it wasn't really me. "Maybe this isn't such a good idea after all, my staying on here. I seem to be screwing up your father's life, now yours, maybe even my own."

"You're not screwing up Dad's life, and you're certainly not screwing up mine. If it's your own life your concerned about, that's another story." She hesitated, and then continued, "I do know that if you don't stay and do what you want to do, you'll always regret it and deep down inside you'll blame Dad, maybe even me, for keeping you from getting something that you wanted. You've never had a real want in your entire life...something just for you. Remember, Mom, you only regret the things you haven't done."

I looked at my daughter. She was right. All regrets are reserved for the missed events of life. "What could have been" will sooner or later embitter reality.

6

On September fifth, Mark loaded his Volkswagen Camper and headed for California. On October first, Frank flew to Brussels. Five days later, Fiona died. Gina and I went to her funeral. When Fiona was buried so was a part of my life, and the void that I felt that fall of 1972 would never again be entirely filled.

Chapter Four

"...long were the
nights of aloneness..."
    Kahlil Gibran

1

The house in Oyster Bay was two blocks from Shore Road. It was said to be an old rum-runners path, but not as famous as Sugar Toms Lane in East Norich. The house was cold in the winter and hot in the summer. It had creaky floors and a leaky roof. I loved the place because I inherited it from my paternal grandmother, Margaret Mary Mullin.

Living without Frank in the big old house in Oyster Bay had mixed blessings. For the first time in my life, I was without family obligations. Whenever any of the nurses decided to go out to dinner, drinks or whatever, I was instantly available. It was a beautiful sense of freedom but, like a pinioned bird, my flight was limited and eventually I had to go home to that empty house and even emptier bed. Life seemed to be made up of good days or good nights. Where is it written that we can't have both at the same time?

2

Surprisingly, I became the fifth wheel in our social group. I was still included in the larger parties, but not one of my friends, not even Jenny, ever asked me home to dinner or even to a movie. Maybe it just never occurred to them, but weekend evenings were the loneliest times of all for me. As I saw less of my married friends, I began seeing more of my single friends. Gina was living with me but we didn't see much of each other. She had her job at the Vivarium and was dating Alex and a couple of other boys. I guess she wanted to be very sure. We both spent long hours away from home. I had a balanced survival kit. School filled me with idealism, and the hospital was my contact with reality.

3

Four West was a small unit. It had originally been designated as a medical unit with one two-bedded room for emergency surgical patients. It somehow developed into a catchall for patients who couldn't be accommodated on specialty units when they were full, patients with personality disorders and patients with poor prognoses. It was a continual challenge; it increased our theoretical knowledge and sharpened our nursing skills.

I was pouring the ten a.m. medications when Dr. Hakim came striding down the hall.

"Good morning, Ms. deMeo, you are just the one I wanted to see."

"Good morning, Doctor, does Mr. Aiello need something?"

"No," he smiled, assuming a confidential tone. "This has nothing to do with hospital business. Jimmy Galletta asked me to speak to you."

"Dr. Galletta? I don't understand."

"He would like to know if you would go out with him." He laughed. "He is too shy to ask for himself. He really likes you. His intentions are quite honorable. He is thinking about settling down." He cleared his throat. "You know, getting married."

"You're joking?"

"No. I am not joking."

"Well, I'm...stunned, flattered. Dr. Galletta is very nice. But I'm married."

"Oh? I, that is, we did not know. You wear no ring. You have been seen at the Meadow Brook having dinner with the other nurses so we assumed you were divorced or something."

"Oh no, I'm married."

"Yes, but are you married-married?"

"I'm married-married-married. My husband is working in Europe and I'm joining him there in June."

"Aha, I see. Well Mrs. deMeo, June is a very long way off."

I finished giving out the meds thinking about Dr. Galletta, somewhat overwhelmed by the whole idea. Imagine sending his friend to talk to me. I was still smiling to myself as I pushed the medication cart back down the hall. Dr. Hakim was at the nursing desk talking to Sally Moore, the Head Nurse. While I was clearing off the cart, he came into the tiny medication room and asked, "By the way, Mrs. deMeo, what do you do after work?"

"I go to school."

"Well, what do you do after school?"

"Study, mostly." I didn't want to tell him that I was working on my dissertation. Higher degrees for nurses were not looked upon favorably by many physicians.

"I know how lonely it can be at times, and you cannot always study. Perhaps we can have dinner one evening and talk. I am very interested in what you are studying at school."

"That's very kind of you Dr. Hakim, but I really don't have the time."

"Ahhh, but we have established that you do have the time, dinner at the Meadow Brook with the nurses, remember? Besides, your personality will suffer if you listen only to nurses' points of view." I smiled at the idea of a surgeon talking about a personality problem. "But no matter, you do not have to go to dinner with me if you think it improper. I understand." He smiled and hesitated, "But if ever you are lonely and would like to talk, please telephone me. Surely there is nothing wrong with talking on the phone, is there?"

"No, uh, that's really very nice of you, Dr. Hakim, but I couldn't do that. I wouldn't think of disturbing you."

"You will not. I live alone." He turned and left.

I was uncertain about him, about his intentions. What was he really saying? Damn it, he was being kind, making a sincere offer. Was I the one with the dirty mind?

"How about lunch, Kate?" asked Sally as she secured her wobbling cap.

"Fine, but let's go early. I'm starved."

Sally was a few years younger than I. She was the epitome of black being beautiful. She was divorced, had two kids, one Beagle puppy, and a boyfriend Tom who was a radiologist in another hospital. He wanted to get married. She didn't. Sally was happy with her life as it was, simple and uncomplicated, and she didn't want any change. I liked being the Assistant Head Nurse on her unit. We shared the workload, the weekends and the holidays.

At lunch I was telling Sally about my conversation with Dr. Hakim, leaving out the part about Dr. Galletta. "You know, Sally, that was really nice of him."

"Ho, ho, ho."

"What do you mean 'ho, ho, ho?'"

"He doesn't just want to talk to you. Can't you see that?"

"Sally, you're misjudging him. What can happen over the telephone?"

"You may be right, but I doubt it. Be careful Kate." Her cap tipped foreword and she pushed it back. "For such a smart lady, you can be pretty dumb."

"Oh, come on, Sally..."

"Just be careful, and don't trust these doctors..." Sally laughed, "especially during a full moon."

"Come on, Sally, you're too young to believe in old nurses' tales."

"You're right, of course I don't believe in them." She pointed her finger at me. "The truth is you have to watch men, doctors or not, during all of the moon's phases."

When Sally and I returned from lunch, Patti Flaherty met us in the hall, hands on hips and tapping her toe.

"Galletta's patient. Mrs. Ulrich." She spoke in a staccato voice. "Again. Yelling her head off. Mary's still with her."

Mrs. Ulrich was a fifty-eight year old woman who was having a gastrointestinal work-up done to rule-out gastritis, ulcers, or hiatus hernia. All routine hospital procedures, but in her case, it was somewhat difficult. The nurses believed Mrs. Ulrich to be psychotic, but the doctors did not. Of course the nurses spent eight hours a day with her, while the doctors averaged less than eight minutes. It wouldn't be the first time a schizophrenic patient outsmarted the doctors.

"She was hearing voices again, and people coming into her room," Patti was explaining, "only this time they were coming in through the ceiling, not the windows. How can I be expected to lock the ceiling?"

As Mary came down the hall from Mrs. Ulrich's room, Sally asked, "Is she restrained?"

"She's okay," shrugged Mary.

Patti and Mary escaped into the elevator in pursuit of late lunch. Before the doors closed I heard Mary's complaining voice say, "Jeeze, Sally and Kate are such old ladies."

I went to check my meds before doing rounds with Sally.

I just about got through the doorway when Sally yelled, "Kate, STAT! I ran out of the room and saw Mrs. Ulrich in the middle of the hallway. She was yelling something.

"Hurry, Kate, hurry, before she gets to the double doors." Sally and I sprinted down the hall. Mrs. Ulrich screamed as we reached for her. We almost got her back to her room when the double doors opened. We turned our heads and looked into the stern face of Kowalski, the Pediatric Head Nurse.

"You are scaring my kids."

Neither Sally nor I tried to explain. We looked hopelessly guilty. Kowalski shook her head muttering, "Damn nuts from Four West. I wish I could legally padlock that fire door."

"This whole thing is ridiculous," stormed Sally. "I'm asking for a psychiatric consultation." She pulled out a consent form and slammed the drawer shut.

"I really don't think there will be a problem, Sally. Galletta is the attending, and after today's outburst, I'm sure he'll sign for a consult."

"He'd better," said Sally with fire in her eyes.

"Who do we use?"

"Sternberg. He's good."

"Aaron Sternberg?"

Sally looked surprised. "You know him?"

"I met him years ago when I was a hospital volunteer, then later as a student in the VA Hospital. He's not just good, Sally, he's fantastic."

Two days later, Mrs. Ulrich was transferred to a hospital equipped to give her both physiological and psychological care. The illustrious Dr. Sternberg was surprised to see me. We went to the coffee shop at three o'clock to reminisce over our days at the VA Hospital.

"I'm disappointed that you didn't become a psychiatric nurse. You have the talent, you know."

"Nice of you to say so, Dr. Sternberg, but..."

"Aaron," he corrected.

"Okay, uhm, Aaron. It was a difficult decision for me. Those days working with you, your psychodrama and all, were the most exhausting days of my life."

"Come on, Kate, you thrive on exhausting situations."

"Maybe so. I'm task oriented and like most nurses, med-surg just naturally won out."

"That's a cop-out. I was sure you were going to choose psych. What made you change your mind?"

I shrugged my shoulders, "I don't know, maybe it was after I discovered that you required an excellent bridge partner during lunch."

"Another cop-out."

"And here comes still another," I said getting to my feet. "If I don't leave now, I'll be late for my four o'clock appointment with my Committee Chair and you know I'm compulsive."

We shook hands formally and I left him sitting there looking myopically at the empty cups.

4

I was happy to be working the weekend since Gina had gone skiing at Great Gorge with Alex. Weekends meant a backbreaking workload because we worked half-staff. It was our solution to having every other weekend off. I divided the twenty-one patients among my team of two registered nurses, one licensed practical nurse and one nurses' aide. I ran the desk, gave medications and took vital signs. As the night nurse was giving me her report, I looked at the ever-changing Kardex of patients.

"...Oh, and keep an eye on Saunders in 422-1," the night nurse cautioned. "He keeps trying to crawl into bed with the women across the hall. He has an order for Thorazine p.o., but I couldn't get him to swallow any."

"Okay, Helen, thanks. I'll get an IM order for the Thorazine. Get some sleep and I'll see you tomorrow morning."

I was making out the assignment sheet when Mr. Saunders came hopping past the nurses' station heading toward another room. I called to him, took his arm and guided him back to his bed. I knew that if I restrained him he'd yell loudly and unnerve the other patients. If I put the side-rails up, he'd attempt to climb over. And if I did neither, he'd hop into the women's room across the hall. I asked Tina, the best nurses' aide in the business, to keep an eye on him until I could get a medication order.

I slammed the phone down.

"No luck, I can't raise anyone. We'll have to think of a way to get him to take his meds."

Patti, Mary and I tried, but neither coaxing nor coercion succeeded in opening our patient's mouth.

"I'll have to keep him with me until I can get an intern."

My decision was not a good one. As I was pouring the medications, Mr. Saunders would empty one medication cup into another, mixing pills, capsules and liquids. His charted diagnosis was vague. Since our census of elderly patients always increased just before the holidays, we worried that families might be dumping their elders. I thought about the differences between normal aging and disease processes—the differences between chronological age and physical age. This was the population I was studying for my dissertation, older adults from sixty-two to infinity. They were all independently functioning and seemed to be aging successfully. I looked at this sweet elderly man and wondered what to do with him. We weren't getting much work done this morning, especially me. At any rate, I was reminded once again that nursing doesn't always deal with matters of life and death. But I did feel like killing Jimmy Galletta. Saunders was another of his patients. Aaron Sternberg was right. I should have been a psych nurse. At least I would have known what I was in for. I also knew that we were in desperate need of a psychiatric unit in this hospital. This was the time for desperate measures. I was willing to try almost anything.

I did.

I borrowed a cleaning bucket and half filled it with water. I grabbed a towel, a washcloth, latex gloves and then I grabbed Mr. Saunders. We headed toward the public telephone booth that was in full view of the nurses' station. I told him that enemy biological warfare had targeted that booth, and he had been selected for the mission to search and destroy. I dramatically poured 60cc's of green soap into the bucket, and then added 30cc's of hydrogen peroxide, which I thought might give my story a little substance. Mr. Saunders saluted me. "Never feed a psychosis" kept running through my head. Oh, what the hell. After checking that no one could see me, I returned his salute, and closed the door of the booth. He set to work, finally contained, and in full view of at least one of us at all times.

During the morning some of the attending physicians came on to the unit to visit their patients. They looked mystified at the action that was taking place in the phone booth and began to question me.

"Don't ask. Just don't ask."

By the end of the morning, all of our work had been completed, and we also had the cleanest public telephone in the hospital. By the time the intern finally arrived, Mr. Saunders was in his own bed, sleeping the peaceful sleep of the innocent.

"You want Thorazine IM for that guy. He's out like a light. What's the matter with you today, Mrs. deMeo?"

"Don't ask. Just don't ask."

I looked past his boyish face and had an immediate urge to kill. Dr. Galletta was getting off the elevator.

5

The following week, Dr. Hakim was at the nurses' station busily writing orders for his patients. As he closed the last chart he looked at me and said, "I heard you had coffee with Dr. Sternberg."

"Not that it's any of your business and besides, not true."

He raised his eyebrows.

"I had tea."

"Okay, then tea. How about having tea with me at three o'clock?"

"Can't," I said pulling his patients' charts down to my desk.

"Some sort of ethnic preference?"

"You know better than that," I replied. "I have to be at school by four and I have all these orders to pick up before I leave."

"After school then?" I looked at his face. It was a nice face. His tight, black curly hair framed his dark Egyptian features. The nice face was waiting for an answer. I was about to explain that I knew Dr. Sternberg from school. Oh, what the hell, why not? "Okay, I'll meet you for tea at the Town House Diner tomorrow night at seven-thirty."

He was already there, having coffee and dessert when I arrived. He rose to his feet, smiling, and when we were both seated he asked if I'd like something to eat. "The pastries are very good here," he suggested.

"No thank you, I'm really not hungry," I lied. "I'll just have a cup of tea."

I was a little uncomfortable and I couldn't think of

anything to say to him. When the waitress brought my tea, it gave me something to do with my hands and a place to put my eyes. He started talking about an emergency tracheotomy we had done together a while back. I remembered it well. He was a good technician–steady, sure strokes with his scalpel. He was also a bit of an idealist and had a reputation for not engaging in hospital politics. He was one of the few surgeons whose consults didn't always end up in the O.R. He believed in surgery to be sure, but he believed in utilizing conservative medical options first. We talked for nearly an hour, a long time to spend over a cup of tea. I felt it was time for me to leave and I said something to that effect.

"It is so early. Why do we not go somewhere for a drink?"

I didn't want to go home. Gina was out. It was fun talking to him, and I couldn't see any harm in having one drink.

"No sense in taking two cars," he was saying as we left, "Leave yours in the parking lot and I will drive you back here later."

It seemed reasonable at the time, but once I was in his car I began to have an anxiety attack. Suppose someone sees me? How will I explain what I'm doing in his car? Suppose there's an accident? What if I'm unconscious, or dead? Who would explain? What would people think? By the time we got to where we were going, I really needed that drink.

Dr. Hakim asked if I'd like something to eat and again I lied and said I'd eaten earlier. I was starving and for some reason I couldn't admit to it. I'd have to drink very slowly if I wanted to stay sober on an empty stomach.

"This is the first time I have seen you without your uniform...Kate. May I call you Kate?" I looked down at my navy sweater and plaid mini skirt, the heavy matching jacket draped over the back of my chair. Nothing special, I thought, but my nothing-special outfit was purposefully planned. My long sandy colored hair was twisted in a bun–the same way I wore it at work. I didn't want to look particularly appealing. I wanted him to think of me as a companionable, intelligent person, and not necessarily female.

"Of course you may call me Kate. And what may I call you?"

"Taf," he smiled, "my friends call me Taf."

"Taf," I repeated, trying it out, "That's an unusual name."

"Allow me to introduce myself," he said with a mock bow, "I am Mustafa Abdul Hakim."

"My God, I am impressed. Well now, my full name is Kathleen Mary Mullin deMeo. And me mother was an O'Reilly," I added with a brogue. "I hope you're equally impressed."

We talked for two hours. I was completely relaxed. He had an easy way about him, soft and gentle. The drinks helped too. I listened to his views on the practice of quality medicine, and he listened to mine on continuing education for all health practitioners.

He drove me back to the diner parking lot and the most aggressive thing he did was to put his hand gently on my back as he walked me across the parking lot. I got into my car, started the motor, and rolled down the window. "Thanks for a lovely evening, Taf. It was really very kind of you."

"It was not kind of me at all. I enjoyed very much being with you. You are a lovely, intelligent woman, Kathleen Mary Mullin deMeo."

I was feeling good when I arrived home. Gina was already there. "Hi, Mom. Where were you? You didn't have any late appointments. Where'd you go? I was worried."

"I'm sorry. I forgot to tell you that we had a dissertation seminar tonight, and then we all went out for a drink." I don't know why I lied to her. All of my good feelings disappeared and I suddenly felt very guilty.

6

Gina and I began meeting twice a week at a Health Club. We'd work out for an hour in the gym, do a few laps in the pool and end up lazily talking in the Jacuzzi. Then we'd shower and go to the local diner for a late snack. Gina and I got to know each other. We were becoming friends. By the middle of December we would transcend our mother-daughter relationship.

7

My dissertation was moving along rapidly but I was pretty well wrung out. I went to see the Director of Nursing. I had already informed her back in October that I would most likely be leaving in June. It had squelched my promotion and now I was reluctant to commit to a definite termination date in case my situation with Frank somehow changed. I asked her about the possibility of working per diem. We agreed to three days a week, which included one weekend a month. In the event that anything did change, I could go back on staff or more likely be promoted to staff educator or supervisor. Sadly, it meant that I wouldn't be working exclusively on Sally's unit anymore. Rather I'd be working anywhere in the hospital where a nurse might be needed.

Christmas was coming. Gina and I had been shopping every spare minute for months. Mark came home and joined our efforts. He went up into the fir grove and cut down a beautiful tree for us. Frank was due to arrive early Christmas Eve.

I drove to JFK and arrived at the International terminal one and one-half hours early. I was a wreck. I leaned against a pillar, staring at the passenger exit, afraid that I would miss him. Two hours and fifteen minutes later, he walked through the door, an even more beautiful Frank than I had remembered. I pushed through the crowd and flung myself at him. "Oh my God, my God, how I missed you."

He kissed me, put his arms around me and guided me through the crowd. "When I saw you standing there," he whispered, "I was happy that I was the one you were waiting for."

Yuletide season 1972 was the best ever. Mary Ellen stayed with us for a few days and Alex joined us for both Christmas Eve and Christmas day. We had a 'trim the tree party' on Christmas Eve. All of our close friends were there— our usual four couple group. Sally came with Tom, and Gina and Mark's friends outnumbered us all.

I worked on Christmas Day in partial payment for my own happiness. Then, before I knew it, it was New Year's and Frank was leaving. He was anxious to return to Brussels. He wouldn't have stayed if he could. He didn't live here anymore.

Chapter Five

"It is when you give of
yourself that you truly give."
Kahlil Gibran

1

School and work went on as usual. One day, late in January, I was assigned to Four West. It was great being back with the old gang. During our coffee break, we were sitting in the kitchen exchanging the current events of our lives. Some people would call it gossip. We called it group therapy. Patti had gotten engaged. Mary was still looking. Sally was her same happy self.

"How's everything with you, Kate? You look as if you lost weight." Sally shook her head in disapproval.

"Yeah I know. It's my dissertation. Hardest thing I ever had to do. I should be finished sometime in the spring."

"Who cares if you get a doctorate? You'll still be a nurse," sniffed Mary. "I think this education stuff is a lot of crap,"

I scraped my chair noisily on the floor to face her. Sally tried to stop what seemed to be an inevitable clash.

"Come on, girls, coffee break is over." We all got up to leave but just before Mary reached for the door, I put my hand on it and held it closed. "Mary, education is not crap. You could go back to school and get your R.N. You'd learn a great deal, make more money..."

"Face it, deMeo, it's crap."

"What's crap is you bouncing on the empty beds with interns." She blanched and looked at me with disbelief. I opened the door and left her leaning against the table.

I walked to the desk and picked up my assignment from Sally, who tried to get a reading from my face. Not being able to detect anything but silent anger, she began giving me a report on my patients.

"There are two with melanoma, Kate. Really sick cookies."

Oh God, I thought. There are ways to die and ways to die. Malignant melanoma was one of the worst. Cancer of the melanin, those tiny, pigmented particles that gave skin its color, the same tiny particles that mobilized to give us our summer tans. Although the amount of melanin under the skin determined how fair or dark we were, the amount had nothing to do with the disease itself. It was caused by over-exposure to the sun's rays and people with light complexions seemed to be the most susceptible. I shuddered, knowing that the Irish are prime targets.

I looked at the thirty-year-old school teacher in the bed before me. I had difficulty removing all of the dressings from the more advanced tumors. They were on her arms, her shoulders and her face. Some of the nodules looked like large pigmented moles outlined in red but many had already begun to ulcerate. Oh Jesus, I thought, if she looks into a mirror, she'll see dark bleeding sores on her face. This poor woman, she's too young to die, too young to die with oozing black ulcers, too young to die an ugly death.

"I'll order up some non-stick dressings..."

"Will they help to cure the sores?"

I couldn't be sure if she pretended not to know or if she genuinely didn't know. "Well, the new dressings will be more comfortable, they won't rub or stick."

Dr. Rizzo walked in. He asked me to prepare an IV dose of Dactinomycin. It was one of the drugs used to inhibit the rapidly proliferating cells of the body, and should therefore attack the cancer cells.

"Is this medicine going to make me better?" she asked, looking wide-eyed from Rizzo to me and then back again. I waited for him to say something. He finished giving the medication and left without a word. That's not like him. What the hell is wrong?

"Be back in a second," I said, following at his heels. "Dr. Rizzo…Peter…one moment, please. That woman just asked you a question. You have to tell her something."

"Why?"

"Because it's unfair not to tell her, unfair to give hope where there is none."

"How do you know there's no hope? Maybe the medication will work. Maybe this will be it, and if it isn't…" he shrugged. "I don't want to tell her she's dying. Do you?" Before I could think of anything to say, he walked away.

"What did the doctor say?" she asked as soon as I reentered the room.

"He said that we would have to evaluate the drug therapy on a day to day basis." Some of the hope faded from her eyes. "I know that's not an easy thing to do," I continued. "Try to be patient. You have one of the best doctors in the business." She smiled and seemed reassured. Who knows? Maybe he's right. Maybe this is the better way.

My other melanoma patient was a thirty-nine year old man. In spite of his illness, I could see that he had once been very good-looking. He had been in the hospital for two months and his melanoma was quite advanced. In addition, one of the tumors was dangerously close to the carotid artery and all we could hope was that he would be comatose before the tumor reached the artery and eroded it.

"Good morning, Mr. Birge," I said, a little too cheerfully.

"Take off these dressings and give me that mirror," he demanded.

I did as he asked and he stared at the large ulcerated areas on his neck. When I tried to take the mirror from him, he resisted. I sat down and waited.

Mr. Birge was divorced. He had a girlfriend who came to visit him daily. His daughter had once been a faithful visitor too. No one had been to see him for weeks. Maybe they couldn't bear the sight of the daily deterioration. He had failed to keep them at his bedside. His anger had made it easy for them to give up on him. His daughter still telephoned occasionally but his girlfriend simply dropped out of sight. He was going to die alone.

Everyone dies alone. Their families avoid the reality of death by ignoring it physically or mentally. Not only patients like Mr. Birge, whose family stays away, but those who have family continually at the bedside. The families, along with the hospital personnel, keep the patient in cheerful isolation. They talk about inane things: the lovely weather, the hospital room drapes, and plans are made for the patient's homecoming. Who gives a damn? The patient doesn't. He goes along with the game because he wants to spare his family. But he has really important things on his mind. He knows he's dying. There's so little time, and so many things will be left unsaid. His family continues the game, believing they are helping him, and the cycle continues.

Mr. Birge finally handed me the mirror. I finished his dressings in complete silence. I had joined the ranks of those who allowed people to die alone.

Last fall, I had been to a seminar given by Dr. Elizabeth Kubler-Ross. She maintained that patients who successfully go through the five stages of grief have a more peaceful death. It seems that all patients go through the first stage, denial, "This can't be happening to me." Many reach the second stage, anger, and ask "Why me?" Some go on to the third stage, bargaining, "Please, God, if you do this one thing for me, I'll never ask anything of you again." The fourth stage is depression, the realization that the signs and symptoms are worsening. The fifth and final stage is acceptance. Not resignation but acceptance, and with this acceptance comes peace.

The main objective, as Kubler-Ross sees it, is to sensitize family members and hospital personnel to the implicit communications of the dying patient and to come to the acceptance of reality together, thereby avoiding much unnecessary agony on the part of the dying and even more so on the part of the family that will be left behind.

The problem is that few of us are up to handling our own feelings about death, much less helping others to do so. Everyone is afraid of dying. But isn't that just another of our learned fears? Man is the only animal said to fear death. Is it because we understand what death is or is it because we don't understand? Death is the inevitable conclusion or extension of life, depending on one's personal philosophy.

I left Mr. Birge's room with a gnawing disappointment in my gut at my own lack of ability to help him. Dr. Kubler-Ross would have recognized that I failed to move Mr. Birge beyond the second stage.

Mary was waiting outside his door. "How come you never reported me, deMeo?"

"There was nothing to report," I replied, walking past her.

"Wait a minute...deMeo...Kate...please. It was that day when I was with Doctor Yang, wasn't it?"

"Mary, I never breathed a word of it. I only mentioned it today because I was angry. I'm sorry. Let's forget it."

I wanted to forget it. Most nurses are women, most doctors are men, and most women have sex with men. If a nurse were going to have sex with someone, it would probably be someone in the hospital. Why not a doctor? For the most part, they're educated and interesting. Hospital morals are no better or worse than any others.

Billy Ting Yang was the most sought after intern in the hospital. Some of the nurses had a four-star rating system on the posted printout of attendings, residents and interns. Sally and I thought they were selecting the best doctors– diagnosticians, surgeons, and bedside manner. Sally and I disagreed with their choices and told them so. Later, we found out that one star meant they'd sleep with him once, two stars, twice and so on. According to the same nurses, Taiwan won first prize in well-endowed exports. One smile or a pat on the ass from Billy would be enough to send them into a state of euphoria.

Billy was not only good-looking, he was so charming that he was the only one who could get away with asking for a mercy fuck. Another intern tried to ape Billy's style with Clancy, the Assistant Head Nurse in Recovery. She dragged him down the stairs and threw him out of the back door. This was the same nurse who put a mugger in the hospital after he jumped her in the parking lot. Clancy had just worked a double shift and it was after eleven p.m. by the time she left the building. The mugger knew our shift schedules–that we were paid every other Wednesday and cashed our checks at lunchtime. He knew a lot about us but he didn't know anything about Clancy.

2

By the middle of February, I was working on a surgical unit and one of my patients had just had a gall bladder removed by Dr. Hakim. I wanted to see him but because it was Sunday,

I didn't think he'd show up. I was sorry that I had extracted a promise from him never to call me at home. His patient wanted to know something trivial and I used that as an excuse to have him paged in case he did come to the hospital. At three o'clock I called reception to ask if he had signed in. He hadn't. I was walking through the lobby with the other nurses, on our way to the Meadow Brook for a drink. I hesitated in front of the phone booths. "Go on ahead," I said, "I'll catch up with you. I flipped through the phone book and found his number. With trembling fingers, I dialed.

"Hello?" It was his voice.

"Hello. Kate deMeo here."

"Well, I am surprised. How are you?"

"Very well, thank you. I hope I'm not disturbing you."

"Not at all. I am doing nothing but listening to music. Do you like Beethoven?"

"Yes, yes, I do but I prefer Chopin." Why did I say that? There was a long pause. Then we started talking at the same time. It was all so awkward. I was sorry that I started it.

"Kate...would you like to talk?"

"Yes," I sighed.

"I'll meet you in the Town House Diner parking lot at seven-thirty. We will go somewhere for dinner."

I dressed carefully that night. I chose a navy blue suit with a maxi skirt and left the lower buttons open to show some leg well above my boot tops. I chose that outfit because Frank hated it and because everyone was still wearing minis. Except for the expanse of leg that showed when I walked, it was rather severe looking—kind of butch. I polished my fingernails, dusted my zygomatic arches with blusher, combed my hair loose about my shoulders and borrowed Gina's coat from her closet.

I arrived at the parking lot at seven-thirty five, intentionally being a few minutes late. His car was already there waiting and I pulled into the empty space along side. I was trembling and I wasn't sure I could get out of my car. As he came around to greet me, I rolled the window down and not trusting my voice, I smiled a hello. He bent forward as if to speak, then kissed me gently on the lips. I was immediately flustered.

"I am sorry," he apologized. "I did not mean to upset you. It is just that you look so beautiful tonight, I could not resist. Forgive me?"

Now I was really flustered. "I have two conditions before we go to dinner."

"I agree to whatever they are."

"How can you agree? You don't even know what I'm going to say."

"Okay, I am listening."

"First of all, we're going Dutch Treat. I'm paying half the check. Secondly, I want to drive. I'm far more comfortable when I'm driving in my own car."

"Not a problem," he said. "Allow me put my car in the garage. It is on the way." I followed him to his apartment. His car vanished beneath the building. A few minutes later, he was strolling towards me, smiling as he offered a choice of restaurants, depending on the kind of food I liked. I chose the one where I though we'd be least likely to be seen.

The waiter showed us to a table where we sat side by side. When he handed us the menus I thought he looked strangely at me. In fact, I thought everyone in the restaurant was looking strangely at me. I hid behind my large menu, convinced that everyone knew I was a married woman having dinner with a man who was not my husband.

"Now, Kate, come out from behind that menu. Suppose someone does see us? We are only having dinner."

I knew I was being childish about the whole thing and I tried to relax. We talked about things related to our work. Then he began telling me a little about himself. He talked about his childhood holidays in Port Said, his schooling in

France, his internship at New York Hospital and finally having
to live outside the United States for five years before he could
immigrate. It all sounded romantic, especially compared to
schooling at St. Margaret's Academy, vacationing in the
Adirondacks, and being a housewife. He said he hadn't married
because he hadn't been in one place long enough, and now that
he was finally settled, he wasn't sure that he liked the idea of
losing his freedom. At thirty-five, he felt he had plenty of
time.

The waiter came with the dessert menu. "Nothing for
me," I said quickly and gave Taf a pleading look. He realized
how desperate I was to leave. He handed the menus back to
the waiter and asked for the check. "Don't forget," I
whispered, "I'm paying half."

I drove him back to his apartment building and we talked
in the car for a bit. "Why do you not come up for a drink? I can
even prepare a cup of tea for you." I was reluctant. I shook my
head. "Come on, Kate, I am not trying to seduce you."

His books and his music were the nicest things about his
apartment and I smiled when I heard Chopin's Waltz in C
Sharp Minor filling the room. He sat on the couch next to me
and poured two small glasses of Galliano, another of my
favorites.

"You're incredible," I commented, "Is this normal
bachelor methodology?"

He frowned. "What sort of a comment is that? I thought
we were friends. I simply enjoy being with you." We listened
to the music and he poured himself another Galliano. "I am
curious about something, Kate. It is purely a philosophical
question." He sipped slowly. "Would you go to bed with me if
you were not married?"

I tried to put myself in a '73 singles sexual revolution
frame of mind. "Yes," I finally answered, "I think I would."

When I finished my drink, I got up to leave and I put
money for my half of the check on the table. He protested,
but so did I. "I wish I had a camera...a beautiful woman

leaving my apartment, leaving money on the table. My friends would never believe this."

We walked to the elevator. He put his hands on my shoulders, and then kissed me gently on the forehead. It did not fluster me in the least. I left the building feeling that I'd conquered the sexual stigma that stands between the male-female friendships. I felt that he really liked me and didn't care whether or not he got me into the sack.

3

As if I didn't have enough on my plate, I let Patti talk me into working with her in a black community–based outreach program. They needed registered nurses to teach health education (that's how they referred to sex education) to underprivileged fifth and sixth grade girls. Patti volunteered us and then, at the last minute, she reneged. Apparently Sally talked her out of it citing that it was a high drug area and not worth the risk for a young inexperienced nurse. Although it wasn't the population I needed for my study, I decided to stick it out. Once I started something, I had to finish or it would be like breaking a promise. The classes were set for two evenings a week, two hours a session. The only word of caution I got from the social worker was that, since it was a high drug area and it was believed that nurses carried drugs, I was not to wear my uniform.

Gina and Sally said it was the worst idea they'd ever heard of. Taf Hakim told me that I was completely out of my mind and that he wouldn't go into that area alone—and he was a man. For God's sake, I argued, these are eleven-and twelve-year-old girls. I made a mental note, however, not to mention the project in my weekly letters to Frank.

At our first session in the Martin Luther King conference room, the small size of the class disappointed me. The social worker in charge had split up the group of twenty into two groups.

"Don't be fooled by the fifth grade label. Some of these kids may be as old as fifteen. You'll be damn lucky if you can handle ten at a time."

I looked at them from the head of the long table. A dark sea of hostile faces. They wouldn't even take off their hats and coats. They just sat there, arms folded, scowling and staring straight ahead.

"I guess we can get started. My name is Kate deMeo. You can call me Kate or Mrs. deMeo."

Silence.

"I thought we'd start by learning the correct terminology, you know, the right words, about our bodies, and in that way we'll..."

One of the faces hidden beneath a wool cap finally spoke, "We got ah own tuh-man-ahl-ogy."

"Okay, fine, but I'd like to help you learn the words that other people use, like doctors." I wasn't sure if I was getting through, or if they even knew what I was trying to say. "Look, all I'm saying is that if you learn the proper words, no one will be able to talk over your head, say things that you won't understand, you know, put you down."

The little girl on my right glowered at me. "You mean you gonna teach us fancy tuh-man-ahl-ogy fo what we already got names fo?"

"Something like that. Only it's not fancy, it's more like knowing two languages."

Two girls at the far end of the table were conferring. Then one of them looked straight at me and said, "You means, if ah gives you some words, you gonna tell us how to say em co-reck lak?"

"Yes. Yes, sure I will."

"Well," she snickered, "What does it mean, co-reck lak, when a dude shoots his load?"

They were all looking at me now. I had their attention and I intended to keep it. "What you're referring to is called an ejaculation."

"Eee-jack-yoo-what?"

"Eee-jack-yoo-who?" They were laughing.

One of them got up and started walking toward the door and said, "Man, ahm goin out and get mahself eee-jack-yoo-ulated."

"Oh no you're not," I shouted, "You're going to get your ass right back into that seat and listen to me. I came here tonight because I thought you'd like to learn something…" I searched their faces for the leader, "something about your bodies…" I remembered the social worker mentioning that someone's sister was having a baby; "about how they function…" Which one is she? I looked at the girl on my right, "How babies are born?"

"She-it, mah sister's havin a baby."

"Wouldn't you like to know how it all happens?"

She looked at the others, took off her cap, threw it on the table and announced, "Ahm lissnin."

They all settled down. Ten faces were looking at me. I tore up my outline for the course and allowed them to pick subjects according to their needs. They picked up my terminology along the way and I picked up theirs. My little leader, Sharene, turned out to be smart and funny. The first three months went beautifully.

4

It was the wettest April ever. My social life was picking up, which helped to speed up my separation from Frank. Gina and I were working out twice a week in the health club and she occasionally included me when she was having dinner with her friends. I'd see Jenny from time to time, and I'd frequently have dinner with Sally and Tom. I'd always have tea or a Coke with Aaron whenever he was in the hospital. He was quite a guy. His dream was to set up mental health satellite clinics around New York. He had interesting theories and I enjoyed listening to him expound on the subject.

I saw Taf from time to time, but only in the hospital. He started calling me something that sounded like Habifti. He said it was a term of endearment in Arabic. I don't know whether it was or wasn't but it made me smile.

"How about dinner tonight?" he asked.

"I have my little girls at six-thirty tonight. I'm learning more than they are."

"Ah yes, your little girls. Well, may I call you when you get home?"

"Okay. I'll be home nine, nine-thirty."

That night everything went wrong. I forgot to put a pair of jeans and a sweatshirt in the car so I went to teach my class wearing my nurse's uniform. No one had ever bothered me before, and besides I reasoned, I'd have a raincoat on.

As I got out of my car, some big guy hooted and chased me through the parking lot. I ran like hell and made it into the building. I went into my classroom, closed the door and sat down in my usual seat. I was shaking.

"Shit, how stupid can I be?" I cried, looking down at my legs, "White shoes and stockings." I looked at my watch. The kids wouldn't be arriving for another ten minutes. Seconds later, someone started pounding on the door. I didn't move. I didn't breathe. He kicked the door off its hinges, entered the room and just stood there, looking at me. Except for recognizing the obvious, that he was big and black, I was too frightened to focus in on him. He walked to the first chair, put his foot on it, rocked it and kicked it over. He paused, then went to the next chair and did the same thing. He kicked his way down the line of chairs towards me. I thought of running for the door, but I couldn't make myself move. He finally put his foot on my chair and began rocking it.

He looked at me, loathing in his eyes. "Man, ah hates yo

ugly white mother-fuckin face."

"You sound angry," I said, "Would you like to talk about it?" I went on talking—not really knowing what I was saying. I used every psych term that I'd ever heard of or read about. He mistook my frozen terror for icy calm.

"You is crazy...crazy honky bitch mother-fucker. Honky nurses is hoes. You is a hoe. Ah don't want nuttin to do with you...crazy honky hoe cunt mother-fucker..." He continued yelling all the way down the hall until he made his way out of the building.

Some five minutes later my kids strolled in, walking right over the unhinged door, never noticing it or that the nurse who dismissed them a half-hour early that evening was similarly unhinged.

I walked out of the classroom with my little leader and casually asked, "Hey Sharene, what's a hoe?"

She giggled, "Man, ah gotta teach you everthin. A hoe is a chick what gets money fo fuckin...oops I mean intercourse." She giggled again. "You sho is a dumb teacher."

"I know. I know. But thanks to you at least I know that I'm not, and never have been, a garden tool. But," I bent down to look at her, "if I had to be a garden tool, I'd rather be a rake."

She scrunched up her face at me. "Huh?"

Once outside of the building, we went our separate ways. I began to breathe the night air and I felt better, dumb but better. I looked around. There was no one in sight, so I headed for my car at a rapid pace. I had almost reached it when someone yelled, "Yo momma, got some peels?" I leaped toward my car. I heard more than one person running across the parking lot. I was shaking trying to unlock the door. Unlock, unlock. I could hear them getting closer. It unlocked. I scrambled into the car and pulled at the door. It wouldn't close. Something was jamming it. The metal part of the seat belt was in the way. As I put my hand down to free it, a large hand pulled the door all the way open. Another large hand dragged me out of the car by my arm. I could hear the sleeve of my coat tearing and feel my knees scraping along the pavement. Two strong arms pulled me roughly to my feet. "Ah axed you somethin," he said slapping me across the face, "ain't po-lite not ta answer."

I just looked at the two of them without really seeing them. My heart was pounding, and I was too frightened to answer. I had a hollow humming in my ears. It was as if I couldn't equalize the pressure.

"You some kinda mother fuckin-dummy?" He slapped me harder this time. I tasted blood in my mouth.

This can't be happening. "Please...leave me alone. I don't have any pills," I answered weakly.

"Gimme yo car keys." He put his hand out, palm up.

Just then the other guy was pulling something out from under the front seat. "Looky here man, whooee, ah found it." They walked a few steps under the streetlight to examine their find, momentarily forgetting me. I dove into the car, slammed and locked the door. They ran to the window and started pounding on it.

"Motor, please start," I prayed. My prayer was answered immediately. I gunned the motor and drove off in a panic. One of them jumped on the hood and slid off after a few yards. He couldn't hold on because he had something clutched in his hand. A black bag. It was vaguely reminiscent of something. As I pulled onto the parkway heading north, I felt safe. I began to laugh. Then I was laughing hysterically. That black bag. It was Mark's. Mark's gym bag. He was home on Spring Break, and he borrowed my car last night. No drugs in that bag, at least I hoped there weren't. Are those guys going to be pissed? The only loss was Mark's smelly gym clothes, and uh oh, his prized Converse high top sneakers autographed by Bill Bradley of the New York Knicks. I stopped laughing. Oh God, is Mark going to be pissed or what?

When I arrived home there was a note on the kitchen table from Gina saying that she was spending the night with her friend Linda. I showered, put Merthiolate on my scraped knees and pulled on a sweater and jeans. I looked into the mirror. My lip was already quite swollen and caked with blood. I threw away my ruined white pantyhose and surveyed my torn coat. I sat down to repair it and I suddenly couldn't bear to be alone. I remembered that Taf said he'd call me. I couldn't wait. I called him.

"What is the matter, Kate? You sound strange."

"I had a bad night, that's all."

"Do you wish to talk?"

"Yes."

"Do you wish to come here?"

He checked out my lip, put ice on it and held it there. He listened to my whole story and never once said, "I told you so." He got up from the couch and made me a strong scotch and water. His quiet empathetic attitude made me feel warm and comfortable.

"My God, Taf, what will I do? I think I'm afraid to go back there."

"Surely you are not considering going back...are you?"

"I have to finish what I started. There's still another week to go."

He shook his head and put his arms around me. "Why? Why do you have to be super-nurse? Kathleen Mary, what ever will I do with you?" He began kissing me on my eyes, my nose, my ears, carefully avoiding my bruised mouth. His hands were under my sweater exploring my breasts. He gently pushed me back on the couch and I could feel his erection rubbing on my leg through layers of clothes. For a moment, but only a moment, it seemed right.

"Wait a minute," I said, pushing him away, "I thought we were friends? I thought you didn't care about laying me?"

"No, I never said that. That is all in your mind. Of course I want to lay you. Look into that mirror Kate, and tell me that you really believe that you are one of the boys." He got up off the couch. "Damn it, as good a nurse as you are, I find you physically distracting to work with. I would never hire you to work for me."

I was crushed by his words. How could I have been so stupid? I got up from the couch and walked toward the door, fighting back tears. I hurt inside and out. I felt betrayed, and I wasn't sure by whom.

"Hey, where are you going?"

"Home," I managed to answer, my voice barely audible.

"Come here," he commanded softly. I turned and looked at his outstretched arms, and at the gold ankh glistening around his neck. "We do not have to engage in sex if you do not want to." He smiled, "I win some, lose some. Come here, Kate, we are friends."

I felt warm and safe in his arms. No one could hurt me. No one could frighten me as long as I was there. We settled on the couch, lying there unmoving, listening to the music. After a while, he kissed me on the forehead saying, "Some day Kate, you will learn that screwing is no big deal." I spent the night in his arms, and in that period of time before deep sleep, I knew that I could never be alone with him again.

Taf had early morning surgery and I was home before eight a.m. I tossed my rumpled clothes into the hamper, took a shower, and set about working on my dissertation. My oral defense was scheduled for the second week in May. I sat in front of the typewriter and tried to concentrate, but my mind wasn't on the dissertation. It was on Taf.

His words kept running through my head. In the cold light of day, I didn't like myself. He was right. I had been leading him on. No matter how honest I thought I had been, or how sexually naive, I should have realized what was happening. I couldn't understand why. Why couldn't we have had a Platonic relationship? A relationship that transcended the bed. I wanted to believe it was possible.

Every time I pick up some sort of a banner, take on a cause, I lose sight of the real world. I can give myself an 'A' in sincerity, but that's where it ends. Even my volunteer teaching project—what made me think that I could walk right in there unchallenged?

Why should they accept me? What had I done to earn it? Causes and wars are not won with sincerity; they're won with realism. My whole approach to everything these past months had been a disaster. How could I work on my dissertation, write about the quality of life when I felt the concrete pressure of overwhelming guilt. I'm nothing but an old fashioned tease and a modern liberal do-gooder all rolled into one. My self-esteem hit an all time low. I didn't think that I could ever look Taf in the eye again, but I knew for certain that I'd have to face the ghetto again tomorrow night.

Gina came home about nine a.m.

"What are you doing home?" I asked, "No classes?"

"Bomb scare. One of the buildings where my class is being held is cordoned off and crawling with police. They told us to come back at two…"

I turned away as she talked and walked over to the stove. She stopped talking. She shouldn't have been home so early. I'd had no time to think about explanations. "Want anything?" I asked. "Breakfast? Tea?"

"What's wrong, Mom?"

"Nothing is wrong. Everything's fine."

"What's wrong with your lip?" She was standing behind me. "Look at me."

"It's nothing. I'm okay. It's just that I have to work on finishing my dissertation. I'm writing the summary, conclusions, implications and recommend…" I could feel my throat tightening. I fought off the tears that wanted to take control. Oh no, I won't cry. I turned and pretended to look for an elusive pot in the back of the cupboard.

"Stop turning away. Hold still." She pulled me around.

"You have a fat lip. Your face is bruised. Mom, what happened?" Gina put her arms around me. I couldn't think of a reasonable, logical excuse, so I told her the truth, all of the unnerving incidents in the ghetto the night before. It all poured out too easily.

"Sit down, Mom. I'll make a pot of tea." Role reversal time. Who could have guessed it would come to this? She sat for a minute before speaking. "Okay, now. Chuck in that teaching class. Get out of it now."

"I can't. I'm committed. It's only another week."

"If you came home with a fat bloody lip last night, what will you come home with next?"

"It was my fault. I shouldn't have worn my uniform. I won't let it happen again."

Daughters want perfect mothers. They don't want human beings that make mistakes like ordinary people. They simply don't want to see the warts.

"God, you are so stubborn. Reconsider, please."

I looked up and shook my head. "And don't tell Mark."

"At least switch cars with me. They may be looking for yours. A 240Z isn't exactly low profile."

"I think I'll lie down for a while. I'm really tired." I went into the den, climbed onto the couch and pulled the knitted Afghan around me.

At two that afternoon, I was in the laundry room when I heard a car rolling in on the gravel. The dogs barked half-heartedly; it had to be someone they knew.

"Hi dogs. Where's your mother? I'll bet she's doing what any red-blooded American woman would do on her day off...laundry."

Jenny headed straight for the kitchen and yelled, "Come out, come out, wherever you are. I'm making a pot of tea and I brought some sinful fattening Danish."

Jenny McMahon was hard to ignore, so I went into the

kitchen knowing I'd have to explain away my bruises. I went through the whole story. It didn't seem so bad now—telling it for the third time.

"Gee Kate, I encouraged you to do this. I never dreamed..."

"Well, obviously, neither did I."

Jenny had the unusual habit of really listening. She locked directly into your eyes and wouldn't let you get away. "What aren't you telling me Kate?" The gold in her hazel eyes flickered.

"Nothing."

"Kathleen Mary, it's a sin to tell a lie." She put her face in mine. "Confess."

"I think I'm involved with another man."

"Only you could make a statement like that. What do you mean 'think?' Either you are or you aren't."

Why did I tell her that? Was I trying to assuage my guilt by confessing? Confession may be good for the soul, but it could be hard on a friendship.

She turned her attention to stirring her tea, and finally asked, "Okay, what about this guy, how involved do you think you are?"

I told her about the entire relationship, never mentioning that he was a doctor.

"You mean you were alone with him only two times, twice," she held up two fingers, "and he never even laid you? Oh Kate, you don't even know what the word involved means." Her eyes softened. "Why the big guilt trip? You have nothing to be guilty about."

"But I have. I used him. I was lonely and I used him. I don't think that I can ever forgive myself for that."

"Listen to me. First of all, in a relationship of any kind, both parties are there because they're both getting something out of it. He wouldn't have been there if he wasn't getting something."

"That's not true, Jenny. I took and I gave nothing in

return...except maybe an advanced case of blue balls."

"He took his chances, everyone does in a relationship. Secondly, he sounds like a nice guy. He must have recognized that you were sincere, or else he would have tried to force the issue."

"Please don't tell anyone."

She screwed up her face. "You know me better than that." Jenny paused, "You know a little heavy duty makeup will do wonders."

I sipped my tea. In spite of her logical comments, her reassurance, I felt enormously depressed. I wanted to smile, but I couldn't quite bring it to the surface.

The following day Sally took one look at my lip and figured out what had happened. "Give it up, Kate, you can't win. Try to understand. I know that you don't think in terms of color, but think of it from the black point of view. We've been kicked around one way or another all of our lives by whites, and in case you hadn't noticed...you're white."

"But Sally, I don't believe it's a question of color. They would have attacked any nurse. Besides, I get along great with my kids now. They trust me, and I think I'm helping them."

"Sure, they've gotten to know you over the weeks, but what about those guys in the parking lot? You were lucky this time, but I wouldn't count on being that lucky again."

I was afraid that she was right, but I remained adamant. I went to meet with my class that night. Gina and I exchanged cars in case someone was looking for mine. I sat in the locked car in the parking lot for fifteen minutes getting up the nerve to make a run for it. When I finally thought it was all clear, I took off for the building, breaking the record for the 100-yard dash.

That night I was ineffectual as both teacher and counselor. I jumped at every noise, shied at every shadow and I left there sick with failure. On the way out, I handed my letter of resignation to the social worker, whose only comment was, "I heard…kids gonna miss you."

5

Five days before Easter I left for Brussels. I bought a new raincoat for the rain capital of the world. Although I intended to stay only ten days, I filled two suitcases and a tote. That was Jenny's influence. She supervised the packing and made sure I had something for every possible occasion.

"Ya sure ya didn't forget nuttin, honey?" asked the airport limousine driver as he lifted my bags up onto the rack.

"Shhh," answered Jenny, winking at him, "she's running away from home."

On the plane I thought about Frank. How he would look? I wondered if he had changed even more. Or if I had? I was so apprehensive that I couldn't eat. I couldn't even get into the book Gina had given me, so I closed it on Jenny's gift, a bookmark inscribed with a poem on friendship. Maybe I'd have a drink and watch the movie. I should have been relaxed. My committee approved my dissertation and copies were given to two 'out-of-department readers.' I was ready to defend.

I opened my purse to pay the flight attendant for the drink when I noticed the envelope that Sally had given me the day before. Her familiar scrawl across the front ordered, "To be opened after take-off." There was a short note enclosed, brief and to the point, a typical nurse's note. "Remember how crazy you are about Frank, so don't do anything foolish that might jeopardize your marriage." Taf flashed across my mind. I blushed, wondering if she suspected anything. "Get a good night's sleep and you'll feel better in the morning." Wrapped in a tissue was a green and white capsule. I put the miniature bottle of Scotch in my bag and popped down the Librium with the water. I curled up in my seat and the empty adjacent one, ready to dream about happy marriages that last forever. The flight attendant woke me the next morning an hour before landing.

I had no idea whether or not Frank would meet the plane. It was a working day. I had his address clutched in my hand as I followed the crowd towards customs. I was walking through a large hall when I heard Frank's voice calling my name. I looked up at the tier above and saw him waving and smiling broadly. I waved back and called his name. I raced for the stairs and we met halfway.

As his white Jaguar sped towards town, he told me of the plans he had made for my stay. During the day, he'd arranged for me to apartment hunt, and the evenings were to be like ten Saturday nights. He had even planned for a weekend of riding. He pulled up to a row of town houses that edged a landscaped pond.

"Welcome to my bach pad," he grinned. It was a handsome flat, very tastefully done—much nicer than Taf's. Why am I comparing? A very uncomfortable feeling came over me.

"You can hang your things in the closet. Here's some drawer space..." He stopped talking, held me for a moment and kissed me. "I'm glad you're here, Kate. I've looked forward to it." I needed him to tell me that.

I could rarely tell what Frank was thinking or feeling. He constantly hid behind a cloak of logic and unexpressed emotion. He rarely lost his temper. There were so many times I wanted to have a good knock down, drag out fight, really ventilate. But that isn't possible unless both parties agree. It's difficult to be in the ring without an opponent. I looked into the handsome face of my business-oriented husband and wondered what I really knew about him after all these years.

"So have I, though I must admit, I feel just a little bit wicked being in a bachelor's apart..." I couldn't finish the sentence and I looked down.

"Good. I'm going back to the office. Try to get some sleep so that you can acclimatize yourself to the time change. See you tonight, honey."

I hung up my clothes. I was sure that I couldn't sleep, so I picked up my book, sat on the bed and began to read. The next thing I knew, there was someone in bed with me, forcing a hand between my legs. For the moment, I didn't know where I was and I struck out wildly.

"Hey."

"Oh, Frank, it's you."

"Who were you expect..."

I kissed him and kissed him. I held on to him much tighter than I normally would have. I needed him to hold me, to kiss me.

He did, for a long while, and then became impatient. "Come on, Kate, enough of this kid's stuff. Let's do it."

We did, but there was something missing. I felt the absence of spontaneity on my part. I attributed it to change of time, change of water, and any other change I could think of. It was not the greatest week in my life. It was no one's fault. There was no blame to be placed. I looked at Frank and saw a stranger. He had long hair, dressed differently, and he ordered dinner casually in French. There was a European air about him. He had a sense of belonging that I lacked. I guess I was the stranger, not he. I was the stranger in his strange land. There was nothing that I could touch base with—nothing except the things I'd brought in my suitcases.

We both felt the strain on our relationship. The evening of the eighth day, Frank came home early. We mutually decided to cancel our dinner plans and stay in his apartment. He put together a menu of cheese, pâté and French bread from his rather sparse larder and unending bottles of good wine from his well-stocked wine cabinet. We sat on his bed eating and drinking. We talked and we laughed. It felt like old times. Wine has a way of helping strangers get to know each other.

"Frank, I'd like to go home tomorrow. I haven't been able to find an apartment and one more day won't matter. I'm kind of anxious to get back. My defense is soon."

"Are you coming here in June to live with me?"

I thought of how easy it would be for me not to come here to live. We each had our own lives in different worlds, but I knew that the alternative to living in Frank's new world was living without him in mine.

"I'll be here, Frank. I don't want to live anywhere without you again."

"I'll give it everything I've got, Kathleen...Kate. I'll give you everything I can. But understand...the only thing I can't give you is newness, the newness that you get in a beginning relationship. We've known each other too many years. You can't fault me there." The air was cleared with confirmed commitment, and we made beautiful, free-spirited love with all of the old warmth and passion.

Frank drove me to the airport the next day. After we made our good-byes, I sat waiting at the gate alone. The flight attendant announced that there would be a one-hour delay due to technical trouble and I groaned. The gentleman sitting next to me began a reassuring dialogue "nothing to worry about...flights are always being delayed due to a technical problem...doesn't mean that the plane is unsafe."

I wanted to cry, but the O'Reilly and Mullin clans didn't cry. Everyone was taught "only babies cry." If you dared to snivel you'd be admonished with "if you come home crying, you'll get something to really cry about." And if you did cry everyone would call "cry baby, cry baby..." I was miserable. I wanted to cry, let it all out. Maybe it was latent childhood, or early menopause. As I clenched my teeth and blinked hard, I knew that above all I wanted to be with Frank.

6

I quickly got back into the routine. Being lost in my work always did wonders for my head, and there's nothing like working with dying patients to put one's own priorities in order. I sent in my letter of resignation. On my last working day, Sally said, "Just leave at the end of the day, Kate. Don't say goodbye." I couldn't say goodbye either. I just slipped out the back door when no one was looking. All of my unfinished business was just about concluded.

Frank called the day before my dissertation defense to wish me luck and give some advice. "Remember, you know your material better than anyone in that room, so when you defend, pause first and reply appropriately."

"I'm always appropriate."

"No, you do things like...'if you turn to page eighty-seven, second paragraph'...You show-off." His advice worked. I passed the orals without any problems or corrections. My committee had been comprised of three geniuses—a nun, a Jew, and a lesbian. They were experts in public health, behavioral research and psychology, and they had allowed me to pick their brains.

The following day I awoke full of ambition. I went through my endless books, papers and copious notes trying to establish some semblance of order. I packed some of the undergraduate textbooks, notes from related courses, and wrote a detailed note to Sally explaining how to get a Bachelor of Science in Nursing.

I looked at my watch. I had to go to school to drop off copies of my dissertation. One was to be sent to Ann Arbor, Michigan for printing and binding. One copy would remain in the library and I would keep one for myself. I thought I'd wait for Gina. I wanted to spend as much time with her as possible. The movers were scheduled to come the following week and I'd be off to Europe. I thought that with the termination of work and school, I'd feel a great loss. Instead I felt great relief. And now without those pressures I was anxious to start my new life. Gina waited in the car while I dropped off my dissertation. That was it. My last official act, since I wasn't staying for graduation. We drove home talking over her plans to move in with Alex and her forthcoming visit to Brussels in July with Mark. We were in great spirits.

7

The day before the moving men came, Gina moved in with Alex. Mark decided his home was California. It made sense since he was at Berkeley. He'd leased a house there and rented rooms to his college friends. On the surface, the kids were okay. Suddenly, I began to panic. Unresolved conflict Aaron called it. I couldn't even begin to sort it all out. I was having a difficult time letting go.

"Frank, I want to stay."

"How long?"

"I don't know."

"Give me a time, a date."

"I don't know."

"Two days, two weeks, two years?"

"I don't know, I don't know, I DON'T KNOW."

Chapter Six

"Much of your pain
is self chosen."
     Kahlil Gibran

1

I slept through the days and stared into the nights. At first my only ventures outside Frank's apartment were the necessity walks of Fiona's dog, Nic, a Bouvier des Flanders. No one had wanted the old international champion after my friend died and I insisted on bringing him with me. He was a calling card to my new life, and a constant reminder of Fiona's strength.

Two weeks after my arrival, Frank took me on one of his business trips to Paris. That evening, we sat at a table on the *Rue de la Paix* sipping *Perrier Menthe*. Later we dined under the stars at the seasonally open-roofed restaurant *Lasserre*. The beauty of the city, the romance of the evening was reaching out to me. Frank was reaching out to me. I tried to touch him across the distance with a smile that came from deep inside of me—my first in a long time.

"Welcome back, Kate," he returned the smile.

Later, in our hotel room, we began making love. It felt so good to be back in his arms. Why had it taken me so long to get there?

"Hurry and put on a condom," I whispered.

"I don't have any. I forgot them."

"You forgot them? How could you forget them?"

"And why the hell didn't you stay on the pill?" he snapped.

"Oh, I see, it's my fault. Well, I have news for you. I had enough on my mind without remembering the God damn pill too."

"You know something, Kate, it was a hell of a lot easier being married to Kathleen."

Oh my God, what am I doing? "Frank," I whispered, "I can think of something else we can do."

"Forget it." He rolled over and turned his back to me.

I lay there in injured silence.

2

Frank continued to travel and I spent days on end never hearing English spoken or seeing a familiar face. I was now a dog walker. Nic and I would spend hours in the *Bois de la Cambre*, walking the paths of his ancestors. I frequently wrote to Gina and Mary Ellen. Jenny kept me posted on the local news and Sally sent me all the hospital gossip. I also called my general practitioner, Bob Jorgenson, and asked him to send me a year's supply of the pill.

"No problem," he said, "but Kate, please remember to take one every day."

Early one morning, Frank was preparing to leave on a two-day business trip. He hadn't intended to wake me but I happened to open my eyes just in time to see him putting something into his attaché case. I sat bolt upright.

"You son of a bitch," I said with all the venom I could muster. "You bastard, you couldn't remember them when you were with me."

He turned around, completely unabashed and announced, "Okay. That was one time I forgot. I always carry them. You know that. It's a habit left over from my Navy days."

Frank joined the Navy after completing his senior year at Brooklyn Tech. He was only sixteen but it took the government over a year to catch up with him. By then, he had already served in both the Atlantic and Pacific theaters. After he was mustered out, he earned a Bachelor's at Columbia University on the G.I. Bill of Rights.

"And just because I carry them, it doesn't mean that I use them."

He left the apartment and left me in a speechless rage. My rage was at his coolness. He had brushed away my confrontation without losing a step. I jumped out of bed, ran to the door and opened it. The iron cage elevator was already descending. I raced to the terrace so that I could see his car leaving the building. I watched his Jaguar emerge. I wanted to do something dramatic–jump over the railing and land on his car. I wanted to hurt him even more than he hurt me. Instead, I went back inside, took his photo out of my wallet, threw it in the wastepaper basket and then went back to bed. An hour later, I plucked the photo out of the wastepaper basket with two fingers, and without looking at it, dropped it in the bottom of my dresser drawer.

Early in our marriage, I had never thought about Frank and other women. Not seriously anyway. I'd always been secretly jealous of his secretaries, their business luncheons, parties and whatever other extra-business activities they shared. Later, when I did consider the possibility, I somehow couldn't imagine Frank with anyone. Yet, he had every opportunity. He had good looks, charm, wit, power, and money–certainly all of the pluses. I wondered if there was someone in London, or Paris–or London?

And now I was living in Frank's apartment–not our apartment, not our home but his bachelor pad. Early one morning, Frank was already at work, and I was getting ready to resume my dog walking routine, when the door buzzer sounded. It had to be either the concierge or the laundress, neither of whom could speak a word of English. I opened the door.

"Hi, I just happened to be in the neighborhood..."

Mark was standing in the hallway. I was overjoyed to see him. He joined Nic and me walking in the *bois*. We watched the birds and the waterfowl around the ponds. We tried to pick out known species from our part of the world and identify new ones from the book Gina had sent me. His presence eased the tension between Frank and me, or perhaps we were just too polite to allow it to surface while he was there.

Most days, leaving a tired footsore Nic at home, we explored the city via the Tram System.

"Where is it going?" I asked.

"I don't know," he shrugged, "Let's find out."

With his own spirit of adventure, Mark was rekindling mine. I enjoyed the tram rides and that day we ended up at the Atomium. The Atomium was a vestige from the Belgian World's Fair in 1958. It represented an atom of iron and the nine spheres were the component electrons. It was 350 feet high. Mark held on to me as the elevator sped to the top. Escalators linked the spheres and their exhibitions illustrated peaceful uses of the atom.

I was getting into our tram experiences and thought it better than going by car. It was safer. Belgian drivers frightened me. It seemed as if men drove using their cars as an extension of their manhood. I didn't want to compete with any of them for road space or join them in their national pastime of four-on-the-floor Belgian Roulette.

During one of our journeys the tram we were riding hit

another tram. The force of the impact threw me backwards and I cracked my head on one of the metal poles. I held my head in my hands as if I was afraid it would fall off.

"Blood is running between your fingers, Mom. Better let me look."

"Scalp wounds always look worse than they are," I said. He forced my hands away. They snapped back again into position. He pulled me off the tram and pushed me into a taxi. At a nearby hospital, a French-speaking doctor shaved and sutured my scalp. The familiar antiseptic smells made me miss working more than ever. I left the room without understanding a word of what the doctor said. I didn't care.

The hospital was very near our new apartment, in the borough of Uccle. It was named after the World War I heroine, Edith Cavell. She was a British nurse working as a matron in a Belgian hospital, and alleged to have helped hundreds of allied solders escape from occupied Belgium to the neutral Netherlands. In 1915, she was arrested, court-martialed, and shot by a German firing squad. The night before her execution she told the Anglican chaplain, "Patriotism is not enough. I must have no hatred or bitterness for anyone."

Mark was waiting in the hall. "You okay, Mom?" He reached out and hugged me.

"You bet I am."

When we reached the street, I thought about "time" having been given the credit for healing all wounds. I suppose it does deserve some credit with regard to physiological wounds. In healthy tissue a wound heals at its optimal rate, and there's no way in which this rate can be accelerated. But all the time in the world can't heal psychological wounds—only the presence of other people does that.

I took the scarf that was looped around the strap of my handbag (a fashion statement of the times) and tied it around my head, hiding my latest battle scar. "Let's walk home, Mark."

Frank was already at the apartment when we arrived. "Where have you two been? It's late. Jesus, what happened to your hands, Kate?"

I looked down at my bloodstained hands.

"Mark, what the hell has happened to your mother?"

"It's okay, honey," I said, "It really is."

We told Frank the story and it no longer seemed so bad. The minor tram accident, the visit to the emergency room brought everything into perspective. I missed working. And I decided to do something about it.

A few days later, we were sitting down to one of my rare home-cooked meals. I wasn't doing too well in that department. The week before, I had picked out what I thought was a chicken in the supermarket. When we couldn't cut it with a steak knife, I realized that *poule de l'annee* must mean tough old bird or stewing chicken. Tonight things looked a lot better. I had picked out a steak. It looked like a steak. I knew it was a steak. The label had *"steak"* printed on it.

"What kind of steak is this, Kate?" asked Frank, after cutting into the meat and tasting it.

"Tastes different," commented Mark.

"I don't know. It's really very lean looking, isn't it? I have another in the freezer," I said getting up, "I'll look." I pulled open the freezer door and read the label aloud, *"Steak Cheval."*

"Ugh," groaned Mark, pushing his plate away, "You'd better learn French, Mom. This is horsemeat."

Frank dropped his knife.

Nic was the only one eating and growing fatter with each mistake. I was making a mental note to sign up for French lessons when the phone rang. "Hello. Gina? Gina, how are you? Are you all right? Are you... Uh huh, uh huh..." Mark and Frank were looking at me. I put my hand over the receiver. "She and Alex want to get married...right away."

3

I was no doubt the first in the history of mothers of the bride to wear an expensive Parisian creation and a Franciscan monk's hair-do. Mark removed the sutures and Jenny helped me conceal my tonsure with flowers and clever hair pinning.

Gina was a beautiful bride. She radiated happiness and I wanted her to be happy for the rest of her life. I watched as Frank proudly walked her down the aisle. He lifted her veil and kissed her. He seemed reluctant to let her go. I understood. I was reluctant, too.

We stayed briefly in New York. Gina was honeymooning. Mark decided to do some climbing in the Tetons with his friend before returning to California, and my mom was going to New Bedford to be with her sister. I was also anxious to leave. I didn't live here any more either.

4

Two evenings after our return, Frank made dinner plans with one of his American clients, Larry Prior, and his girlfriend, Chantal. Larry was Frank's age and Chantal–she was young, maybe twenty, twenty-one, but she looked sixteen. Although her mother was French and her father Italian, Chantal was Belgian. Her parents had met in Brussels and had decided to settle in neutral territory and bring up their daughter as a European. Chantal was petite, with short dark hair and warm brown eyes. She was decidedly French looking with that French air of perfection.

In spite of our language difficulties and our age differences, we hit it off right away. She spoke French, Italian and Flemish fluently. Her English was not that good but as compared to my French, it was great. I had just enrolled in a French language class at the *Université Libra de Bruxelles* and we struck a bargain. I would help her with English and she would help me with French. At the time, it seemed that I would get the better part of the deal.

Frank and I began seeing more and more people socially. I was trying to fill my calendar, do whatever I could to keep busy, and we spent our leisure time soaking up European culture at museums, castles and folklore festivals.

My favorite was the *Grand Place*. It was the heart of Brussels, both geographically and spiritually. The buildings were ancient guildhalls of the Middle Ages covered in pure gold leaf. The perfect Gothic architecture had just one flaw, an off-center door in the main tower. The legends are that the architect committed suicide by jumping off the tower when he realized his error–or that the gentleman that hired him had thrown him off.

The *Grand Place* has many other attractions. We enjoyed the flower market, with vendors wearing sabots, the giant chessboard with live costumed participants. Each of the knights was astride a black and a white horse. Everyone knew that the game was over when the Black Queen curtsied to the White King.

The first time I saw the *Grand Place,* it was two in the morning and after two glasses of wine. I stood in the middle of the square and looked up at the navy blue velvet sky. I lowered my gaze to the glittering gold Gothic buildings. I twirled around on the Belgian block surface, the same surface that had been trod upon in the Middle Ages. It was one of the most beautiful sights I'd ever seen. It was a magical moment.

Behind the *Hôtel de Ville* (in the *Grand Place*), we found the *Mannekin Pis*, a bronze statue of a small boy sculpted in the 17th century. The boy is known as Brussels' "Oldest Inhabitant." The *Maison du Roi* displays his various wardrobes from countries all over the world. I wasn't happy to see that the costume from the United States was that of a cowboy. The Belgians must have thought that all Americans were cowboys. The *Maison du Roi* was also called the King's Breadhouse because bread was sold there during the 12th century.

5

After two months in Europe, I was experiencing a cultural change. I was coping beautifully with the communal toilet system. I'd reached a point where I could walk coolly past a man who was utilizing a urinal, enter a half-door stall and urinate uninhibitedly. Not bad, considering that until recently I ran the tap water if I thought that I was too noisy. Why I'd been so uptight over a simple biological function, I'll never know.

One of Frank's clients, Robert Gilles, invited us to a cocktail party at his large country place north of the city. As we crossed the foyer on our way to the salon, the stately Christine Gilles and her husband greeted us warmly.

"Would you like to wash your hands, *Madame* deMeo? It was a long drive from the city."

"*Oui, merci, Madame* Gilles," I smiled.

She ushered me gracefully towards a door off the foyer, opened it and gestured. She smiled. I smiled. We both did a lot of smiling. We had to. Neither of us could think of anything to say. She had exhausted most of her English with her opening lines and the only French I could remember was *bonjour* and *merci*. So I *merci-ed* again, walked into the room, locked the door and looked around. Oh shit. She really did think that I wanted to wash my hands. There was nothing in the room but a washbasin, little soaps shaped like strawberries and a raft of monogrammed guest towels. For a moment I considered using the washbasin. It would have required some difficult gymnastics even if I had been taller. I ran the water, pretended to wash my hands, crumpled a guest towel and left. Unfortunately the running water had only served to increase my kidney perfusion.

I walked back to the salon. Guests were milling around, still others arriving. Everyone was engaged in the normal cocktail party chitchat, in a least four different languages. People were introducing themselves, shaking hands—buon giorno, gutentag, buenas dias. I nodded and smiled a lot.

I heard someone use *comment allez-vous* as a greeting. With that added to my *bonjour* and *merci*, I'd have to smile a lot more to make up for my deficient vocabulary. My jaw was beginning to ache and I was sure that I looked like Alice's Cheshire cat, when I spotted Frank talking with a group of people. I joined them, nodded a hello and looked at the pretty blonde-haired woman on his right. Women have an innate ability, upon entering a room, to single out their competition and, at the same time, assess the men who are interested in them. The blonde had huge boobs and seemed to be hanging on to Frank's every word. I had no idea that his views on brand equity were so fascinating. It was true that Frank would have talked business with anyone, any time, any place, but the blonde with the boobs made it all the more pleasant for him. I tried to follow what he was saying but the pressure on my bladder was now putting pressure on my brain.

I found my hostess and asked, "*Où est la salle de bain?*" Oh God, was it *de* or *du*? Who cared? At least I'd found three more French words. She looked puzzled. Then Madame Gilles, still smiling, regally escorted me to the most beautiful bathroom I'd ever seen. I wasn't smiling anymore.

The room was totally mirrored from floor to ceiling. There was an Olympic-sized tub in the center of the floor, two matching washbasins and a bidet, in what my hostess described as *Copen Bleu*. But where the hell was the toilet? A plumbing error? I doubted it. Christine wasn't the sort of woman to permit an error. I think that I might have used the bidet had she not been there. Maybe she was under the impression that I wanted the grand tour. She was opening a secret door behind one of the mirrored panels. Well, this is it, at last. I peered through the door in disbelief. Jesus, Mary and Joseph—a sauna.

Didn't these people urinate? I knew that they did. I learned that in NUR 101. They couldn't possibly reabsorb their urine in some strange way, could they? Like Urea Frost?

No, they urinate. Everyone does. I learned that in BIO 101. So does the lovely Christine. The question was where. I had to muster up some sort of communicable French and find out where it was hidden.

"*S'il vous plait, Madame* Gilles," I ventured, "*Où est la W.C.?*" The blank look told me that I'd struck out. Was it my pronunciation, choice of words, grammar? I didn't know and I didn't have time to find out. My bladder had reached beyond its limit. Then I remembered the concierge's little boy holding his crotch and jumping up and down. Good God, what was it he had said? Substituting *Madame* Gilles for *Maman*, I said, "*Madame Gilles, je dois faire pee-pee.*"

She raised her eyebrows. "*La toilette?*"

All at once, Christine understood the urgency of the situation and led me rapidly to another room equipped with a real honest to goodness toilet.

I shouted, "*Merci*," slammed the door with one hand and pulled down my pantyhose and bikinis with the other. I sat luxuriating through what seemed like a five-minute non-stop stream. I didn't care what it sounded like. All I felt was beautiful, blessed relief.

6

Shortly after the Gilles' party, Chantal and I were lunching together. I told her I had decided that I'd been sitting around long enough.

"It's been almost a year since I left New York. I've done all of the tourist things. Taken language courses at the *Université Libre de Bruxelles*. I've written some articles based on my research on aging, which will soon be published, and I've been working on a book."

She wrinkled her brow. She was trying to keep up with my English. I slowed down. "I'm bored out of my mind, tired of being a kept woman. But most of all, Chantal, I miss nursing. I'm going to get a job."

"It is not possible to do this," she said, her large brown eyes widening, "not possible for a stranger."

"Foreigner, not stranger," I said, correcting her, "Maybe so, but I'm going to give it 'the all-American try.'"

"All-American try, Catleen. *Je ne comprend pas.* What means 'all-American try?'"

Chapter Seven

"Work is love made visible."
                Kahlil Gibran

1

Most buildings in Brussels are very old and very beautiful. The buildings of the *Hôpital Sainte Gudule* were just very old. I was sitting on a creaking bench facing a door marked *Directrice*. What the hell am I doing here? How do I have the nerve to ask for a job? Chantal is right. I am a foreigner. I haven't a work permit, a Belgian license, and I can't even speak the language. My few lessons at the *Université Libre de Bruxelles* hadn't exactly prepared me for this interview—unless of course I was asked to open the window, close the door, or count to twenty. Unhappily, I doubted that any of those actions would be required of me this morning.

Even attaining this interview was a little dishonest. Chantal did the telephoning. She didn't exactly say that she was me, but then she didn't exactly say she wasn't.

"*Madame* deMeo?" queried a formidable starched and veiled

woman who appeared in the doorway.

The bench let out a groan as I shot to my feet, and with my best accent I recited, "*Oui, c'est moi.*"

"*Entrez, s'il vous plaît, Madame,*" she gestured toward the door. As we took our seats on opposite sides of her disturbingly bare desk, she introduced herself as *Mademoiselle* Dauphin, *La Directrice des Infirmieres.*

"*Mademoiselle,*" I started and then hesitated, feeling disrespectful calling her *Mademoiselle.* My Irish Catholic conscience was genuflecting again. I'd never addressed a nun as anything but Sister, except for Sister Mary Jerome during my dissertation defense–and only when she insisted. I tried to think of the correct word in French, then rather than take the chance on coming up with the wrong one, I braced myself against my background and began again. "*Mademoiselle...*" Why should I feel guilty? She introduced herself as *Mademoiselle,* didn't she? If I considered myself a liberated woman, then why would I not allow her the privilege of being a liberated nun?

"*Mademoiselle,*" I started for the third time with complete confidence, and went on in rather loud halting French, enhanced with flourishing gesticulations. I was trying to communicate that I was a damn good nurse from New York. I proposed that she allow me to work in the hospital's intensive care unit for a couple of months, without pay. Then if they liked my work, they could pay me–if not, ask me to leave. No hard feelings. A simple business proposition. An equitable one I thought.

She stared at me with astonishment. An instant later, *La Directrice* was on the telephone making important sounding noises in rapid French. Either she'd accepted my offer or she was calling the psych unit to have me committed or worse, the American Embassy, to have me deported as an undesirable alien. After the third phone call she ushered me into the next room, shook my hand in the Belgian one-pump style, and left me with another stranger. I didn't know who she was or what was expected of me. I looked at the woman behind the desk.

She was about my age, raven haired and very attractive.

"Do you prefer that I speak English?" she asked. Her voice was friendly and her English made it seem even more so.

"Oh yes, please do," I replied with obvious relief.

"First I help you to fill out this paper."

I think I got the job...

"The hospital will arrange for a work permit."

I did get the job.

She handed me a schedule of appointments for the remainder of the week along with cards of introduction. I looked at the list. It seemed simple enough.

mardi, 09 heures, Blood test & x-ray at Ste. Gudule.

mecredi, 14 heures, Minister of Education.

jeudi, 10 heures 30, Minister of Nursing.

vendredi, 15 heures, Physical, Le Médecin de Travail.

"...and finally," she said, "you may report to this office on the Monday next at nine o'clock with a lock for your *vestiaire* and comfortable shoes. The hospital laundry service provides the uniforms and bonnets. How do you say bonnets in English, 'caps?' Yes? It is usual to begin at seven o'clock, but *Mademoiselle* wishes personally to introduce you to the *Service— Soin Intensif-Réanimation.*"

"Why do you call her *Mademoiselle?*"

"Because she is not married."

"Yes, I realize that, but in the States we call nuns 'Sister.'"

"Nun? I do not under...Oh, do you mean *Religieuse?*" She was laughing. "Why would you think *Mademoiselle* Dauphin is a...a nun."

"Well, she wears a veil..." I was beginning to get the feeling that another cultural curve was coming my way.

"*Madame* deMeo, in our country, nurses may choose to wear a veil like *Mademoiselle*, or a bonnet like they do in your country. Many of the older nurses prefer a veil. A nun, how amusing," she continued to laugh.

I was not amused. To think that I'd spent all of those years being educated by Dominican Nuns and now I couldn't even tell a nurse from a nun-nurse. I smiled at my own bad pun and finally there was nothing to do but laugh along with her.

"My name is Simone Lacroix. If you have any problem, please call on me. *Bonne chance, Madame.*"

I thanked her and left the office walking two feet above the ground. My feet suddenly came to a screeching halt and crashed onto the cracked tile floor. "Hey, wait a minute," I asked myself aloud, "how come this was so easy?"

"It is very difficult to find nurses willing to do the hard work of intensive care, and above all, without pay," echoed a now familiar voice into the empty corridor.

I didn't care about the money. I needed to work as a nurse. Unlike Florence Nightingale, who had a "calling from God," I just had a calling. I believed that a good nurse could make a difference. I was a good nurse. And now I had the opportunity to bring all of my education and experience to *Ste. Gudule.*

I couldn't wait to tell Frank the good news. I drove straight to his office and asked the receptionist if I could telephone him from her desk. She put me through.

"Frank deMeo," announced his business, nothing-but-business voice.

"Hi, it's me. Are you busy?"

"I'm never too busy to talk to a good-looking broad with big tits. What do you have in mind?"

"Lunch if you're not already booked."

"Nothing I can't break. To tell you the truth, I'm intrigued. You've never asked me to lunch before. Only problem is that I'll have to be back early for a meeting. How soon can you get here?"

"How about twenty seconds?" I said, hung up, and ran back to his office.

We slid into his favorite booth at his favorite restaurant.

"Okay Kate, I know you're high on something. What's happened?"

I sat smugly, sipping my wine. Then I put the glass on the table and looked Frank squarely in the eye. "I have a job," I announced. "A real job. At *Ste. Gudule*. Forty hours per week. I start Monday."

He looked surprised and happy. I related the whole interview, exaggerating the French and my cultural catastrophe to make him laugh. Things are always funny in retrospect, never when you're living them. I left out one very small detail, but his business acumen picked up on it immediately.

"How much are they paying you?"

"I was afraid you'd ask that." I filled in that small detail and vigorously began to defend my position.

"Whoa, not so fast. I'm not criticizing you, honey. I think it's a great idea you're getting your foot in the door that way. As a matter of fact," he laughed, "they don't know it but I would have paid them to give you a job."

I'm sure he would have. He wants me to be happy. Besides, if I'm happy–he's happy.

"I know that you haven't been happy not working. You don't exactly mark time quietly." He leaned across the table and kissed me, then raised his wine glass in a toast, "Happy Nursing."

2

The tech who took blood from my arm on Tuesday morning was an artist. She had to be in order to get into my small veins with the first stick. My first impression of *Ste. Gudule* was a good one.

Next stop radiology. A routine P.A. and Lateral, full front and side view–a mug shot of the chest. The technician pointed out a two-by-two curtained cubicle and I removed everything from the waist up. I looked around for a hospital gown or some kind of cover up. There was none. I could hear the technician's voice calling, "*Madame* Moo-lan, *s'il vous plaît, Madame* Moo-lan, *s'il vous plaît.*"

I had no way of knowing that, in Belgium, a woman never loses the identity of her maiden name. Her *nom de jeune fille* legally remains on all documents for life. I thought it was a great idea, but I wished that I had known about it a little sooner.

The cubicle curtain pulled open and the technician stood there glowering, "*Madame* Moo-lan, *s'il...vous...plaît.*"

I grabbed the curtain and held it in front of me, "deMeo," I said, "*Madame* deMeo."

He held up a card between his face and mine. It read Mullin, Kathleen. He gestured wildly for me to follow him to have my film taken. I too gestured wildly that before leaving my refuge I would need a hospital gown, or something. Things were not done that way at *Ste. Gudule.* The technician was impatiently tugging at my arm, then pulled me out of the cubicle. There was a bench filled with men, also waiting to be x-rayed. They were baring their chests too but somehow that fact did little to alter my feelings. I folded my arms in front of me and I flushed with embarrassment. I couldn't understand the injustice of it all. In the States, I had always sent my patients to x-ray covered from their ears to their toes. The technician was roughly trying to pull my arms down and push my unyielding body into position against the machine, which was in full view. I had obviously incurred his wrath.

Stay cool, I advised myself. You're over-reacting. He isn't the least interested in your boobs. His only real concern is in finishing his x-rays and going to lunch. Right? I realized my analysis was incorrect when he gave me an appreciative smile accompanied by a raised eyebrow while x-raying my lateral. That just made the return trip to the cubicle, past the bench of waiting men, even more difficult.

The next two days of appointments with the ministers were uneventful. The Minister of Nursing couldn't understand why a nurse would need a college degree, much less a Master's and a Ph.D. The Minister of Education, after seeing 'Dean's List' all over my transcripts, advised me, with the wisdom of his years, that it was not a good idea to be on anyone's list.

I was beginning to have my fill of the differences in cultural attitudes when, on that Friday, Chantal and I had lunch with some European women.

After I told my x-ray story, a Swedish woman replied, "Oh, you Americans are so concerned about anyone seeing your bodies. What makes it such a big thing with you? Everyone has a body and they vary just as faces do, and I don't see you covering your face."

The real shock was yet to come. That afternoon I had an appointment for my physical with the *Médecin de Travail*, the official doctor who signs all the work permits. At three o'clock, while being ushered towards another cubicle, the nurse reached inside my blouse and slapped a Tuberculosis Patch Test strip on my chest. She instructed me to remove all articles of clothing except underwear, shoes and stockings. As we came closer to what looked like a telephone booth, we were overwhelmed by heavy body odor. It must really have been deadly because the nurse had me wait while she ran off to get a can of aerosol deodorizer. She sprayed the room thoroughly, then pushed me in and closed the door. I gasped, clutching my throat with my hand. That wasn't a deodorizer. That was bug spray. The combined effects of body odor and bug juice encouraged my brain to tell my nose not to breathe. I held my breath as long as I was able. When my lungs rebelled, I opened the door a fraction to catch a bit of air.

An unseen hand on the outside, slammed the door admonishing, *"Madame, s'il vous plaît."*

I was sure that I was turning blue. Damn her, she left me to die alone of respiratory failure. Then I noticed another door in the cubicle. I decided to try it. Anything was better than not breathing. I cracked the door a fraction of an inch. Another unseen hand slammed the door shut. This time it was from the inside. It was mine.

"*Madame, s'il vous plaît,*" barked a man's voice. That door opened directly into an office.

I slumped down on the bench, pulled off my blouse and held it over my nose. I cautiously tried inhaling. Ahh, that's better. The filtering aspect of the material and the fragrance of my perfume helped some. At least I could breathe the toxic aerosol without pain. I thought that I might as well finish undressing. That way it would be easier for whoever performed the post mortem.

I stripped down to my delicate blue lace spit-through bikinis and bra. I've always had a thing about underwear. I suppose that too is part of my legacy from my mother, Mary Ellen. At an early age, she instilled in me the absolute dread of being hit by a car and taken to the hospital wearing imperfect underwear. I never worried about being dead or maimed, only of the embarrassment of being caught in undesirable undergarments. Over the years, I exaggerated Mary Ellen's instruction into designer bras and panties of beautiful fabrics and colors. When I worked on accident victims in the ER, I never had time to notice anything except their trauma. It's funny how these things take root in childhood. It no longer mattered how it all started. I enjoyed wearing pretty lingerie. It felt good next to my skin and it made me feel good all over.

There was a rap on the door that led to the office and a voice instructing me to enter. I rose tentatively to my feet, surprised to find that I had survived the hospital gas chamber. I automatically grabbed the oversized cape-like toweling that was hanging in the cubicle, enveloped myself and walked through the door. I faced a fairly good-looking middle-aged man who was sitting behind a desk, looking as if he were too busy to see me. He had to be the doctor. After some paper shuffling, he spoke without looking up, "*Bonjour. Vous êtes...Madame...Moo-lan."*

"deMeo," I answered, "no Mullin. *Je suis* Madame deMeo. *Je suis*, eh, no... *Je* was, you know, past tense, *Mademoiselle* Mullin." I waived my hand over my shoulder in an attempt to indicate past tense. I couldn't get used to being called *Madame* Mullin. It was a total contradiction in terms. Anyway, I had been a deMeo longer than a Mullin.

He gave me a patronizing look as I was trying to decide on my name, then resumed, *"Madame* Moo-lan..." He asked a few questions, grunting here and there, then asked me to go into the adjoining room for a physical examination. Upon entering the room, he pointed to some pegs on the wall. I realized that I was still holding my oversized shoulder bag, so I hung it on one of the pegs. I followed him to the end of the room and set myself on the edge of the small examining table.

"And where do you think you are going?" he snapped in near-perfect English, "To a ball?"

"I don't understand." I couldn't figure out what I had done, why he was so angry or what he was talking about.

"This," he said, fingering the terry towel, "is supposed to be an evening wrap?"

"No, it is not an evening wrap," I started slowly, understanding his implication. "It's a drape, a drape that is utilized during patient examinations."

"Are you suggesting that drapes are used in the United States?" He pronounced it drapps.

"I'm not suggesting," I fought back with cool conviction, "I'm telling you. In the United States we protect our patient's privacy during any examination, x-ray for example, whenever necessary." I was still bristling from Monday's episode.

"You will tell me nothing of the kind. I lived and worked in the United States for one year." His voice had increased another decibel.

"Really? Well, I lived and worked there a lot longer than that. I was born there."

The whole thing had evolved into a small, childish war. I

was furious. I had not raised my voice, but more than likely, my blood pressure.

"Very well," he said as he deliberately walked to the window and sat on the sill with folded arms. "You may walk back to the peg, hang up your DRAPP, and only then shall I proceed with the examination."

"Really?" I said, sliding off the table with a closed mouth smile, "and you my good doctor can go..."

"I think you should consider that I am the only person qualified to sign permits of work," he interrupted, "and I am a very busy man." He looked at his watch adding just the right ingredient, pressure.

I stood there hesitating, my id, ego and superego battling for the custody of this situation.

My id said, "Just tell him to go fuck himself, Kate. You don't need this job. You don't need any job."

My ego countered, "Better not, Kathleen, he won't sign your work permit and you really want to work."

Neither of them listened to my superego hovering in the background saying, "Besides, Kathleen Mary, it's socially and culturally unacceptable to tell someone to fuck themselves, especially a doctor...and coming from a nurse. Tsk, tsk."

Oh shit, what'll I do? It would probably be better for Frank if I forgot the whole thing right now. Bad enough I stayed in New York his first year here all because of nursing. Now that I'm living here, how will it look for the wife of the Executive Vice President to be schlepping to the local Bellevue every day? *Le Médecin de Travail* looked at his watch again, increasing the pressure. I could feel the vasodilatation. Damn.

Let's keep it real, Kate, my ego was still fighting.

I really want this job. I have to work as a nurse.

I walked to the peg and hung up the article in question, half expecting to hear a big band playing "A Pretty Girl is Like a Melody." I could feel his gaze on my back. You were wrong, Mary Ellen. I've just been run over by a truck. I'm in the hospital wearing my beautiful underwear and I am embarrassed. Damn him anyway. Well, I refuse to be intimidated. I paused, pretended I was Jenny, drew a deep breath, straightened my back, threw my nose into the air and attacked the space between the table and me. It wasn't until I sat down that he slowly got off the windowsill and walked toward me.

He checked my blood pressure. "Your *tension* is elevated," he commented with what I thought was pleasure. It didn't merit a reply. Next he checked my heart and lungs. When he began putting his things away, I thought he had finished. I started to leave when he put a restraining hand on my shoulder. He asked me to stand at one end of the room with my eyes closed, arms outstretched, walk directly back to him and touch him at the opposite end of the room.

"What for?" I asked, dumbfounded.

"It is to test your equilibrium," he answered with an absolutely straight face. "Do not open your eyes, or be afraid of falling. I will be sure to catch you."

I started to say something but my winning ego interrupted by saying, "walk."

I walked.

"Good," he said, after I had completed his directive. "Now turn your body with your back to me and touch your toes." He put his hands lightly on my hips and I instinctively flinched.

"And this is routine for, Scoliosis?"

"Yes, that is correct."

"Don't you think you're standing a little close?"

"*Madame.* If you please."

I touched my toes. He was standing so close that as I bent, my posterior brushed against him. I felt sick and I returned to an upright position on his command.

"That is all. *Fini. Merci.* Thank you, *Madame* Moo-lan."

I grabbed my shoulder bag and ran back to the cubicle without the terry wrap. I couldn't get out of there fast enough. Okay, I had my God damn examination by *le Médecin de Travail.* He'll sign my papers and I'll never have to go back there again.

Once back in the apartment, I stripped down all the way and stepped into a bubble bath filled to my chin. I closed my eyes and allowed myself to sink below the water level. After a few seconds, I pushed my head up through the hot sudsy water, feeling cleansed. The whole scene upset me. I'd never had a physical like that before, and I'd never witnessed one like it as a nurse. Maybe that Swedish woman was right. Maybe we do make a big thing of our bodies. But I really didn't know where the puritanical American left off and the right to personal privacy began. There had to be some middle ground where I could tread comfortably.

3

Working at *Ste. Gudule* was different. Like our clinics, the patient's doctor was the luck of the draw, but unlike any medical facility in the United States, there was no such thing as a release form signed with knowledgeable consent. Patients were subjected to whatever tests, surgery and treatment *le médecin* decided upon. No questions asked. Malpractice laws did not exist. *Les infirmieres* (the nurses) did not need to carry insurance coverage because nurses simply followed doctor's orders and were protected by the system.

The *service* where I was working was called *Réanimation, Réa* for short. The *Chef de Service* was *Monsieur* Anton, an unsmiling little man with cold gray eyes. *Madame* Descamps, the *Chef des Infirmieres,* was his complete opposite. She was kind to everyone and gave reports with the drama of an Italian opera. She was heavyset and did rounds noisily in her clogs.

Réa was broken up into a five-bed *Cardiac Chambre.* Four of the beds were in one room and the fifth in a secluded area out of view of the rest of the *service.* This private room was frequently reserved for dignitaries, celebrities and royalty and their dossiers would be labeled *Madame* or *Monsieur* X. There was a four-bed *Respiratoire Chambre*, and three single-occupant rooms clustered together at the opposite end of the hall. Any diagnosis might be found in any room regardless of the label. There was a single utility room, a storage room, and a kitchen. *Le bureau* was the office and there was a very small doctor's room with a desk and bed for whomever was on night duty. The equipment and the facilities were obsolete and some of the procedures bordered on the primitive.

I quickly discovered that it wasn't just my own personal experience. Patients were not draped routinely during an examination. It didn't seem to matter which part of the anatomy was under scrutiny. The patient was entirely exposed to whatever elements were there. The staff would gather around to voice their opinions or to make comments—including the cleaning people.

My basic problem had nothing to do with the hospital but rather with my inadequate knowledge of the French language. During my first week, I gave a cardiac patient a slice of salt-free bread when what he really wanted was a bedpan. It left the staff howling with laughter, the patient wondering how Americans use a slice of bread, and me realizing that I'd have to gain some control over the language.

Marie Louise gave me my first practical lesson. *"LE pain,"* said Marie Louise as she held up a loaf of bread. *"LA panne."* She pointed to a bedpan.

"But the pronunciation of *pain* and *panne* is the same," I moaned.

"LE sel," she poured salt into her hand from a shaker. *"LA selle,"* she delicately held her nose and pointed again to the bedpan.

"They sound alike too." How can such a beautiful language be so confusing? In English, articles are always neuter. In French they are masculine or feminine, and *le* and *la* before a word can be of extraordinary importance. Now I fully realized what I had done. The unwitting patient wanted a bedpan for a bowel movement and the witless nurse had given him a slice of salt-free bread. But if you stopped to think about it, *le* and *la* made no sense whatsoever. For example, vagina (*le vagin*) is masculine and penis (*la verge*) is feminine. How can I possibly have faith in such an illogical language? But I was not in the least bit discouraged. I had nowhere to go but up.

In the meantime, I thought I'd be okay if I stuck to medical terminology, but that turned out to be confusing too. Martine asked me to assess a patient's PVC. I reported that I found no signs of PVC's (Premature Ventricular Contractions), but I did note that the Central Venous Pressure line had not been turned off properly. She looked puzzled. I knew something was lost in the French to French translation. We finally sorted it all out. It seems that she really had wanted me to assess what she called a PVC, but to her it was the Pressure Venous Centrale. In the U.S. it was Central Venous Pressure (CVP). Who could have guessed that they'd call a CVP a PVC.

"Then what do you call a Premature Ventricular Contraction?" I asked.

"Extra systole."

I nodded. That was the first bit of logic that I'd heard in this language.

I began picking up phrases much the way a child does. I never knew exactly what I was saying, but I learned which sounds elicited certain responses. With this method, my French was not developing into the well-bred garden variety, but rather, a weedy idiomatic *Bruxellesoise*. My very first phrase was *"tu me casses les pieds,"* the French equivalent of "you're busting my chops." And they were, they really were.

4

Frank was happy in his job. He traveled to the major capitals of Europe, and he was even happier now that I was caught in something of my own. I'm sure he was genuinely concerned about my feelings but I think, most of all, it assuaged any guilt he might have had over his own freedom.

With the passing weeks I found myself changing. I was consciously aware of the fact that I was a desirable woman. I suppose it was Taf who first made me realize that. On the Continent, the mature woman was in.

I remembered way back when Jenny used to tease me about never recognizing a pass. Even at fourteen, Gina could read a pass at twenty paces. Once when we were waiting for our old Woody station wagon at the car wash, a man who was also waiting pointed to the book I had under my arm and asked, "What's so interesting about Hong Kong?"

He displayed a cavalier smile, and pushed at the book with his index finger. After I gave him a three-minute history lecture, he nodded and walked away.

Gina shrugged and said, "Really, Mom, do you think he was burning for the facts on opium and tea in 1841?"

I don't suppose I'd ever really thought about that either. I'd always answered questions literally. I responded to everything as if I was answering Sister Brigid's questions in a classroom. A habit from childhood—a lifetime away.

When I thought about my earliest recollection of my grandmothers, I realized that they had been my first lesson in the differences between physiological and chronological age. Kathleen Mary O'Reilly wore a black dress and shawl. She spoke with a brogue and her long hair was pinned up in a bun on the top of her head. There was always a pot of dark bitter tea brewing on the stove and her many cats purred, stretched and lazed about in their good life. Margaret Mary Mullin couldn't have been more different. She wore plus fours and bobbed her sandy hair. She lightly rouged her cheeks and mouth, and she drove her own car. She was so American that she looked and behaved as if she were a member of the DAR.

Mary Ellen, my mother, said that she didn't act her age, but Margaret didn't care much what anyone thought. As a matter of fact, Mary Ellen looked and acted more like Margaret Mullin than she did like Kate O'Reilly.

Martin Malachy Mullin was a good dad. I never knew my grandfathers, so Marty took on that role too. He and Grandma Margaret used to surreptitiously give me candy treats or sips of coffee from their cups. I never did like coffee, but I went along with their game because I loved them. These were our little secrets and were to be kept from Mary Ellen at all costs.

Marty made his living, and a decent one at that, as a horse trainer. He worked for J. Howard Adams, who gave my dad unconditional authority, not only with the training, but also the buying and selling of his horses. They raced their horses primarily at Belmont and Santa Monica. When I was ten years old, he took me to a horse auction and told me that I had to sit still and be ever so quiet. Horse after horse was paraded out on a taut lead line. I waited for Dad to bid, but he just sat there with his pipe clutched between his teeth. I was surprised to find that he had not only bid, but had bought two horses that day simply by making the smallest gesture with his briar pipe. When one of the horses from that auction became "Filly of the Year," everyone shook Marty's hand and slapped him on the back. Mr. Adams gave him a bonus. I was pleased that I was there when he bought her. That was the same day that I saw Fiona Jones for the first time. She was at the auction with her husband.

"Mr. Mullin," she waved as she cast her eyes toward me, "Can she sit a horse?"

Marty took off his cap and replied, "Yes indeed, Mrs. Jones. Good enough to keep up with the exercise lads when they're racing for beers. My girl has earned herself a Coca Cola or two."

"I'd like to take her foxhunting, with your permission of course, Mr. Mullin."

Dad bent down and put his craggy face close to mine and

looked me in the eye. "Would you like that, Kathleen Mary?"

And so began a beautiful friendship. Fiona would eventually take over where Grandmother Margaret would leave off.

Horse trainers are a hardy lot but Marty had a soft side–he wrote poetry. My mother was his inspiration. He wrote tributes to her physical beauty that he carefully penned on the fly-leafs of books. She was the kind of woman who knew what she had and carried it confidently. She also voiced her opinions citing adages and clichés. Her favorite was "children should be seen and not heard." She was as strict with me as he was lenient. Mary Ellen had very specific ideas as to the proper behavior of children. I studied voice, dance and piano. I was never permitted to miss Sunday Mass or Holy Days of Obligation and that included St. Patrick's Day. I had to stand tall, walk with a book on my head, lift up my feet as I walked, and enunciate clearly. I was the only child in first grade that could pronounce "pumpkin" and "chimney" correctly. My mother saw to that. Even at a young age I recognized the dichotomy of her child rearing. How could I sing, enunciate clearly, and for that matter, play the piano if I was not to be heard?

"You'll be breaking many a heart, Kathleen Mary."

"For heaven's sake, Marty, don't tell her that. You'll spoil the child." My mother shook her head, and then dismissing him, she said, "Let me put a curl in your hair, Kathleen Mary." My hair had little tendency to curl, but my mother fought hard–even against genetic predisposition.

"She may have your good looks, Mary Ellen, but she has the coloring of the Mullins–the sandy hair and the bright blue eyes," proffered Margaret. "You know, a good stallion stamps his get," she nodded with authority.

"You mustn't say those things in front of her, you'll swell her head for sure," came the eternal Mary Ellen admonition.

"Proud of her you should be, Mrs. Mullin," declared Sister Brigid, Principal of St. Francis Xavier Roman Catholic School, "skipping a grade again—not a thing but A's on her report card."

I waited for Mary Ellen to add the part about not saying it in front of me. She didn't. I guess she forgot. She just smiled her pretty smile. Not a big toothy one. It was the big toothy smiles that belonged to the Mullins. Margaret joked that the Mullin front teeth looked like tombstones.

Instead Mary Ellen said, "Tell Sister you'll do even better next term." I did as I was told, but I wondered what I had to do to better all A's.

Good, better, best,
never let it rest,
'til your good is better
and your better, best.

Why, I wondered? But I really didn't have to ask. It was so I could bask in the warmth of their praise and snuggle in the security of their approval. Reinforcement in every corner. The ultimate in complete creature comfort.

Then one day, I had the first of what were to be many rude awakenings. Sheila McCarthy, who was thirteen years old, suddenly turned on me in the gym locker room.

"I hate you, Kathleen Mary."

"Hate me? How can you hate me? I go to church, say my prayers...Sheila, we're best friends."

"You're the only girl in the class with real bosoms and gets the curse every month. Worst of all, the boys think you're pretty and they always throw snowballs at you."

I stood there defenseless with the Kotex bulge showing through my panties, wondering why they call it the curse if it's so enviable, and why getting pelted with snowballs was such an honor. My eleven-year-old mind was having difficulty trying to sort it all out. Sheila was blinking hard to hold back the tears. She was utterly miserable. I looked at her toilet paper stuffed bra standing away from her red freckled chest and felt a momentary sense of power in being disliked for all the wrong reasons.

It had never occurred to me that people might not be pleased with themselves. It would be many years later that I would remember this incident with Sheila. It was when I was working per diem, and assigned to the Recovery Room. A patient was brought in from the O.R. having had a breast augmentation. Less than five minutes later another patient was brought in and put in the bed next to her—she had just had a breast reduction. As I took the vital signs and checked the dressings of one and then the other, I wondered why we couldn't all be happy with the way we were.

I didn't want to be like anyone else. But more than that, I wanted Sheila to be my friend. She was right. It wasn't fair for some people to go through life with certain advantages. I wasn't really sure who it was that decided what were advantages and what were not. I supposed it was God. But that couldn't be, God was fair.

That evening, Sheila called to remind me that we were going to the nine o'clock Children's Mass. That was her way of making-up. Once in the church, we took our place in one of the pews up front and to the left of the altar—the Blessed Virgin side. The boys sat to the right—the Saint Joseph side.

Both sides were heavily dotted with Dominican nuns, who were there to maintain compliance.

Sheila whispered, "I'd like to sit on the boys side."

"Shh," hissed a nun.

We tried to avoid putting our full weight on our knees while we prayed so our knees wouldn't end up looking like Herbert Hoover's face. Herbert Hoover knees were a Catholic girl's syndrome. But if Sister caught us with any part of our backsides resting on the pew, we could expect a hiss at best or a cuff on the back of the head at worst. But it was mostly the boys who got cuffed—girls got hissed at, poked with a finger and on occasion a single loud clap. That usually led to major confusion because we knew if a nun clapped her hands loudly once, it meant we were to genuflect.

To this day, if I hear anything that resembles a clapping sound, my right knee begins an involuntary break toward the floor.

Last I heard, Sheila took her final vows at the Sisters of Saint Joseph's novitiate in Brentwood. I guess she finally got to sit on the boy's side.

Chapter Eight

"And all work is empty save
when there is love..."
                Kahlil Gibran

1

By the first of June, *Ste. Gudule* and I were getting it all together. I got into the swing of working some days from seven to three without lunch, other days from seven to eleven, then a huge lunch and back at three until seven. The twelve-hour night shift ran from seven to seven, and seemed even longer when I was scheduled to work four additional hours that morning too. A sixteen-hour day in intensive care was ludicrous. If we were lucky, we had every other weekend off. So far, I hadn't been lucky.

2

I was working in Cardiac the second half of my split shift. I was alone. Martine, who was working in one of the single rooms, called for me to help. Her patient was a recent transfer and I had no idea as to the diagnosis or the nursing situation. As I walked into the room, I noticed that both nurses wore isolation gowns and gloves. There was no isolation sign on the door and since they hadn't said anything to me, I concluded that the gowns and gloves were to protect their uniforms from the blood.

Blood coated the room. It had soaked through the bedding and was dripping onto the floor. Bloody footprints traced their movements to all corners of the room and out into the hall. Martine asked me to hold the patient on her side while they changed the bedding. I looked down into a wound that ran from the patient's waist in back of the iliac crest, to mid-thigh. It was at least four inches wide. I had never seen anything like it before. It was an earthquake of human flesh. There was a hand towel stuffed into the huge fissure in an attempt to stifle the blood. It wasn't until I noticed the familiar green of the oxygen tubing that I realized what I was looking at. It was Clostridium Welchii—Gas Gangrene, an anaerobic Gram-positive bacteria that causes severe infection.

"Jesus Christ," I whispered to Martine, "I haven't the protection of isolation clothing."

"You will only be here for a little minute," she shrugged.

Thanks a lot, I mumbled to myself. "How did it happen?" I whispered.

"An injection."

"An injection?"

"The needle was perhaps not too sterile."

"Oh my God," I breathed. "Where I come from, there are no degrees of sterility, just as there's no such thing as being a little bit pregnant. It is or it isn't, you are or you're not." The patient was dead within six hours.

As a result of that experience, I fought even harder for sterile technique. Occasionally I'd win a battle. I ran around as the self-appointed infection control nurse, handing out sterile gloves, bars of soap, even stealing sterile gel from the supply service. I washed my hands so often it looked like a daily performance of Lady Macbeth.

Throughout the hospital I was known as "The American" and my language mishaps entertained the personnel. There was good ambiance among the nurses, who for the most part chose to ignore the French-Flemish language rivalry. Most of the doctors, whom we professionally addressed as *Monsieur*, walked around as if God handpicked them. The system fed their egos, and the nurses did a lot of feeding too. If a doctor gave an order, they obeyed as if the voice of the Omnipotent had been heard.

One morning, *Monsieur* Anton gave an order for 40mEq KCL, three grams of potassium chloride, for one of my terminal patients. I started to put the KCL into a new IV bottle that I was about to hang. Anton stopped me and told me to put it into the tubing that went directly into the vein. I shook my head at my inability to comprehend his order. I was positive that I misunderstood him. If I put the KCL directly into the vein, I'd kill the patient. Damn language barrier. Again I began to put the KCL into the IV bottle. Anton blew out his cheeks and stalked out. Moments later, Marie Louise came into the room and patiently explained that since there was no hope for that patient, *Monsieur* Anton expected me to push KCL directly into her vein, terminating her life.

"I can't do that," I blurted out.

She looked surprised and asked, "*Pourquoi pas?*"

"For starters, it's illegal."

She explained that although it was not totally legal, it was an accepted practice. "Just do it, we all do. Especially when we need the bed."

"*Je ne peux pas.* I can't."

"Do you want me to do it for you?"

I couldn't answer yes or no, so I simply said, "*Je ne sais pas, mais je ne peux pas.*"

I excused myself and walked down to the end of the hall to the toilet. Alone in the tiny room, I tried to analyze my feelings. In the States, I had been one of the foremost advocates of "plug pulling." It might be argued that one method is merely an extension of the other, but I didn't believe that. This was different. It was an overt act. Why did everything have to be in extremes? Either the use of heroic measures to sustain life in terminal cases—or committing an overt act to end life. One thing I knew for certain was that I could never bring myself to actively end a human life.

Shortly after my third month, word got out via Marie Louise that I was working without pay. I tried to explain my rational, how money was of secondary importance to the need to work, but this seemed to be an alien concept to my Belgian friend. I suspected it might be alien to Jenny and my girlfriends back home too.

"...and don't repeat those ideas to anyone else or they will think you are crazy," concluded Marie Louise, tapping her finger to her head and mouthing the word *folle*.

She reported our conversation to *Madame* Descamps, *Chef*, who in turn, decided that I was being exploited. She and her staff marched menacingly to the office of *La Directrice* and demanded equal pay for equal work for the American. It was supposed to be kept secret from me. I hadn't seen anything like it since five thousand nurses marched on Albany to support the Nursing Practice Act.

Later that day, I received a telephone call from Simone Lacroix. "*Allo, Catleen, ici Simone.* It seems you have many friends up there."

"Oh?"

"I cannot explain it to you, but *Mademoiselle* Dauphin has put through an order for you to receive pay."

"I can't believe it. *Chouette! Merci bien*, Simone."

"One thing you must understand, the paper work takes a

very long..."

It didn't matter. They had decided to pay me. I was elated, but I had little time to think about my own good fortune because events were happening all around me and I was about to experience more lessons in life.

3

Our private room had been reserved for the American President Robert Norris. It was merely a precautionary measure in preparation for his Brussels visit on the twenty-fifth and twenty-sixth of August. President Norris was strong and healthy. A military person who made the arrangements determined that Anton would be the doctor and I was to be the president's nurse. His decision, according to the staff, was based on the fact that my English was the best on the service, but I think it was because I had a New York State Registered Professional Nurse license. Had he researched my politics, he might have thought twice about his decision. Happily, President Norris never needed our services. Just as well that he didn't. It would only have served to increase the accusations and criticisms of American policy by the staff of *Ste. Gudule*.

I was annoyed when some of the nurses began to ride me about corruption in the United States. They mentioned Lockheed in general and Watergate in particular. But as an American, I countered with the argument that only in the United States of America could two journalists print the truth and perhaps even topple a President, whereas in Belgium, a Prince could hide behind his monarchy.

I found that royal asses resembled everyone else's when I had to give an intramuscular injection into a Royal's posterior gluteal site. The most difficult part was learning to curtsy and then back out of the room through the double door without dropping the contents of the medication tray or bumping into unseen objects along the way. I never really became proficient with that particular task. My excuse to Marie Louise was that "Americans didn't know how to retreat." I was never assigned to royalty again.

4

Late in September, the hospital began humming with news of an *étranger* assigned to our service. Jean-Claude Karambuku. In addition to his Christian name, it was rumored that he had an unpronounceable tribal name. Much of the excitement stemmed from the fact that he wasn't from Zaire (formerly Belgian Congo), but from Rwanda, east of Zaire, somewhere near Lake Victoria. He had studied medicine at the University in Moscow and had come to Brussels to further his education. In addition to his native language, he spoke Russian and French. He reminded me of Sally's boyfriend. He had the same large frame and the same ease when he smiled. I liked him immediately. As the weeks passed, I found him to be an intelligent, dedicated doctor, kind to his patients and without airs of self-importance. After one month, I became one of his many supporters.

5

It was a beautiful fall day. I slept late and planned to spend my day off doing a little shopping and having a late lunch with Chantal. I was making a cup of tea when I noticed small spots of blood on the kitchen floor. Thinking that Nic had stepped on a bit of glass, I examined his paws. Finding nothing, I thought no more about it until I went to fill his water bowl. There were droplets of blood all around. I checked his mouth and found a small sore on his gum adjacent to the large canine tooth. It looked all too familiar. I telephoned a veterinarian and arranged for an immediate x-ray. Then I phoned Chantal and asked if she could arrange to go along with me. I picked her up at the little decorator shop just off Avenue Louise and headed out toward Genval.

"I'm happy you're coming with me, Chantal. I don't want any language mistakes today."

"You think it will be bad, don't you?" she stated more than questioned.

"Yes, I do. I'm sure it's malignant. At best I think it can be surgically excised. I don't care how Nic looks, as long as he's comfortable. Anyway, what really worries me is that if the cancer has already metastasized to the jaw bone," I swallowed hard, "I'll have to put him down." She didn't understand. I took my right hand off the wheel, made a fist and turned my thumb down. "*Comme tuer.*"

"But Catleen, it is not possible. He is so healthy, so gay."

"Joyful," I corrected. "I understand what you're saying, Chantal, but what would I be giving him? A few months? I couldn't bear to see him suffer. And why should he, when I can prevent it. He is my responsibility and I must do what I feel is best for him."

Nic was anesthetized and the x-rays taken. I studied the films and saw the small pencil like lines and dots of cancer marching from the existing visible site straight down into his mandible, then flanking left and right. It was too far-gone for even radical surgery.

I looked at the Belgian doctor of veterinarian medicine. "*Monsieur*, I wish you to overdose him now while he is still under the effects of anesthesia." I turned to Chantal to ask her to repeat my request in clearer French. Tears were running down her cheeks and I realized that my French had been all too clear.

"How can you do this thing, Catleen? He does not appear to be ill. What do you know from looking at a film? How can you be so sure?"

"The only thing I know for sure is that it will not go away. Soon it will invade his lungs. He will deteriorate rapidly. It's better to terminate his life now before he experiences pain." I gave Nic one last hug and removed his collar. I kept swallowing and avoiding Chantal's eyes in order to hang on to my own emotions. Fiona had been in agony but there was nothing I could have done for her. Nic was not a human being and I had full power and authority over the quality of his life. But just being sure of doing the right thing is not enough salve for the conscience. I drove home with a sense of despair, bearing the burden of supreme judge and realizing that my last link with Fiona had been broken.

It rained the next day. It rained a lot in Brussels. The difference with this day was that Nic was not there to help me greet it. His nudging with his nose always made me smile. But not today. Or any other day. He was gone and with him the unconditional love he provided. I wandered around the apartment collecting all the reminders of Nic and tossed them into the trash. I would never have another dog. I made a cup of tea and looked out of the window at the gray sky.

6

Late in November, near the end of the shift, Martine and I walked into le bureau together. She fell into the chair behind the desk and stretched her long legs. I looked at her red shoes. I couldn't get used to the idea of nurses wearing anything but white. We were supposed to keep to black or brown shoes or clogs, but other colors crept in from time to time. I still wore my white nurses' shoes, but I did succumb to wearing beige pantyhose, mainly because white was not available in the shops.

I took the thermometers from the small tray I was carrying and returned them to their place on the shelf. Unhappily, thermometers were community property, all resting together in an alcohol filled cup. Happily, the oral, which we used axillary, and the rectal were usually separated. I was never quite sure which bothered me more—the idea of a thermometer going from armpit to armpit or from rectum to rectum. I spent a good deal of time washing thermometers and changing what I hoped was a seventy percent aqueous solution of ethyl alcohol, and then hoping they'd be undisturbed for thirty minutes.

7

The following Saturday, a woman was brought in bleeding from the nose and mouth. *Monsieur* Karambuku examined her. The thin forty-year-old *Madame* Gaspar had a history of alcoholism and cirrhosis of the liver. A Baxter of 1000cc of 5% Glucose and a naso-gastric tube was ordered. IV's were called Baxters (the manufacturer's name) and were pronounced "Back-staire."

Marie Louise started the IV and I passed the NG tube through *Madame* Gaspar's nostril and into her stomach. I irrigated with normal saline, a solution of 0.9% Sodium Chloride. The return was bloody and the bleeding would have to be controlled. *Madame* Gaspar was understandably apprehensive. It's frightening to see one's blood coming from a place that cannot be controlled by compression dressing. Marie Louise and I took turns holding her hand and trying to reassure her.

Madame Gaspar didn't fit the profile. My experience had been that cirrhotic patients were usually men over fifty and the mortality rate was high. I never thought much about it, but this woman made me remember its devastating proportions. Many Belgian patients' chief complaint was something they called "*crise de foie*," liver problems, which they claim, is brought on by an over-indulgence in chocolate. Unfortunately alcoholism was not on the decline, and I didn't think the consumption of chocolate was either.

The following day, *Madame* Gaspar's abdomen was enlarged and firm. I called it to the attention of *Monsieur* Karambuku. He nodded silently as he palpated the area. When he had finished, he motioned me outside. I followed him into *le bureau*. He sat behind the desk and began writing in her dossier. I knew that she had esophageal varices, varicose veins of the esophagus, and that her abdominal symptoms were probably due to leakage of capillary fluid into that cavity, but I was curious as to what his recommendation would be. He handed me the dossier. I read it quickly, stopped at Tamponade and read on to Portacaval Shunt, a surgical procedure that decreases the portal pressure and consequently reduces hemorrhage danger from the esophageal and gastric varices.

"*Aux Etats-Unis*, this surgery is used?" he asked.

I nodded affirmatively and closed the dossier. Now *Madame* Gaspar's life was in the hands of *Monsieur* Anton and the surgeons of *Ste. Gudule*.

That evening we went to dinner with Chantal and Larry. Chantal was radiating happiness. Her brown eyes were sparkling as she said, "We have an announcement. You wish to say it, Larree?"

He shook his head, grunted a throaty "Uh, uh. You tell 'em, honey."

"We have decided to marry," she announced without further prompting.

Frank ordered Dom Perignon and we toasted their happiness in French, Italian, English and American.

"When is the big day?" I inquired.

"Well, it's not exactly set," drawled Larry. "We figure a couple of months or so. Meantime, Chantal's gonna move in with me." He hugged her. "That right, baby?"

The three of us continued drinking champagne throughout dinner. Larry switched to gin saying, "What I wouldn't give for some good ole sour mash."

He and Frank lapsed into a business discussion, and when they were sufficiently engrossed, Chantal switched to French. She didn't want Larry to hear our conversation.

"What do you think, Catleen?"

"I'm very happy for you."

"*Non*, apropos moving into the apartment with Larree."

"Why not? You love him, don't you?"

"Oh, Catleen, that is American thinking. We do not move in with…we do not go to bed with someone we wish to marry. It is only to go to bed with someone else, but never, never with the one you wish to marry."

"Chantal, if I were going to sleep with someone, I'd sleep with the one I loved. I can't imagine denying him sex until marriage and in the meantime sleeping with someone else solely for sex."

"*Alors*, you are so American. We will see. I shall move in the end of next month and I hope to set the date of marriage for the first week in June."

"Hey, what you gals parleying about in français?" demanded Larry.

"Drink your gin," I smiled, sipping my champagne, "and let's get on with this celebration."

8

At ten minutes before seven, I was listening to the night nurse, *Madame* Smets, tell me about their busy night. "…and finally *Le Neuf* expired. Poor old soul," she sighed. "We never did get to bathe any patients, *Madame* deMeo."

"It is not important," I said, watching the staff straggle in, one by one. What a way to begin a split shift, I thought. Of all of the shifts, this was the one I like the least. Four hours on—four hours off—four hours on. It made the day seem endless.

Smets had already sent the two other weary night nurses home and was impatiently awaiting the arrival of the charge nurse. A flaxen-haired young man stuck his head in the door and said, "Sleep well, Smets, see you tomorrow night."

"Now there's a nice young doctor...Flemish. His name is Willem Goosens and he's just been transferred to *Réa*."

Finally, at ten minutes past seven, *Mademoiselle* Follet sauntered in. She would be taking charge of the service today in place of *Madame* Descamps, who was enjoying a well-deserved day off. Rumor had it that *Mademoiselle* Follet slept with *Monsieur* Anton. They deserved each other and the thought of those two going at it amused me no end. She took the report with a stone face, far different from the animated *Madame* Descamps. I glanced at the assignment sheet and found that I would be working *Respiratoire* with Martine and Paul. We gathered all of the necessary supplies for patient care and headed into the room. Only three patients—numbers, six, seven and eight. One empty bed—that was patient nine. Should be an easy morning, I thought.

"Only one EKG for us," said Martine looking through the orders. "Oh never mind, it was for *Le Neuf*."

Le Neuf referred to the patient in bed number nine. All patients were labeled according to their bed number, and the article *le* or *la* signified man or woman. They wore no identification bands around their wrists.

"Why don't you take the blood, *Madame* deMeo?" Paul suggested formally.

"*Mais oui*," I answered, picking up the first carrying case of test tubes. "How are you this morning, *Monsieur* Maus?" I asked, walking over to Bed 6. *Le Six* was a sixty-two-year-old man with a tracheotomy. He grimaced when he saw the tubes for blood. I couldn't blame him. He'd been here quite a while with pulmonary emphysema, thanks to a two pack a day habit. We were in the process of weaning him off the respirator. He was doing fairly well–even walking a few steps. Now he was mouthing words of protest. He didn't want any more blood taken. It wasn't that I was good at lip reading in French or even in English–I just knew how anyone, including myself, would feel under similar circumstances.

"I'm sorry I have to stick you this morning, *Monsieur* Maus, but I don't need very much blood and I'll do it quickly. *Ca va?*"

I looked at his purple, bruised arms. His veins had been used a lot but they weren't bad. I knotted a *garrote* on his arm and palpated a prospective vein, rubbed the site with alcohol and went in with a number 19 needle, using my thumb as a stopcock. As I felt the needle go into the vein, I changed the angle, slowly advancing it in the lumen. I removed my thumb from the back of the needle and the blood immediately surged through and into the test tube that I held beneath it. I unsnapped the rubber *garrote*. I smiled to myself, remembering when I had been introduced to this method. I'd thought it barbaric, and I was sure I'd never get used to it. I had always taken blood in the States with a vacuum tube or a syringe. It was neat and clean–untouched by human hands. The *Ste. Gudule* method required a great deal of dexterity plus a cooperative or comatose patient in order to keep to a minimum any blood that might spill on the sheets, the patient, the floor–and oneself. Now here I was, able to catch the blood in one tube using one hand, while agitating an already filled tube with the other. The adaptability of human beings never ceased to amaze me.

"That's it, *Monsieur*, all finished," I said as I pulled out the needle and pushed a four by four against the site, exerting pressure with my finger. I looked at him and smiled, "*Pas mal*, wasn't too bad, was it?"

He rolled his eyes upward, blew out his cheeks and rocked his head from side to side. He was a nice old gentleman and I found myself becoming quite attached to him.

Next I went to *La Sept*, *Madame* Gaspar. Her nasogastric

tube had been attached to low suction and the bottle was bright red with blood. As fast as she was transfused, she would lose an equal amount or more. Her bleeding problem was in a delicate balance and the scale could tip at any time. Karambuku was still pushing for surgery, but Anton resisted, opting for rest and a conservative approach. *Madame* Gaspar was becoming increasingly anxious, but tranquilizers were part of the hospital milieu.

By the time I reached Bed 8, Paul and Martine were finishing up. I looked at the elderly man with pneumonia. He was becoming more and more debilitated with each ensuing day. "And don't get blood on the clean sheets," Paul teased.

"Don't worry, I'm not going to get blood on them," I answered, looking at the patient's arms. "Look at those veins. Go in there with a needle and they'll pop and collapse. I'm not taking his blood."

"But you must try."

"Why? He has bad veins and I know that I won't be able to get any blood."

"I'll do it," said Paul.

"*Pourquoi?* Why must you try? You can't get in there either. I'm calling a doctor to go into the femoral."

"No," he said, already preparing the arm.

Paul tried twice, Martine once. The patient had large swollen lumps on his arms. I left the room with the other tubes of blood and put them on the pick-up counter for the lab. I stuck my head into *le bureau* and told Follet that we were unsuccessful in getting blood from *Le Huit*. She threw me an annoyed glance, got up from behind the desk and walked directly to Bed 8. "What's the problem?" she asked, looking at Paul.

"No problem, just no blood."

She touched the three swollen areas of the patient arms and said, "I can see that everyone tried."

"I didn't."

Paul caught my eye and put his finger up to his lips. I blew through my lips Belgian style and mouthed a *tant pis* at him. It all escaped Follet as she was attempting to get into *Le Huit's* vein. She tried, and tried, and tried. She wanted very much to be the hero of the day. Finally, defeated, Follet left the room, leaving the patient with a pair of lumpy arms. A few minutes later, Karambuku came in and successfully took femoral blood in a matter of seconds.

After we had finished morning chores, Martine and I went into the kitchen for a coffee break. Karambuku and Anton were arguing over the medical management of Madame Gaspar.

"You must understand, *Monsieur* Karambuku, that she is a poor risk for surgery."

Anton against surgery? What a surprise. Usually, any patient was a candidate for an exploratory laparotomy, just to give his boys a little practice.

"I am not arguing that point," said Karambuku, "but poor risk or not, the amount of bleeding increases with each day. It is imperative that the bleeding be controlled or she will die. We must do something. May I once more suggest an esophageal tamponade?"

Anton's face was pinched. "No, I cannot approve of that either. It is also a risk. In my opinion..."

Paul appeared in the kitchen doorway and asked, "What about my coffee?"

"Come here, I've finished my tea," I said, sliding off the stool and passing him in the doorway.

The *Respiratoire* room was quiet. The only sound was the faint hum of the nebulizer blowing the steamy air of a bronchodialating medication toward *Monsieur* Maus' tracheotomy. I was adjusting the flow of the IV of *Le Huit* when I heard a slight cough coming from the direction of Bed 7. I stopped and held my breath. I heard it again, louder.

I turned towards *Madame* Gaspar's bed and yelled, "Karambuku, *vite!*" With each successive cough, the blood spurted from her mouth and nose as if someone was punching holes in a transfusion bag. Karambuku was there within seconds. I was pumping up the pressure cuff to get a reading, while doing my best to reassure her. But how do you reassure someone who's choking on their own blood? Martine and Paul were waiting for directions. Anton hovered in the background, silently observing.

Karambuku turned to him. "Perhaps I may have your permission for a tamponade, *Monsieur*, as rapidly as possible, *s'il vous plaît*."

The hemorrhage had to be controlled by exerting pressure on the cardiac portion of the stomach and against the bleeding varices by a double balloon tamponade. *Monsieur* Anton worked swiftly in obtaining a Sengstaken-Blakemore, and it looked fairly new. Karambuku checked it over by immersing it inflated into a tub of water, much like checking an inner tube for a leak. When he was satisfied, I pushed it into a bucket of ice. Martine had already carried out a medication order. Paul brought in a portable fluoroscopy machine and connected it. Karambuku explained briefly to *Madame* Gaspar what he was about to do. We were ready.

I looked at *Madame* Gaspar and wondered if she was ready. She was sitting in a sea of blood, looking out at us from somewhere behind her glassy eyed stare. I handed the lubricated tamponade to Karambuku, and removed her nasogastic tube. *Madame* Gaspar clutched my hand and wouldn't let go. I looked into her eyes and read all the terrors of every patient I'd ever seen. A bed surrounded by professionals, all executing their skillful life-saving techniques, concentrating, too absorbed for a word or a gesture of reassurance. Karambuku began passing the tube through her nostril.

"Breathe through your mouth," we choused, "it will be easier." The tube was descending down the esophagus. "Swallow, swallow. *Avalez, avalez*." We choused in two languages.

The tube reached the stomach. We were all observing the path of the tamponade on the screen of the fluoroscope.

Karambuku had just started to inflate the stomach balloon when we lost the picture.

"*Merde,*" Paul complained under his breath, desperately trying to retrieve the picture.

Karambuku looked at the blank screen for a moment and then continued unruffled. He inflated the stomach balloon somewhere between 25mm. and 30mm. Hg. as measured by the manometer. Then he pulled the end of the tamponade, gently exerting force against the cardia. We exchanged glances as he started inflating the esophageal balloon. Although his demeanor remained calm, tiny blisters of perspiration broke out on his forehead. Martine quickly mopped them away. Without the benefit of fluoroscopic control, there was always the possibility of rupturing the esophagus. None of us would have wanted to be standing in his shoes. We were all watching him now, including Anton.

Madame Gaspar had by now dug her fingernails deep into my hands. Karambuku continued increasing the esophageal balloon pressure and then abruptly stopped, nodding that he felt it was sufficient. He put traction on the tube. Paul hooked up the gastric suction.

"It is over, *Madame.*" Karambuku reassured, "It went well."

We all stayed and held our collective breaths for the next few minutes. *Madame* Gaspar began to breathe normally and gradually relaxed her grip on me. Karambuku silently left the room, but we knew he'd be only a call away.

Once we had made *Madame* Gaspar as comfortable as possible, I stayed for the next hour monitoring her vital signs. As a precaution, I taped a pair of scissors to her bed. There was always a danger of the counterweight pulling the tube into the oropharynx and consequently asphyxiating the patient. At the end of the first hour, I was irrigating the stomach tube when *Monsieur* Karambuku and Paul came back into the room and stood beside me. The color of the return had decidedly changed. The bleeding had apparently been checked. We all hugged each other and beamed at *Madame* Gaspar. Her eyes smiled back at us saying it all.

I was sitting at Frank's usual table in *Les Chirubles*, on *Rue Royale*, waiting for Chantal. It was December third, her birthday and my treat. I had just worked seven to eleven and I had to be back to work from three to seven. I looked at my watch. Fifteen minutes before noon. I was early and Chantal would be late. I rubbed my hands and wrists. I could still feel *Madame* Gaspar's fingernails burning into the over-scrubbed flesh of my hands.

"*Voulez-vous un apéritif, Madame* deMeo?" asked the charming hostess.

"*Non, merci, Madame. je prend…l'eau gazeux, s'il vous plaît.*" I wished that I had the afternoon off. I'd like to have some wine with lunch and be able to really celebrate Chantal's birthday. This was my tenth sequential working day and I was looking forward to having tomorrow off. The club soda was placed before me. I took a large swallow of the cool sparkling water. It tasted good. I leaned back and looked at the copper coal-scuttle filled with fresh flowers. I enjoyed the hushed atmosphere of the small green room. It was quite a contrast to my hectic morning. I closed my eyes.

"Catleen, Catleen. What are you dreaming?" Chantal was sliding into the booth next to me. "*Bonjour,* my dear." We kissed on the cheeks three times in the Belgian fashion. "*Kier, s'il vous plaît, Madame,*" she ordered.

"*Bonjour, comment ça va?*" I asked automatically. Then I toasted to her birthday with my club soda. "*Heureuse Anniversaire,* Chantal. How does it feel to be so young?"

Her brown eyes darkened to black. "I am no longer young. I am old…soon too old to be married."

Oh God, I thought, what brought this on?

"I am not happy," she continued, "Larree does not agree to the date of the wedding. What must I do, Catleen?" She sighed deeply and leaned back. "I don't think he wishes to marry at all. He simply enjoys having the convenience of a woman without any of the responsibility."

"Oh, come on, Chantal, I'm sure it will all work out. Maybe he..."

"Hey, what are you two doing at my table?" Frank was standing over us smiling. "Mind if we join you?"

"Not if you're paying the check, we don't."

He slid into the booth opposite us, followed by a tall, good-looking young man he introduced as Guy Peeters. Frank had Guy transferred recently from the Amsterdam office to Brussels. The presence of the two men immediately perked up what started out as a rather dismal birthday celebration.

While Guy and Chantal rattled on in Dutch and French, Frank looked across the table at me. "By the way, Kate, something's come up. I have to fly to London tonight. I'll call you tomorrow and let you know when I'll be back."

"*Merde*," I replied without thinking.

"*C'est bien français,* Catleen," laughed Chantal.

She seemed to have forgotten her problems, at least for the moment, and was enjoying her twenty-fourth birthday.

Shortly before three, I was in the lift at *Ste. Gudule.* So was Follet. We rode in detached silence. As the doors opened onto *Réa,* I followed her out, and Martine was getting in. "*A demain,*" she waved, hurrying past me.

"*Pas moi,*" I called after her, "I have the day off."

"Good," she answered, and as the heavy lift doors closed on her, I heard a muffled, "See you. Bye bye."

Paul and I walked counter clockwise around the *Respiratoire Chambre,* and he began the report on our patients. Bed 9 was still empty. Bed 8, *Le Huit*–the old man with pneumonia–after an unexplainable sudden drop in his blood pressure, had expired. *Madame* Gaspar, in Bed 7, was sleeping. If no bleeding occurred in the next few days, the tube would be removed, and *Madame* Gaspar would have won the first round.

Paul was looking at *Monsieur* Maus in Bed 6. "I did not wish to wake him so I left the medication for you to give." He handed me the meds as he talked. "It is Geomycin…to be mixed with this ampule of sterile water in a syringe and put down his tracheotomy."

"Down his trach?"

"Yes, it will make him cough, so you must quickly plug up the tracheotomy in order to keep the medication in there for a bit. Then later you must suction him. He doesn't like it very much."

No wonder he doesn't like it. It's like drowning. I wouldn't like it either. I looked at the small vial of Geomycin in my hand. I rolled the clear ampule of water in my other hand automatically checking the label. I looked closer. Paul was preparing to leave.

"*Attend, s'il vous plaît*, Paul." I followed him out of the door. "What is this Mag Sulfate for?"

He looked puzzled. "No, that is not magnesium sulfate, that is sterile water." I handed the ampule to him. "*Merde.*"

We both realized what had happened. The sterile water, the normal saline and the magnesium sulfate all look alike, all clear 5cc ampules kept in identical plastic bins next to each other on the bottom shelf.

"*Mon Dieu.* Do you know what I did this morning? I mixed all the penicillin with Magnesium Sulfate thinking it was sterile water."

"That explains the sudden drop in pressure of *Le Huit*."

"Oh my God. He died and it's my fault," moaned Paul squeezing his eyes closed, "very bad."

I silently agreed. The patient probably arrested. I shuddered at the thought. Paul went on agonizing. Both of us were aware that there was no such thing as malpractice in Belgium, but he didn't want anyone else to know what had happened.

"Don't tell. Don't tell anyone. He was going to die in a few days anyway."

I nodded. "Tell you what, Paul, why don't I put a label on each of those bins and it will help to remind us all, and prevent it from happening again."

He gave a half smile and disappeared into the stairwell. By five o'clock, the two remaining patients were holding their own. *Madame* Gaspar's bleeding was still in check.

I looked around the room. The hospital was old but our unit had been recently renovated. The stark rooms, with their large windows, allowed an abundance of light and, when it wasn't raining–sun.

Monsieur Maus had engaged me in a game of Dominos in partial payment for his cooperation when I tried to drown him with Geomycin.

Suddenly, Follet thundered through the doorway. "Who put labels on the plastic tubs containing the five cubic centimeter ampules?"

She didn't have to ask. She already knew. American printing as well as handwriting has a style all its own and there's nothing European about mine. "Godzilla," I mumbled.

"*Qui?*"

"I did," I admitted.

"I thought so."

Clever girl.

"*Alors*, go into *le bureau* immediately and remove those labels. They are an insult to our intelligence. Do you think we do not know the difference between those ampules?"

Follet turned on her noisy clogs and left. *Monsieur* Maus was staring wide-eyed throughout the entire exchange.

At twenty minutes before seven I went into *le bureau* to wash my hands. I thought I might try to talk to Follet. I wanted to clear the air. I didn't like working in the midst of a cold war. I pushed myself up on the table that was against the wall. I watched her sitting at the desk. She didn't look up.

I started casually, saying, *"Je suis fatigué."* I was tired and that wasn't the half of it. I was sick and tired. The entire day had been a crock of shit.

Finally, she looked at me through narrowed eyes, pursed her lips and sniffed. How could anyone so young, act so old? Follet and her pursed lips got up from the desk and left without a word. I sat there staring at the clock.

9

Brussels awoke one morning to an unusual sight. Snow. It confounded the natives and snarled the traffic, but it was a breath of home to this New Yorker. It took almost an hour instead of the usual twenty minutes to get home from work that day. I didn't mind at all. My first salary check had been deposited directly into my checking account at the *Société Générale Banque*. It was only about half of what I made in New York, but I was delighted. It was one hundred percent more than nothing and just in time for Christmas. I couldn't wait for Frank to return from Milan to tell him the good news. I decided to tape my bank statement to his shaving mirror where he couldn't help but see it.

As I got off the lift, I heard the ring of the phone. I hurried to answer, hoping that Frank might be returning earlier than expected. Not very likely, so don't get your hopes up, I cautioned. Could be a wrong number. Well, even a wrong number isn't all that bad when you're home alone.

"Hello, Kate?"

"Yes?"

"Aaron. Aaron Sternberg."

"Aaron? Aaron, I can't believe it. Where are you?"

"The Amigo Hotel in beautiful downtown Brussels."

"I still can't believe it. How did you find me?"

"Sally, who else?"

"Oh Sally, how I miss her."

"Yeah," he paused, "actually I called to invite you and your husband out to dinner."

"Oh? That's nice of you, Aaron, but Frank is in Italy on business."

He paused again, "Well, I am a stranger in town...alone. Would you consider having dinner with me?"

"I thought you'd never ask."

We met at *Aux Armes de Bruxelles,* a restaurant on *Petite Rue des Bouchers*, just off the *Grand Place*. It was frequented less by the tourists and more by the locals. Aaron gave me a kiss from Sally, and then he filled me in on all the hospital news. I unburdened months of working frustrations on him. It was unbelievably satisfying, talking to someone who understood my concerns about hospital policy and procedures. I stopped talking for a moment and looked at him. "Oh Aaron, I am sorry. I've been going on about myself and I haven't even asked what you're doing here."

He pushed at his glasses with his index finger and shrugged. "Nothing really. I just delivered a paper in Paris, decided that I'd like to see Brussels, took the train up and here I am."

I coaxed him into telling me a little about his paper and then he lunged into a discussion of the Yom Kippur War and Kissenger's foreign policy. We argued over the rates of malpractice insurance. He thought it too high. It was high, I agreed, but after my working experiences in Brussels, I tried to convince him that too high is better than none at all.

Half way through dinner and a half-liter of wine, I knew that he wanted to go to bed with me. At the end of dinner and a liter of wine later, I knew that I would.

Chapter Nine

"My eve is in truth
my dawn."
    Kahlil Gibran

1

W e walked back to the hotel through the tiny streets, neither of us saying a word. I stamped the snow off my boots as we entered the lobby of the Hotel Amigo. Aaron guided me to the elevator, gently cupping my elbow with his hand. My body was alive with excitement.

He took my coat. Then, my head took over and the misgivings began. Maybe this isn't at all what he had in mind. Oh God, suppose I have misread him? How do I go about getting out of this gracefully? I listened to the penetrating silence.

He cleared his throat. "It's a nice room." He nodded as he spoke. His voice was strained and he made a sweeping gesture with his hand.

"Oh, yes. Really nice. The Hotel Amigo is considered to be Brussels' most charming luxury hotel."

"Would you like something to drink"?

I shook my head no.

"Kate, I..." He was still standing close. He touched my face with his fingertips. He brushed at some wisps of hair on my forehead. He kissed me timidly and held me as if he were afraid that I would dissolve in his hands. He touched my breasts and suddenly I had this incredibly ebullient feeling. It was the excitement of illicit sex–the excitement of sinning. Aaron was trembling as he clumsily tried to open the buttons on my blouse. I wish I could have believed that it was passion, but I think he was just nervous. So was I. He hadn't even been able to negotiate the first button. How long should I let him struggle?

I pulled back and looked at him. "Shall I take off my clothes?" I asked, trying to sound casual–even worldly.

Aaron's eyes widened. He nodded, automatically adjusting his glasses. I began a slow strip, partly calculated because he was an appreciative audience, but mostly because of my own insecurity. His eyes never left me and he was breathing audibly. I hesitated before unhooking my bra. I wasn't sure that I could do it. I turned my back to him and finally tossed it aside with what I hoped looked like complete abandon. I stood there riveted to the floor in my Gucci print bikinis. I turned toward Aaron with my hands covering my breasts.

Aaron pulled off his clothes and put his glasses on the bedside table. At the same time he ordered, "Take off your underpants."

"No. Uh, uh, not my bikinis. They stay." I stepped back defensively, forgetting my breasts and flattened my palms against the delicate material.

"Okay," he said quietly, "it's okay. You don't have to, it doesn't matter." He put his hand out to me and then enclosed me in his arms.

I furtively glanced at his penis. "Good God, you're circumcised."

"Of course I'm circumcised," he looked down as if to validate it, "What did you expect?"

"It's just that I haven't seen a circumcised one before. Uhm, well never...like this."

He leaned his weight in the direction of the bed and we tumbled stiffly onto it. He made a gallant attempt to pull down my bikinis but I adamantly resisted.

"Jesus, Kate, we can't do anything if you keep your underwear on."

"I know, I know. I'm trying." And I was trying, but I never realized how difficult it would be.

After an hour of foreplay, which had to be some kind of a record, I looked at Aaron, feeling as if I gotten him there under false pretenses. If grades were to be given out, I would have failed at Extra Marital 101. I couldn't fail. I had to get a good grade.

I kissed his lips, and then started sliding down his body. I lifted my gaze. He lay there, absolutely still staring at the ceiling. He surprised me with a rapid orgasm, and except for some constrained panting, he was almost inaudible. It was strange. With Frank, there was never any doubt. He was noisy. I was noisy. I assumed everyone was. Why wasn't Aaron? Maybe it wasn't very good? Maybe he didn't like it?

I took Aaron's silence negatively. I pulled the sheet around me and over my head like a shroud. "It wasn't very good, was it?"

"It wasn't?"

I groaned.

"I thought it was great, but what do I know, I never had oral sex before."

"Aaron, please, no jokes."

"I'm not joking." His voice was matter of fact.

I peered out from behind the sheet and looked at his face. Good Lord, he was serious. I pushed myself into a sitting position. He was leaning against the headboard tracing the pattern on the spread with his index finger. He gave me a half smile and said, "Anything other than an occasional missionary position in a dark room is considered lewd and lascivious by my wife."

Jesus, Mary and Joseph, I didn't want to hear about his wife. "Come on Aaron, you're a doctor and I know doctors. You guys hit on us every day."

"You don't know me."

I wrinkled my nose.

"No, you don't know. Listen, Kate, I worked hard putting myself through med-school. I was totally goal-oriented. I had little time or money. When I finally finished, when I had some time...I don't know," he forced a laugh, "the nurses seemed to prefer surgeons. Those bastards got all the action." He thought for a moment, "You know, whenever I'd say hello to a nurse, she'd carefully word her response, afraid that I was psyching her out. People in general find it difficult to be themselves around a psychiatrist."

"Aren't you being just a tiny bit thin-skinned, Dr. Sternberg?"

"No, not at all." He turned and looked at me. "The trouble with you is that you tend to think in terms of your own head, but that's not the way all people view things. You're one of the few who deal first in terms of people, and then go on from there. That's nice, Kate, admirable even, makes for a great nurse but that's not the real world. I think you know what I'm trying to say." He looked embarrassed. "I don't know why I'm telling you all this. I'm the shrink, not you."

"Well you always said I was a good psych nurse."

"I thought you needed a shrink when you didn't take that job at the VA hospital." He hooked his arm around my neck and pulled me to him.

"You know a good one?"

"Yeah." He kissed my forehead and effortlessly slipped off my bikinis.

Aaron made love slowly and tenderly as if to expand each moment. His touch was light, more of what I would have imagined a woman's touch to be. It was different than it was with Frank. With Frank, there was always intense, wild excitement that culminated in an exhilarating climax. I assumed my sexual response with any man would be the same. The whole thing with Aaron surprised me. It was a quiet, floating, dream-like sensation, an ethereal experience but I didn't have an orgasm. I always have an orgasm. I was orgastic before I even knew what orgastic meant. I was orgastic before women learned that they were supposed to worry about frequency and duration of orgasms. Aaron didn't seem to notice, or if he did, he never mentioned it.

It was close to two in the morning when I looked at my watch. "Oh my God." I jumped up and started dressing. Aaron lazily rolled over and watched.

"Aaron?"

"Yes?"

"You were trembling before. You know, when we started. You were nervous, weren't you?"

"No, not at all," he said. His tone became serious. "I just wasn't sure you really wanted to. And I thought maybe you had too much wine."

I nodded. I did have too much wine. I needed that wine to seep below my cerebral cortex into my inhibitory center. I liked Aaron. He was safe and I was curious. I wanted to know what it would feel like with someone else and the opportunity presented itself. It happened simply because it was the right time and place in both of our lives.

As I drove back to the apartment, the streets were deserted and it was still snowing lightly. I watched the blades of the windshield wipers efficiently pushing the snow aside into slanted lines. I didn't feel guilty. I felt strangely euphoric.

The phone was ringing as I put my key into the latch. "Oh God." I raced to answer it. "Lo," I mumbled, trying to sound sleepy.

"Hi. I just wanted to be sure you got home okay."

"Thank you for your concern, but I am quite capable."

"Yeah, I know. I suppose I really wanted to say goodnight, and goodbye. I'm leaving tomorrow."

"I know."

"I'll call or wri…"

"You don't have to say that. It isn't necessary. You don't have to say anything."

"Will you stop telling me what I don't have to say?"

"Okay." My voice relented, "Have a safe trip."

"Goodnight, Kate."

"Goodbye, Aaron."

2

We welcomed the 1975 New Year with an open house party. Frank posted an invitation in the reception room of his office and I did the same in *le bureau* of *Réa*. Open house parties are always fun. Hordes of people come, many of whom are not invited.

"Hi, honey," greeted an American voice, while leaning one hand on the wall behind me, "and who might you be?"

"I'm your hostess, 'honey.' Who are you?"

"Scuse me." He backed up two steps and dissolved into the crowd.

"*Cherie*! Catleen, *ici*." Chantal was frantically waving from across the room. She held onto Larry's arm as they worked their way through the wall-to-wall crowd.

"*Quelle ambiance*," she smiled, holding on to Larry's arm.

"Where's Frank?" asked Larry, as he gave me what he called an American, right-on-the-lips kiss.

"I've no idea where you might find him. You're welcome to try but I suggest that you fortify yourself with a drink and wait. Sooner or later, you're bound to bump into him."

I wondered where Frank was. I had the urge to tell him that I loved him. It was partly to assuage my ever-present guilt. I finally caught his eye some twenty paces away, raised my glass of Moet et Chandon and mouthed 'I love you.' With a nod of his head and thumb pointing at the door, he signaled a "let's blow this party." I smiled and nodded an exuberant yes as he was swallowed again in the crowd, but I stopped when I heard the lift door open behind me. I turned, automatically smiling to greet another guest. It was *Monsieur* Karambuku.

"*Bonsoir, Madame* deMeo." He kissed my hand.

"*Monsieur, bienvenu.*"

He accepted champagne from a passing waiter. I drained my glass and quickly replaced it with another.

"*Monsieur, comment ça va.* How are you? We rarely see you anymore."

"I am well, *Madame*, and I wish to thank you for your kind invitation."

Marie Louise had spotted Karambuku and was heading our way. She shouted above the din, "*Monsieur* Karambuku."

He turned and extended his hand. I stepped away as they melted into the crowd.

"Catleen. Who was that beautiful African?" cooed Chantal, as she and Larry prepared to leave.

"African? Oh? Which one was that?"

"There was only one at the party and he had his eyes on you, *chérie*," she murmured in my ear as she kissed me goodbye.

"Don't be silly, you French flake," I whispered.

Hours later, after the last of the guests left, Frank and I were getting ready for bed. "Good party," I said, kicking off my spiked-heel shoes. "I had a great time."

"Great party," agreed Frank, unbuttoning his shirt, "who was that black guy?"

"He works at *Ste. Gudule*. I told you about him. Good Doc. Anyway, he will probably leave the country soon. Anton wants him out. He's on permanent nights and Anton will never allow him to be in charge. Chalk up another loss for patients, like *Madame* Gaspar, and another victory for hospital politics."

"Hmm."

"What do you mean, hmm?"

"Just hmm."

"You know, tonight I wanted to reach out and touch you," I said, changing the subject.

"Try harder. I'm a lot closer than you think."

3

She was lying on the cold tile floor in the corner of the room, her right foot caught up in the tangled bed-sheet. IVs and medications had been cut. She had become just another terminal patient to be avoided. Paul helped me to put her back into bed. Her lips were cracked and dry. After a fruitless search for glycerin on the medication shelf, I found a cocoa butter suppository. I melted it in the palm of my hand and put some on her lips as gently as I could. There was nothing else to be done for this forty-year-old Caucasian female, slipping away centimeter by centimeter, fading breath by breath. I undid my fist. What was left of the cocoa butter was slipping through the cracks between my fingers.

Madame Gaspar died on St. Valentine's Day. Although I was not a stranger to death, I'd never become accustomed to it. With each patient's passing, I felt a sort of tremor, a sadness, an undefined hollowness within me. But I did think about the person who once lived in that body, the person who breathed life, who was once young, strong, happy, and in love. Now that person was no more. Nothing was left except the outward sign, the sole remainder of our fragile existence.

Embalming didn't exist in Brussels as it did in New York, so the nurses had the unpleasant task of stuffing all of the body cavities with wads of cotton. I hated jamming cotton into the nares, mouth, rectum, vagina and wounds with long, ugly metal forceps. Sometimes their eyes would pop open and stare at me in protest. I'd quickly close them with the tips of my fingers, trying to avoid the accusation I saw there. In New York, I frequently had difficulty winding the gauze around the head and chin so that the jaw wouldn't gape open. Sometimes it helped to tip the head forward a little. The most difficult part for me was tying the identifying tag on the great toe. In Brussels, the worst was putting on the clothing. Only what would be seen was necessary. Then clean sheets. The top sheet would have exactly five pleats. Not four or six, five was traditional. The room had to be neat and all the clutter removed as if to deny that the illness ever existed. *Madame Gaspar* would be, if only for the next few days, receiving more attention dead than alive. Everything had to be in perfect order, peaceful and serene. Okay, *ça va*. It's was time for the family to view the body.

4

It was a typical March evening as I walked through the gates of *Ste. Gudule*. I huddled against the dampness.

"Kate. Kate. Over here." A heavily bearded man was waving from the doorway of a cafe across the street. He darted into the street as a car screeched and pulled to the side in order to avoid hitting him. He jumped back.

"Just wait there on the walkway," I yelled, "You'll get yourself killed."

I crossed over to meet him. "Aaron? Is that you inside that beard? You look like Sigmund Freud. What are you doing here?"

He pulled me into the cafe. "I've been having kidney perfusion. I've been sitting here drinking coffee for over four hours waiting for you to come through that gate."

"You're lucky it wasn't my day off."

"I knew you were working. I saw your car parked up the street."

"But what are you doing here? You're the last person I expected to see. What a surprise. What's with the beard? Did you deliver another paper?"

"Sit down. I have to talk to you. Uh, would you like to order something?"

"Yes, please. *Vin chaud.* Hot wine."

"Hot wine?"

"Uh huh, it's good. You'll like it."

He beckoned the waiter, "*Vin chaud, s'il vous plaît, Monsieur,*" and put up two fingers.

"Well now," he turned his attention to me, "and how have you been?" His tone turned professional.

"Very well, thank you, and you?"

"I've been well also. Yes, very well, very well."

The waiter set the hot wines on the bare oak table. Aaron waited for him to leave before speaking again.

"Kate, I'm taking a consulting psychiatric assignment in Louvain."

"Oh? Uh huh."

"As I see it, there's a good opportunity there for preventative medicine in my field. Matter of fact, there seems to be a lot of support..." He was losing the professional edge to his voice. "Strangely enough, it's called the anti-psych movement."

"My, that is a strange name, isn't it?" I didn't bother to hide the sarcasm in my voice.

"Aren't you going to ask me why Louvain?"

"No, Aaron, I'm not. I don't think I want to know. How far is Louvain from Brussels? A few kilometers?"

"It's only for a few months," he continued, "my family will remain in the States, of course."

"Of course."

"It's something I've always wanted to take a crack at. What do you think, Kate?"

"I think it's nice."

"Nice?"

He leaned forward across the table, pushing his untouched hot wine aside. "NICE? I rearrange my life for you and you say it's nice?"

"Wait a minute. Just one damn minute. First of all, I didn't ask you to rearrange your life for me. And secondly, I don't believe that you did it for me. You rearranged your life for you and then dragged me into it."

"Do you know what you're doing, Kate?" He pushed at the nosepiece of his glasses with his index finger. "You're ruining a great friendship."

I sat back and sighed. "Obviously I already did that at our last meeting," I responded with genuine sadness in my voice.

"Kate, please. I have less than twenty-four hours here."

"Don't lean on me Aaron."

"Look, I'm not trying to break up your marriage, or mine. I'm not trying to steal you away from your husband. I just want to see you."

He put his hand across the table in an attempt to touch mine. I drew back.

"Can I see you again?" He said softly and gently. The switch to his therapeutic voice made me feel as if I were on his couch.

"I...I..." I started to speak. Instead I gulped my wine and pushed the glass away. "I have to go home now."

5

I awoke in his arms. It was almost five a.m. I snuggled against his paunchy body and made myself comfortable. Aaron was taking the afternoon flight back to New York and I was due at the hospital at seven.

He gave me a hug. "You know, I remember the first time I saw you. I'll never forget it."

"Well, how could you? I'm sure you were impressed by my bountiful brains, beauty, and boobs, though not necessarily in that order."

"Wrong, but not that I didn't notice. I was impressed by the way you handled yourself. You were a natural." He rolled over on his side and leaned on his elbow. "Remember Wally?" He went on without waiting for an answer. "Whenever new students arrived, he'd pick out the most vulnerable looking candidate he could find. His line never varied. 'Are you a nurse?' he'd ask. Once eye contact was made, he'd go in for the kill. 'Gee, Nurse, can you get me my meds? It's easier getting a blowjob around here than it is to get medications.'"

"I remember. He was with the Nam group. All on hard stuff." I looked at Aaron. "Did he really say that to all the nursing students?"

"He certainly did. And I'll never forget the look on his face as you stood there looking so innocent in your plaid mini-skirt and knee socks..."

"Hey, Sternberg, you asked me to dress that way just so I could play the daughter parts in your psychodrama."

"Yeah, and without batting an eyelash, you replied, in a soft, sweet voice, 'Well, that seems reasonable since meds have to be signed for under federal law and blowjobs do not.' The poor bastard almost went into shock. You know, Kate, you were the first and only student to pass the 'Wally Test.'"

"The 'Wally Test,' huh? It wouldn't surprise me in the least if you put him up to it."

"Hey, would I do a thing like that?" he asked, feigning indignation.

"Yes, you would. As a matter of fact, I've never forgiven you for putting me in your damn 'hot seat,' then asking me to name the sickest person in the room while surrounded by eighty of your patients. You know, Aaron, I considered naming you."

"You're kidding?"

"I didn't have the guts or I would have."

He laughed uncertainly. He couldn't be sure if I was serious or not. Neither could I. We both pushed down in the bed and settled on our backs.

After a few minutes of silence, I remarked, "You know, Aaron, it bothers me that the nurses here are not required to be educated in psych."

Aaron shook his head, "You're kidding? They're not?"

I shook my head at him. "I get so angry when I see how some patients are treated, the decisions that are made. Some psych nurse I turned out to be. I'm so God damn frustrated."

Aaron rubbed he eyes and reached for his glasses. "Your problem is simple enough to diagnose." He paused professionally, "In the States you were able to give your opinions, reasons, logical assumptions. You were able to ventilate."

"But I do here too."

"Partially true, but it's not the same. First of all, you're trying to live in a different environment, bucking a different system. More important, you're bucking it in another language. You know as well as I that it's difficult enough to communicate in your own language…"

"And I'm trying to do it in kindergarten French. Not much satisfaction in that. Poor prognosis, Doc," I sighed.

"I don't know…depends." He took off his glasses, kissed me, and moved his hand to my thigh.

6

The spring that followed kept all of Northern Europe blanketed under cold, wet weather. Frank continued to travel and I continued to work at *Ste. Gudule.*

"Come on, Kate, why don't you take some time off and come with me," urged Frank. "It will do you good, and it will be fun for both of us."

I did have vacation time coming to me. Belgian nurses

were allocated a great deal of holiday time but it wasn't always easy getting it. We had to apply, in writing, and even then it could be canceled or changed at the whim of our dried up old Director of Nursing. I did apply, in writing, for the first ten days in April in anticipation of going with Frank, but I had made a classical American error. I had asked for days 4/1, 4/2, 4/3, 4/4, 4/5, 4/6, 4/7, 4/8, 4/9, and 4/10 (April 1st to April 10th). So guess what? They gave me January 4th, February 4th, March 4th and so on. In Europe, the day was given first and then the particular month followed. 1/1 was January 1st. Who knew?

"There's always some reason why you can't come along," said Frank, "If it isn't work, it's school. It's always something."

He was right. It was always something.

"Frank, I can't get the time right now, but I have lots of time coming to me–over a month. All of the other nurses fight for July and August. I'll have May or June for sure. How about then?"

"I can't," he said, "I have to be in New York tomorrow, and you know that May and June are my busiest months, preparing for the July exodus." He put his arms around me and held me close.

"Maybe we can figure out a way to get together…"

He pushed me at arms length and looked at me. "Has your time schedule changed in the last few seconds?"

"No, but."

"Neither has mine," he said as he pulled me close again, kissing me on the top of my head, "end of discussion."

"Frank, I still want to talk about it."

"Why? Either you're coming with me or you're not. There's nothing to talk about."

"Stop treating this like a business discussion. Stop treating me like your business."

"I'm not treating you like my business. It just doesn't make much sense to go around in circles talking about something that has a known conclusion."

"You are treating this like a business discussion. You're the employer and I'm the employee."

"For Christ's sake, Kate."

"I expect more than that from you. I think I'm having a crisis or something. I want empathy. Can't you relate to that?"

"Crisis? Hell no, I can't relate to that at all. I don't have crises...I give them."

I sulked and he was angry.

"Look, Kate, I don't want to argue with you," he put his arms around me, "why don't you take time off when you can and get away somewhere by yourself...or with one of your girlfriends."

Maybe he had already found someone who had the time. "I don't know. I've never done that before. I'll have to think about it."

Frank went off to the States without me. Six weeks later, I headed for Greece. Alone.

Chapter Ten

"...the fruitless and the fruitful
all entwined together..."
        Kahlil Gibran

1

It was the middle of May as I walked through the marble-white complex of Hellenikon Airport. I hoped that the Mediterranean winds would discourage tourists and reduce the risk of meeting anyone I knew. I counted on the Greek reputation of being somewhat casual with airport formalities. It was usual for the well dressed, with American passports, to be quickly passed through customs. I was feeling enormously guilty and I couldn't decide whether to try an aloof-sophisticated look or a charming smile as I waived the distinctive green-covered passport. Maybe it just turned into a guilty grin because the customs man smiled wickedly as he passed me through.

He knows. He can tell. Customs people are good at that. Don't be silly. He can't know. He doesn't know. Aha, doesn't he? I continued arguing with myself as I walked rapidly towards the exit, dragging my suitcase. I had to escape from the terminal and the all-knowing eyes of the customs man.

"Excuse me, Miss, may I help you?"

I jumped out of my skin. "God damn it, don't do that."

"Don't do what, Miss? I only want to help you with your luggage."

"Get away from me."

"Hey, you've got me all wrong."

"Get out of my way. You can't do this sort of thing in Greece."

"What sort of thing? Excuse me, Miss, but you have the wrong idea. I was going to offer to share a taxi with you."

"Don't be so damned funny when I'm so damned nervous, Aaron."

"Aaron? Who's Aaron? My name is Morton Radakewitz, but you can call me Morty."

"Stop being such a jerk, Morty," I hissed.

The customs man was walking towards us. I smiled brightly at him and walked into the glorious Athenian sun.

The warmth of the climate and the people made a deep impression on me. We rented small separate apartments at the *Ariane* on *Timoleontos Vassou*. Our plan was to come and go at different times, always meeting outside. Our days would be spent sightseeing. Our nights were to be spent making love. It was supposed to be a happy, make-believe time for both of us.

At the end of the second day, it was my turn to be the first one back at the *Ariane*. I left Aaron at the Acropolis Museum absorbing the works of Phidias.

"Good afternoon, Misses. How do you enjoy your stay here?" The owner of the *Ariane* was a kindly old gentleman named George Socrates Theodopolous. I instinctively liked him and chatted with him whenever the opportunity presented itself.

"Everything is just wonderful, Mr. Theo."

"It is good that everything is wonderful for you, because I am taking away your rooms."

"Taking my rooms? You mean my apartment? I don't understand."

He moved his head from side to side while saying yes, which confused me even more.

"But you can't do that. I have a paid reservation."

"Your money will be returned."

"You can't do that. Where would I go?"

His eyes twinkled behind his thick glasses. "Perhaps the American gentleman will share his rooms with you?"

I was totally unprepared for this. "What a perfectly dreadful thing to suggest."

"Ha. Misses, never become an actress or a spy. You would not only never win an Oscar, you would be shot."

"As a spy?"

He looked thoughtful. "Maybe even as an actress."

I put my handbag on the desk and leaned on my elbow. "That obvious, huh?"

"You cannot even fool the cleaning woman."

"Well, I've heard that chamber maids are the most difficult to deceive."

"Ha! Not this one. She is very easy to fool. I know... she is my cousin."

"I feel terrible."

"Why should you feel terrible? It becomes more practical this way. You save money. You don't run around the halls in the middle of the night opening and closing doors. You save energy..."

If I couldn't even fool old Mr. Theo and his cousin, then apparently the only one I was fooling was myself.

"Come outside," he beckoned, "we will have a glass of Retzina. It will make you feel good."

We crossed the street and seated ourselves in white openwork chairs under a green and white umbrella.

"Two Retzina," he ordered.

"Oh no, please, I'll have a cup of tea."

"Tea? You really are ill."

"No, I'm not."

"Then why do you want tea? In Greece people drink tea when they are ill."

"It's just that I don't care for Retzina." I couldn't very well tell him that I thought it tasted like shellac.

"Okay. You do not have to drink Retzina." He fingered his worry beads. "We will have coffee instead. Good Greek coffee."

Coffee? I don't drink coffee. The waiter put two small cups of dark coffee before us. Now I really will be sick. I watched Mr. Theo sip the hot brew with unbridled delight. He smacked his lips as he put his cup down.

"Ah, good. You like Greek coffee."

It was not a question. It was a statement. I couldn't hurt his feelings. I couldn't be the Ugly American. I sipped the coffee delicately. I sampled some more. Not bad. It tasted a lot better than I ever thought it would. "Yes, Mr. Theo, you're right, good Greek coffee."

I spied Aaron walking up the other side of the street and I waved to him. He ignored me completely. I called his name. He hesitated before crossing over and approached the table warily.

"Hello, Mr. Theodopolous. Uh, Miss," he nodded.

"Sit down, Aaron, and have a cup of coffee. It's delicious."

He sat down stiffly and rubbed his beard, as if he was asked to ponder some great question.

I turned and faced him. "You want the good news or the bad news?" He didn't answer. "Well, the bad news is that we've been caught." He looked uncertain. "And the good news," I continued, "is that I can make a cup of coffee any time of the day or night in your apartment." He hesitated, then smiled with relief.

I moved in without delay, and that was the beginning of my disenchantment. Aaron was fun to be with, but in small doses. I didn't like living with him in the same apartment. He was always there, ever present. I never felt that way with

Frank. I could live happily in a closet with him.

That evening we left the *Ariane* together. We went to *Tourkolimano* for dinner, and selected our lobsters from one of many stainless steel drawers where the catch of the day was kept. We crossed the street and selected one of the tables under the awning. I looked out at the fishing boats. The night was mild and comfortable. I held my arms with my hands and sighed loudly. Except for some free-floating anxiety, all seemed right with the world.

"What's a nice Irish-Catholic girl like you doing having dinner in Greece with a Jewish psychiatrist?"

"Stuffing myself with lobster and Retzina."

"I thought you hated Retzina."

"I thought I did too. Every day I surprise myself a little more. My taste buds are either developing or deteriorating with age, or maybe it's the Gods from Mount Olympus."

"Of course, it's the Old Olympus syndrome."

"Hah, remember that?" I said, licking my fingers and grabbing Aaron's barely-eaten lobster. I couldn't allow a picked-over cephalethorax to go to waste. "On old Olympus top most top, a Fin and German viewed some hops."

"That's not the way I learned the cranial nerves."

"Of course you did, Aaron. Everyone does."

"No. Everyone does not. Just because you learned them that way doesn't mean that everyone did. I learned them quite differently." He cleared his throat in preparation for his forthcoming recital. "Oh, oh, oh, to touch and feel a girl's vagina, so hot."

"You're making that up." I put Aaron's lobster down and began cleaning my sticky fingers.

"Nope."

"Well, it's disgusting."

"I don't think it's disgusting."

"What are you telling me? They teach women one way

and men another? You're telling me that there's not only a double standard for sexual morality and aging, but even a double standard when it come to teaching mnemonics?"

"Tsk, tsk, Kate, you sound angry."

"I'm not just angry, I'm pissed. Chauvinist crap. I'm sick of it. Besides, I could make up something equally as vulgar."

"Go ahead," he extended his arms in a magnanimous gesture, "give us a mnemonic for the feminists' sisters and put us MCP's, male chauvinist pigs, to shame."

"Alright, I will. Give me your pen." I used the napkin to write out the first letters of the twelve cranial nerves. I thought for a minute, and started, "Okay, how's this?" I scribbled as I spoke, "Oh, oh, oh, to tongue and fuck a guy's very solid hard-on." I smiled victoriously and pushed the napkin toward him.

"Feel pretty self-satisfied?"

"Uh huh, yes I do."

"Why?"

"I think that I proved something."

"What do you think you proved?"

"That women are equally capable of chauvinism, of having equally dirty minds..."

"Why'd you feel that you had to prove it to me?"

"I don't know. Except maybe, anything to support the fact that equality between the sexes can exist, and...I just plain got angry."

"I noticed." He reached for my hand. "The last angry woman."

Good God, that's what Frank calls me. I pulled my hand away.

It had been a pleasant five days. We snuggled down into the double bed on our last night. I wondered what I was doing in Greece with a New York shrink. It was no longer curiosity on my part. That was satisfied if not by our first encounter, certainly by the second. It surely was not the sex.

"It's been a great vacation, Kate. I enjoyed it. I don't want it to end, but it's a nice memory." He kissed me on the tip of my nose.

"Why am I here, Aaron?"

"You sound painfully serious."

"I feel painfully serious."

"Do you want a personal or professional opinion?"

"Both. Then I'll judge for myself which I can live with."

He smiled. "I'm not sure that I can separate it out anymore...my affection, my love, my need for you may color my thinking."

"So what is it?" I went on, ignoring his preface. "Am I of an age, a time in life? Do I need to be reassured of my...I don't know...my desirability?"

"I don't think so. You've already discovered that. Confirmed by most men that you come in contact with, at work, socially. You don't need me to tell you. I think you already know. But it's not all that simple, you're not all that simple." Aaron folded his arms behind his head and breathed deeply. "I believe the basic ingredient that I bring to our relationship is friendship..."

"Ohhhh, Aaron," I groaned, "Bull."

"What do you mean, bull? It's not bull. Listen, smart ass, it's not unlike your relationship with Sally, Jenny or even Gina."

"You forget one small item. S-e-x."

"Okay, so there's sex. But you never orgasm with me. You hold back just enough to salve your conscience. The old 'don't go all the way' Catholic School attitude." He rolled over and looked me in the eye. "Maybe you still have to retain some of the old Kathleen for Frank. You have an image with him that began when you were how old? Fourteen? Fifteen?"

"Thirteen."

It was at a Knights of Columbus dance. Sheila McCarthy and I were supposed to be at the Confraternity and I saw

Frankie deMeo for the first time. He was seventeen and the best looking boy I'd ever seen. He made me feel something I never felt before. It was a *coup de foudre* and I was in love. I was aglow just thinking about him.

"I met him at thirteen, began dating him at fifteen, and I married him at seventeen." I stopped and thought a moment. "That's part of what I don't understand. That should be a plus. Time-in is always a plus, isn't it? Time-in should make the relationship between Frank and me the best of all...which theoretically negates my being here."

"It should and it does in some ways, but not in others. Don't forget we began a relationship in a different era, as mature people, not kids. We've approached each other at an adult level. We expect different things from one another. Don't you see, Kate, different starting points have different rules, different expectations."

"I'm confused," I laughed. "Was all that professional or personal?" I wanted to lighten things up. We were getting into areas that I wasn't sure I wanted to get into.

Aaron remained serious. "I'm confused too, but I guess that professionally you have an unfulfilled need which is probably not sexual, but rather, is manifested in intellect and personality..." His voice trailed off and he became thoughtful for a moment. "Personally, I think that you're trying to hold on to some of the old Kathleen Mary, not so much for Frank as for yourself."

"So big deal, I have Catholic hang-ups."

"Yeah, and I have Jewish ones. Everyone has some kind of hang-ups."

"I needed a shrink to tell me what I already knew?"

"You pays your money and takes your chances," quipped Aaron.

Aaron wasn't talking about analysis; he was talking about our relationship. He was a mind-fucker. He always tried to get you on his couch. Ordinarily, I would have enjoyed the intellectual challenge, but I was uncomfortable. I never thought of myself as lacking in self-confidence, but maybe the answer to my total life is simply that I'm insecure.

"Aaron, do you think I'm insecure?"

"No."

"No? What do you mean, no? Psychiatrists aren't supposed to say no."

"Okay, yes." He put his hand on my leg.

"Damn, I'm serious." I sprang to a sitting position.

"Okay, okay, seriously...you're one of the most God damned secure women I know. Too secure."

I glared at him. "Persons. Secure persons."

After a long silence, Aaron began, "You're here because you need me. You need to be with me."

"Bull."

"Bull? Again? What is this, a conditional reflex?"

Ignoring him, I went on, "Yeah, pure bull, Aaron. I know why I'm here."

"If you know all the answers, then spare me your questions," he commented more hurt than angry.

"Come on, be realistic. I'm here...yes, I'm here because I wanted the experience of having sex...having an affair or whatever. A lot of women think about going to their grave having known only one man. It bothers them, whether they admit it or not. I'm equally as sure it would never have happened had I remained in the States."

The truth was that Aaron's appeal rested in the fact that he was safe, comfortable, and by trade, a good listener. Aaron didn't comment so I continued. "There was this guy, one of Frank's clients, at a dinner party. He told me that women who would never dream of being unfaithful in Athens, Georgia would find it easy to be promiscuous in Athens, Greece. Maybe that's what they mean about birds not fouling their own nest." I sighed heavily at my own attempt at analysis. "You angry?"

Aaron lifted his gaze. "No, not really. Guess I'm lucky I happened to be a bird." He pulled me on top of him and cupped my breasts with his hands. I rolled over on my side. "Not tonight, Aaron."

2

"*Vite! Vite! Le Six!*"

I recognized the nascent hysterical pitch of a student. We all began to move at once. I ran to Bed 6 and saw the student staring at *Monsieur* Maus. He was lying on the bed with a nebulizer aimed at his trach. He was ominously silent.

"*Il est mort, il est mort,*" she sobbed.

Everyone sprang into action, hooking up leads to the cardiac monitor, feeling for the carotid pulse, and placing an ambu bag over his nose and mouth.

We respectfully parted as one unit when Anton arrived. He listened briefly with his stethoscope, gave two precordial thumps and began, one-two-three-four-five. Martine gave a burst with the ambu bag. One-two-three... A respirator was rolled in and hooked up.

Anton raised his arms. "Attention," he commanded. Everyone obeyed and stood back from the bed as he placed the paddles on the body. I moved back, pulling the still-running nebulizer with me. As I went to turn it off, I thought that I noticed a peculiar odor emitting from the vapor. I turned as I heard a collective sigh. I knew that they had gotten a heartbeat. *Monsieur* Maus seemed to be responding.

"Bring the nebulizer back here *Madame. Vite.*"

"I think you had better check it out before..."

Follet grabbed the nebulizer and aimed it at his trach.

"*Monsieur,* that's not distilled water in there." As I spoke *Monsieur* Maus arrested again and the team once more flew into action.

"Attention," Anton commanded. He raised the paddles in the deliberate hesitating gesture of a conductor about to create a symphony out of the assorted animate and inanimate objects before him. The electrical discharge jolted *Monsieur* Maus into an imitation of momentary life. Even the monitor awoke. But *Monsieur* Maus relaxed and returned to his still state and the monitor joined him. There was no more life to be found in either.

Willie walked in. I asked him to check out the solution in the nebulizer.

He sniffed. He tasted. "*Mon Dieu!* I think it is some kind of cleaning fluid." He looked around. "Who filled this nebulizer?"

No one had? It could have been anyone, including Gabby, the nurse's aide. He checked out the liter containers of distilled water, which were kept in the storeroom along with cleaning fluids of different types. The solution in the nebulizer turned out to be carbon tetrachloride. Willie suggested to Follet that all of the containers should be separated and labeled.

3

On a Friday, late in May, Chantal and I were hurrying down the long corridor in *Zaventem Aeroport*.

"You are too good to me, Catleen."

It was good of me, and for some reason it was a lot easier to explain to Frank than to Aaron. Frank was on a business trip in Monte Carlo and we planned to meet there late Sunday afternoon. We had finally worked out a way to spend time together. Aaron was disturbed over my being away so long. He was beginning to act more like a husband and Frank was beginning to act more like a lover.

"I am so ex-cee-ted."

"Excited," I corrected.

"I cannot wait to see Maman and Papa. It has been months since Papa's transfer. Oh Catleen, it is all sooo sooo ex-cee–tating..."

Chantal and Larry had finally set the date. I too was ex-cee-tated. I could barely believe it was all happening, but here we were, on our way to Rome to break the news to the entire Vasari family.

"...and if only Laree would have made his mind before they left Bruxelles. I hope we arrive before they depart for Lake Como...or is it depart to Lake Como? All this English is very tea-aring...*fatigue*...it hurts my head."

She smiled provocatively as she placed her handbag on the customs table for inspection. I watched with amusement as she flustered the young agent. She giggled as he struggled with the catch, then she said something to him in Flemish that made him blush a bright shade of pink.

We made our way single file through the metal detector, boarded the plane at a nearby gate and sank heavily into our seats. After a few minutes of silence, I turned to Chantal and inquired, "*Ca va,* my dear?"

She answered in French. I guess all of that thinking in English really had been tiring for her. "I'm frightened now. Maman will be totally agreeable, but Papa...I don't know?" She began chewing on her cuticle. "He won't like Laree very much. Laree is sooo American."

I felt myself bristle a little. I wondered what connotes 'sooo American?'

"Catleen, you must be the one to talk to Papa. He will love you, and also you have much experience with Italians."

"Me? You're out of your gourd. I'm just your basic, ordinary, everyday friend. I'm not working on Papa. You get Mama to do that. That's what Mamas are for."

"Oh Catleen," tears brimmed in her large brown eyes, "suppose he says *non?*"

"Then do whatever you want to do anyway. You're of age for heaven's sake. You have your rights." I shifted uncomfortably in my seat. "What is it Chantal? What's bothering you? I've never seen you so edgy. Is it really Papa?"

She leaned back and closed her eyes.

At DaVinci Airport, two good-looking young men who were roughly Chantal's age met us. I assumed they were her cousins. They exchanged greetings Italian style—voluminous kisses, phrases, gestures, and embraces. I stood by, quietly enjoying the spectacle of Italian opera.

"*Scusate.*"

I turned to my left as I felt someone tug at my suitcase.

"*Scusate,*" repeated a serious faced young man who looked as if he had posed for Raphael.

"No, thank you," I said, looking at the beautiful sculptured face, the high cheekbones, the dark curly hair. He was the reincarnation of an old master's painting. I tugged back on my valise. He let go and then made another attempt to grab the handle.

"Chantal, how do you say 'get lost' in Italian?" Not that I really wanted him to get lost. It would be nice to be picked up by a stranger in Rome, this particular stranger anyway. Chantal and the two young men turned to me.

"Allo Catalina. I am Angelo." Angelo embraced me. "And this is my friend Stefano." Stefano embraced me. "And that guy who is trying to help you with your valise is my brother Vittorio."

I suddenly felt very foolish and relaxed my hold on the suitcase. Vittorio didn't embrace me.

"He's a little shy," offered Stefano.

"I'm very sorry, Victorio, I didn't..."

"Vittorio," he corrected.

"That's what I said, didn't I?"

"VEE-tor-io," he repeated.

"So I have an American accent, don't you find it charming?" Americans find French and Italian accents charming, but no one finds an American accent charming.

"It is of no use, Catalina," volunteered Angelo, "he speaks barely a word of English."

I pointed to my valise and said, "GRA-tsye, Vee-tor-io." He flashed a magnificent smile, revealing evenly spaced white teeth. I felt my breath catch in my throat.

Every last one of Chantal's relatives must have been invited for dinner to celebrate her forth-coming marriage. I found an inordinate amount of people named Zia and Zio until I finally figured out that it meant aunt and uncle.

Everyone was somewhere in the middle of what I thought to be the sixth course. I'd lost count, fallen behind, and I guessed that I may have made it through the third.

"Papa says you must eat. You are too thin," interpreted Chantal. "You look as if you will break in half…like a twig."

Someone refilled my wineglass for the umpteenth time. I lost count on that too. They were all high on *vino* and life. I know I was.

Later that night, Chantal and I shared a bedroom on the third floor. "Happy?" I asked.

"*Chouette,*" she laughed softly. "Hey," she asked, reaching for the light switch, "how do you like Vittorio?"

"Yummy," I breathed into the darkened room.

The light flashed on again. "Oh, Catleen, what means… yum-mee?"

"Double *chouette.*" The light went out again and we giggled like adolescent girls at their first pajama party.

Breakfast was a comparatively silent affair. The Visari's had already left for Lake Como. Zia Teresa, the maiden aunt, stayed on as the chaperone. Chantal and I were going to spend the day sightseeing. Stefano and Vittorio would act as our guides. The four of us walked up and down the Seven Hills of Rome. It was all for my benefit. I was the tourist. We dined out of doors that evening in the Piazza Navona. While savoring risoto and vino, I gazed at the fountain of the Four Rivers. Vittorio combined the history and the folklore of the Piazza with Chantal softly translating. The beauty that Bernini had created and the warmth of the wine contributed to the fairy-tale quality of the evening. It was well after midnight when we finally arrived back at the house on *Via Veneto*. Zia Teresa called down from the head of the stairs.

"She's telling us to go to bed," Chantal giggled.

"Good idea. Let's go," said Stefano grabbing Chantal, who giggled again.

Zia was hysterically funny standing there at the top of the stairs in her long opaque night robe and gray plaited hair. But I suppose, with all of the wine I drank, almost anything would have struck me funny. She cuffed Vittorio on the ear as we passed her on the stairs.

"*Eh, basta, Zia.*" He didn't seem to think it was funny nor did I. I decided that I didn't like her at all. The four of us continued our climb to the third floor Stefano and Vittorio noisily climbed the stairs to the fourth floor.

Moments later there was a light tap at the door. It was Stefano and Vittorio with two bottles of wine.

"Shhh," cautioned Chantal, "the old witch has big ears."

While Stefano was busily opening the wine, Chantal guided me into the corner of the room.

"Catleen?"

"Catleen, what?" I asked suspiciously.

"This is my last chance to see Stefano alone."

"Stefano?"

"Stefano was my first boyfriend."

"Chantal, you're getting married," I whispered, "in three months."

"Catleen, please," she whined.

"Well, where am I supposed to go?"

She smiled. Her liquid brown eyes twinkled mischievously.

"Oh, no," I said, "oh, no, you don't."

"But, Catleen," she pouted, "He really likes you. He has spoken of no one else to Stefano since you have arrived. You would make him so happy if you would go to his room."

It amazed me how fluent her English became when she wanted something.

"No way, you French flake, I'm not going to anyone's room with anyone. I'm staying right here."

"Please?"

"No."

"*S'il te plâit.*"

"*No.*"

"*S'il te plâit,* my dear one."

"*S'il te plâit* yourself, Chantal."

"Then perhaps you will go downstairs and have a very large cup of tea. Give me a little hour. Is that too much to ask? Please?"

"Okay," I relented. I waved "*Ciao*" to Stefano and Vittorio who were quietly drinking and talking between themselves, and quickly left the room.

I made my way down to the kitchen. I lit the fire and put up a kettle of water. I found a cup, settled myself at the large table and looked around the kitchen when the sound of padded footsteps came through the doorway behind me. I turned in my chair and felt a vague pang of disappointment. It was Teresa. I began to explain that I was about to have a cup of tea but she wasn't listening. She was raving and I couldn't understand a word; I understood quite clearly though when she turned off the burner under the teakettle. She pointed upstairs. She was taking her duenna role a little too seriously. I decided not to confront her. When in Rome...

I went through the hall and up the steps, two at one time. I was breathless when I reached the bedroom. I tapped at the door. God, Chantal was going to be pissed. No answer. Pissed or not, I knocked firmly. No answer.

"Please, Chantal, let me in." I pounded on the door. "Let me in, God damn it."

"Psst, Catalina." Vittorio was rapidly descending the stairs from the fourth floor. I started towards him and stopped halfway. I was totally confused. What am I doing running

around in the middle of the night like an idiot? Vittorio
reached me, grabbed my wrist and pulled me toward the stairs
to the fourth floor while I pulled toward Chantal's room. We
heard a door creak open from the second floor.

"*Zia*," he whispered.

We put on a burst of speed, running up the stairs and into
the nearest room. We leaned with our backs to the door and I
looked into a twin-bedded room. I started to laugh, but he put
his finger to his lips, cautioning me to silence. He pulled me to
the far bed, pushed me in and piled the bed linens loosely on
top of me. I watched from under the thin sheet as he rumpled
the other bed. There was a loud knock on the door. Another
knock at the door.

"Vittorio," Zia's voice rumbled.

"*Si, Zia*." Vittorio answered in a sleepy voice while
stripping off his clothes.

He threw open the door and stood there more beautiful
than Michelangelo's David, the light from the hallway
enhancing his silhouette.

"*Mamma mia*," screamed the stricken Teresa throwing her
hand over her eyes, but not before taking a good look at
Vittorio and catching with her peripheral vision the lumpy
form of whom she thought to be Stefano asleep in the other
bed.

The door slammed, the lock turned and Vittorio slipped
effortlessly back into his trousers before turning around. By
the time he reached the bed, I was convulsing with laughter.
He put his hand over my mouth, caressing my lips. "Shhh," he
cautioned with a smile.

He turned on the bedside light, reached under the bed
and produced a bottle of wine and two glasses. We drank
together as co-conspirators. We tried to communicate
verbally. He went over to the large old desk in the other side
of the room and returned with small copybook, much the
same as children use for their written lessons. He opened it
shyly and revealed its contents. Words–words that he had

been collecting a few at a time. He had been trying to teach himself English. It had been his secret and now it was ours.

"*Bella* Catalina. Bee-oo-tee-fool."

I hope that's not prophetic, but then again you may be right. Aloud I said, "*Bella Vittorio.*"

"No," he frowned.

"Oh yes you are, you just don't know it."

He frowned again, and ran his finger down the pages and stopped. "Man."

"Right. You man. You Tarzan," I said pointing my finger at him, "And me Jane," I laughed.

"No *bella*. Man," he insisted.

Well, who could argue with that?

As we continued our word game, Vittorio inched his way close to me. His right arm and the right side of his body were lightly brushing mine. I felt tingly and breathless. I held up my left hand and turned my jade ring around so that it looked like a wedding band. I pointed to the gold band and to myself, trying to indicate that I was married. He smiled, nodded, pointed to my ring finger and to his own third finger, left hand. Why you devil you, I should have known. I'll bet your wife is at Lake Como with the rest of the clan.

Now he put up two fingers, then with his palm flat and his hand out in front, indicated two small heights from the floor.

"Oh, I get it. You have two children."

"DU-e FI-lye," he enunciated while pointing to me.

"Aha, two girls." This language thing is getting easier all the time.

"TRE," he pointed to my abdomen and shrugged his shoulders.

Oh, aha, wow. I hope this means his wife is expecting their third and not that he intends to impregnate me. Not to be outdone, I too put up two fingers, then indicated one small height with my outstretched palm, and then impulsively made a cradling motion with my arms. He smiled. He understood. "One, UNO, boy…one UNO girl," I said pointing first to him and then to myself for clarification.

He smiled and took my hand. Oh boy, here it comes. No, he was writing something with his finger on my open palm. I didn't get it. I gave him a puzzled look. He pointed to my eyes and then to his palm. I watched carefully as he started writing again. What a way to communicate. Just when I thought it was getting easy, it got harder.

"Three. Zero. Three zero. Thirty." He was pointing to himself.

He's telling me he's thirty. I really don't want to know. I'm only going to feel guiltier. He's so young. Oh Jesus. He was holding up his hand in front of me like a slate board. He wanted me to write. He wanted to know how old I was. My God, how do I get into these things? I don't want to tell him how old I am. Well, there's only one thing a nice Irish Catholic girl can do in a case like this. Lie.

It's a sin to tell a lie, Kathleen Mary. Oh yeah, it would be a bigger sin not to. Go ahead and lie, Kate, and make it big. I put my long pointed finger on his palm and started to write slowly and deliberately. I drew a three, hesitated and then drew a two. I watched his face. He didn't bat an eyelash. Shit, I could have lied even bigger. He took my hand and kissed it with the courtly passion that only an Italian-Italian could bring off. Then he turned my hand around and kissed the palm. I didn't know that the palm was an erogenous zone, but it was somehow deliciously obscene.

Vittorio poured me another glass of wine. He pushed the beds together, then took a blanket from one of the beds and wedged it along the crack between the two. He put the bedside lamp on the floor and put his shirt over it to diffuse the sharp lighting. He was incredibly efficient. I had the feeling he had done this before. I didn't care.

The first time he penetrated me, I groaned with pleasure. He stopped and looked very serious as he searched my face.

"Catalina," he whispered heavily, "no good?"

"Yummy," I whispered back closing my eyes.

I waited for more. He didn't move. God, don't stop now. I opened my eyes and looked up at his expression of confusion.

"Vittorio. Good. Yes. *Si*." He still hesitated. "Vittorio, *va bene*," I smiled.

He resumed his thrusts, the gold medallion around his neck keeping rhythm like a metronome. I thought he might have won the medal in the Olympics. Vittorio was a sexual athlete. He could have easily won seven gold medals in the Olympics if they had his category. After we utilized all of the known positions, he invented new ones, positions that I thought would have been totally impossible. My favorite event of the evening was when he stood up on the bed and hoisted me up by my ankles with his strong hands. Every time he'd thrust, he'd pull up on my ankles. It was wild and exciting. I'd never been screwed standing on my head before. It's amazing what a little wine and a lot of lying can do for one's physical abilities. Those two variables along with being in a foreign country helped to provide for a complete sense of abandon. I was grateful however, that I didn't tell him I was twenty-five. Who knows what may have been in store for me?

I kissed him on his sculptured lips and he kissed back. He slid his hands under my ribcage, and with his strong arms he bench-pressed me. I stiffened my body. We held the pose several seconds. Then he slowly lowered me on top of him until our lips met.

5

Chantal and I collapsed sleepily into our seats. I had hoped that it wouldn't be a full flight so that we might spread out a little. I was exhausted. Between Greece and Rome, I felt as if I'd been on a sexual safari.

Chantal was busily rummaging through her bag. "*Le voilà.* Here, Catleen, he gave me this for you." I tore open the small envelope she handed me and Vittorio's familiar gold medallion fell out. I picked it up and examined it. It seemed to be an ancient Roman coin bound in gold filigree.

"I don't understand." I looked into the envelope for an explanation and pulled out a letter. I unfolded the pages and stared intently, trying to focus on the words. "Jesus, Mary and Joseph, I can't read this. It's in Italian."

"No problem, Catleen. You forget, I am fluent in Italian. I shall read it for you."

"Oh no you won't," I said, clasping the letter to my chest and pulling back in my seat. Chantal and I had not discussed the previous evening. I didn't know what the letter might reveal and I wasn't about to take any chances.

"Give," she ordered, wiggling her fingers at me.

"I can't."

"*Alors,*" she puffed out her cheeks impatiently, "who is it that you wish to translate for you? The Italian Embassy? Frank?" I winced with what felt like real physiological pain. "Really Catleen," she said grabbing the letter, "I should think that you would trust me." She pouted. "I trust you with my life, my very life," she added with a dramatic flair.

"It's not a question of trust, Chantal, it's just...I don't know."

She began to read, her voice in a confidential whisper, "My darling Catalina, I have not before felt for a woman what I have felt for you. I knew from the moment that I saw you at the airport that I was destined to fall hopelessly in love with you..."

"He's kidding around," I interrupted, laughing nervously.

"*Silence,* Catleen. It is beautiful. Uhm, he is in love with you, *oui.*" She found her place and continued, "I have thought of nothing else but how we might be together, but I realize the impossibility of such a dream. We have responsibilities, particularly I think of your little baby..." Chantal looked at me and wrinkled her brow. "What little baby?"

"Go on, go on, Chantal."

"So that you may never forget me, so that I may be continually in your thoughts, I give you my medallion. It has been in my family for generations..."

"I can't accept that. This is crazy. This whole thing is insane."

"Hush," she admonished and continued, "I wish you to wear it next to your heart. Perhaps one future day it may bring us together again. Vittorio."

"Oh God."

Chantal took the medallion out of my hand. "It is sooo beautiful, *très magnifique*."

"I can't accept this. It's too expensive, too personal, too family, too involved. I can't accept this."

"What will you do? Send it back? No doubt he has already explained it away. You will only succeed in getting him into trouble. Is that what you wish?"

"For all I know, he has a drawer full of medallions," I sighed, "Chantal, what can I do?"

"*Très facile*. You keep it. He wanted you to have it. *Alors*, you keep it." She smiled and settled back in her seat. "I would very much like to hear about your last night." She laughed, "Baby? You have a baby?" She leaned close and put the medallion around my neck. "*Mon Dieu*, Catleen, you must have made a very large impression to receive such a gift as this."

I still had no intention of discussing my evening and without meeting her eyes I replied, "I've no idea what you mean. I had a cup of tea and fell asleep on the living room sofa." I met her eyes with a vestige of truth, "I even tried to get into your room...if you remember."

Chantal stared me down and I fingered the filigreed edge of the medallion. "I can't keep this. What would I tell Frank?" I took it off.

"*Ca va*." Chantal plucked it from my hand and placed it around her own neck, "*Alors,* I shall wear it."

When we arrived at Zaventem, Chantal tried to persuade

me to go home with her. "But you have hours before your flight. We can have coffee or something with Laree."

"No, I don't think so, Chantal. I don't want to hassle the traffic and I'm paranoid about missing planes."

I waved goodbye until she was out of sight. Then I sat on a bench in the nearly deserted Gate 28. I put my head back and closed my eyes. I was tired and happy and I knew why. I relaxed and drifted away with my thoughts.

6

"Catleen, awake."

"What on earth are you doing here?" She didn't answer. "Chantal, *qu'est qui se passe?*"

"I am coming with you. I don't know where else to go. I just met with Laree." She chewed at her cuticle. "I do not wish to marry him."

"Why not?" She didn't answer. "Come on now, you just have a case of pre-marriage jitters." She still didn't answer.

"It is finished with Laree. I think I knew for a long time. It was a complete charade." She put her hand on my arm. "It is okay if I go with you, Catleen?"

I called ahead and left a message at Frank's hotel in Monte Carlo letting him know that I would be arriving at Nice and that Chantal would be with me.

Monte Carlo was a business trip for Frank and I surely didn't expect him to be at the airport; I didn't expect to see Guy Peeters either. As soon as they spied us, in the crush of disembarking working Moroccans, they rushed towards us, Frank carrying red flowers and Guy pink ones. They loaded our arms until we could hold no more. That gesture, along with taking time out from business, made us feel very special. People stared, wondering who we were. Chantal gamboled towards the exit, holding Guy Peeters' arm.

The week sped by. While Frank and Guy spent their days

in meetings, Chantal and I wandered around the quiet countryside. Evenings were spent dining with fascinating people and gambling at the Casino. Nights were for making love. Frank was always in a state of arousal and that made the sex even better. When Frank asked about Chantal and Larry, I pleaded ignorance. Ignorance was wonderful. It meant that you didn't have to deal with anything.

Frank finished his business and he and Guy were ready to return to Brussels. They had their jobs to attend to and that held a high priority in both of their lives. I still had some holiday time left and I wasn't ready to go back. Neither was Chantal. I rang Marie Louise.

7

St. Tropez was glorious in June, the innocent beginning of the season. There were few bodies on the Pampagalo Peninsula and even fewer on Liberty Beach. The bodies were pale, the sand was abundant and the water was blue and clear. You could smell the delicious purity of the air and hear the quiet.

We had been on the beach most of the morning when we decided to have lunch and explore the shops. We donned our swimsuits, fashionable cover-ups and sandals and trudged through the hot sand.

"*Pamplemouse* tonic," ordered Simone and we all followed her lead.

I looked around. "My God, there are all beautiful people here."

"Not like Zandvort," they all laughed.

"Zandvort, I don't get it."

"The Dutch, Catleen, are culturally different than the French," Simone explained. "They have lunch in the nude."

"You're joking."

"No, she's not. It's really quite shocking to see people

dining or waiting in line for a table stark naked."

How could I have been so stupid–falling asleep in the afternoon sun? My back was tender enough, but the usually unexposed parts of my body were going to be sheer agony.

Frank had been trying to talk me into a *St. Tropez* holiday for years. Not I, I'd never take off my clothes. Chantal, Marie Louise and Simone talked me into it in about twenty seconds. Marie Louise suggested that I wear a gold chain around my waist if I felt too naked. I did. It seemed okay. No men were there, at least, no men that we knew.

It was fantastic swimming, splashing ankle deep in the blue water. We spoke French and eavesdropped on the fully clothed Americans who hid behind their sunglasses and beneath their brimmed hats while commenting on our bodies. The men were always complimentary though frequently crude. The women were never complimentary but always genteel.

I took a shower hoping that the cool water would ease the pain of my sun-burned boobs and butt. I patted myself dry and gently pulled on my bikinis. Then I wrapped myself in a towel and left the tiny bathroom.

"*Pauvre* Catleen," sympathized Marie Louise from the hall.

Poor me is right. I nodded in agreement, trudged to the bedroom and carefully placed myself face down in the bed, one of the positions that I obviously had assumed earlier under the sun.

Marie Louise loved *St. Tropez* and had invested in a small apartment. She and Simone Lacroix shared one bedroom and Chantal and I shared the other. There was a pullout couch in the living room to accommodate an overflow of guests. The bathroom and kitchen were small but efficient. Best of all, it was near to the boat basin and the main street of the port.

"Catleen?" Marie Louise called from the doorway, "I have some very special ointment for after the sun. Shall I put some on you?"

Anything will be an improvement. "*Oui*, Marie Louise, *s'il vous plaît*." I raised my body just high enough to rid it of the towel, and I groaned with every movement. Marie Louise knelt over me and squeezed some of the lotion onto my back. My body stiffened at the shock of its coolness on my burning skin. She began to rub with an extraordinary gentle circular motion. She had the most incredible touch. She worked her way slowly from my shoulders down. By the time she reached my waist, I was spellbound. I'd had sun tan lotion put on me before by Frank, but it never felt like this. Is this touch a specialty of Marie Louise? Is this a nurse's touch? Do I have it? Maybe it's a woman's touch. "Whatever it is, it's wonderful."

"*Quoi?*"

"*Rien.*" I didn't want her ever to stop. I thought that this must be how a cat feels when being stroked. My body was responding like a cat. I wanted to purr. She reached my bikinis and started to pull them down gently with one hand, while continuing to apply lotion with the other. It feels so good. Don't stop. Don't ever stop. I never felt so—I don't know. How do I feel? I feel good, warm. Warm all over. Marie Louise was rubbing my bottom with the most sensuous touch I'd ever experienced. No man ever made me feel like that with his touch. Don't stop. I'll lie here forever if you keep doing that.

"*Pauvre,* Catleen. You soofering much?"

I smiled at her English. "*Oui,* I am soofering much." I was suffering more than she knew. My body was enjoying some brand new feeling. My head was analyzing the feeling. Come on, Kate, you got sunburned and your friend is trying to be helpful. Granted, you shouldn't feel like this, but stop analyzing everything you do and feel. Relax and enjoy it. As Jenny would say, "If it feels good—do it." What's wrong with getting a backrub?

"I have finished here, Catleen. Why do you not turn over and I will do your front."

Why can't I just lie here and enjoy my back rub? Even that can't be simple. "I don't think I can. I hurt too much."

"Oh, I will help you." She put her hands under my shoulders and started to roll me over. My body responded with complete ease. My bikinis tumbled from my ankles. Marie Louise lifted my ponytail off of my shoulder. I trembled at her delicate touch. I looked up into her warm brown eyes, her blond hair tumbling forward as she rubbed the lotion into my chest. The flat of her hand glided over my breasts and nipples. They responded to her touch. Somewhere in the background, I could hear *Claude François* singing. I wondered who left the radio on.

9

"No. Absolutely not. I'm not meeting you." It was the day before Aaron was to leave for the States. The months had flown by rapidly. "I can't keep this up. It has to stop. I've become more and more nervous and my guilt is beginning to weigh more than I do. Besides, I'm too old for these shenanigans."

"Come on, Kate."

"It's wrong. It's just plain wrong."

"It's not wrong, I don't feel guilty. You're perseverating."

"Oh, come on."

"No, I don't feel guilty and I know why I want to be with you. It's simple. You're my fantasy."

"Oh please..." I was beginning to realize that Aaron and I were galaxies apart.

"Kate?" He waited. "Kate?"

"Have a safe flight, Aaron." I returned the phone to its cradle.

Chapter Eleven

"And in the sweetness of friendship let there
be laughter and the sharing of pleasures."
Kahlil Gibran

1

IT had been a while since Aaron left Brussels. He kept in
touch. I didn't–except to include him in my "give my love
to" list at the end of my letters to Sally. His words were light
and friendly but there was an open "miss you–come back to
New York" theme. I thought about him from time to time and
I told myself that I regretted nothing. But I wasn't sure that I
believed me.

I'd been busy, between the hospital, collecting research
data for my book, and our social life. The days raced by like a
horse in a dead run.

Frank and I had been developing a relationship–whatever
that meant. We'd begun to recognize each other as individuals
with individual needs. He was treating me like an adult and I
was acting the part. I wasn't sure when or how it started but
we were able to communicate better, and at a higher level.

We had been doing more things together. I'd begun to realize that Frank was my husband, not my father, and he realized that I was no longer a little girl and that I hadn't been one for years. I may have learned something about relationships from Aaron.

Frank's career and earning power had continued to climb: new promotions, new responsibilities, new campaigns. He was always ahead of the times and everyone else. Although we both had academic degrees, he had an MBA and business was considered a far more erudite course of study than nursing. I was feeling some of my old inadequacies.

The rain was falling softly onto the kitchen terrace. Frank and I sat at the table having coffee.

"I wish I could make some real money."

"Why?" Frank looked surprised. "What do you need money for? You don't even spend what you have now."

"You don't understand."

"Well then explain it to me so that I do. I catch on fast."

"Salary–dollars and cents–just happens to be THE outward sign of worth, strength...equality."

"If you're in competition with me for earning power, forget it, you can't make it. I've had a twenty year head start and I picked the right business to be in."

"You're wrong about one thing, Frank. I've never been in competition with you or anyone else...I'm alone in the arena...all by myself...just me." I sighed, "As for the head start, you're right, but it's not fair."

"Lot's of things aren't fair, but it happens to be a fact of life. Face it and live with it."

Whenever we argued it was principle versus end result. Frank looked ahead to the consequences. He always seemed to see the bottom line clearly. I didn't. I thought if the principle was right, then the conclusion would be, too. I should have learned something from my ghetto experience. And yet, I was acutely aware of the second element of Tort Law, which deals with foreseeing the consequences of any action or inaction. As a nurse, I had no problem foreseeing the consequences of anything I did or failed to do while caring for a patient. As a woman, it was not all that clear to me.

The hospital and the August heat were wearing me down and more than likely driving my blood pressure up. I vowed to continue to stick with it. Perhaps it had become some sort of *cause célèbre* for me. It was the system that was so frustrating, not the job. When I was alone with my patients, God was in her heaven and all seemed right with the world.

2

Chantal and Guy Peeters eloped and were married by the Mayor of a small village in France. Chantal assured me that he wore a colorful sash and a silk top hat. She and Guy were ecstatic. According to Frank, Larry Prior wasn't all that broken up about Chantal. He had a new twenty-two year old girlfriend. It seemed that Larry's philosophy was that "women are like Kleenex; when you use one, another pops up in its place." I wondered what happened when the box was empty. Or maybe it was never empty for a man?

Willie removed the stethoscope from his ears. "D*ix huit / dix.*"

"Eighteen over ten. What are you crazy? *Ce n'est pas possible.* Jesus, that would be 180 over 100."

"Catleen, your tension is too high."

"It wasn't a couple of months ago."

"There are three things you must do immediately. First, take off weight, second stop smoking, and third avoid the use of table salt."

It was nice to know that we read the same books. "The problem is, Willie, I weigh 112 pounds. That's about 51 kilo. I don't smoke, and I don't use salt."

"You know," Willie scratched his flaxen head, "it could be the pill. Yes, you know, that's what I think. It's the pill. You must no longer take the pill."

"I can't do that. The pill is like Dumbo's feather. I can't fly without it."

"Dumb? You think the pill is dumb?"

"Oh, no. Never mind," I smiled and shook his hand, "*Merci,* Willie."

I put in a call to Bob Jorgensen, my general practitioner back in the States. He told me to get off the pill. I told him that I couldn't. "If I go off the pill, I'll have a stroke."

"If you don't go off the pill you'll have a stroke." That was a sobering thought. "Have your blood work drawn and call me with the results."

3

I looked down at the still form on the bed. She had short red curly hair and a sprinkling of freckles across her nose, making her appear younger than her fifty years. She reminded me of Sheila McCarthy, or at least what Sheila probably looked like today. Deborah Ralston had been vacationing with a group of American women when she apparently had a Cerebral Vascular Accident on the Paris-Brussels express. Except for the information listed in her passport, we knew nothing about her. I pulled over a chair and sat down.

"Hey," I patted her arm, "Hey Debbie, can you hear me?" I picked up her hand and began to rub it gently. Debbie…Deb, what do they call you? "Deborah, wake up."

"*Qu'est qui se passe, Madame deMeo.*"

I didn't bother to meet Anton's beady eyes. We were in the midst of a war. *"Rien de tout, Monsieur."* I started to rise.

"Assayez-vous," he said pleasantly.

I bent closer to her face. "Debbie, wake up. I want to talk to you." She stirred. Her mouth opened, but there was no sound. "That's it. Try again Deb, I'm listening." Her eyes lazily opened.

"Merci, Madame deMeo." Anton shoved me aside. His pleasantness was short lived, since I had apparently accomplished what he wanted from me. He looked at me coolly and added, "Have you not other duties to perform?"

Deborah Ralston mumbled something unintelligible. Anton bent his small body stiffly towards her, clasped his hands together and asked in English, "Yes Misses, what is it that you speak, Misses?" The green eyes blinked at the heavy French accent and closed in retreat.

"It's okay, Deb," I elbowed my way back into position, "I'm an American nurse."

"What did she say, *Madame?*"

"I don't know, *Monsieur.*"

"But you speak English?"

What was she trying to say? I sure didn't know, but I did know that if I awoke in a hospital in a foreign county, I'd be just a little more comfortable if I heard someone speaking my mother tongue. I made up my mind that Deborah Ralston would receive all that I could give and more.

Later that morning, Marie Louise stuck her head in the door. *"On y va* Catleen. *Une bonne tasse de café bien chaud."*

Deborah was resting comfortably, so I pulled myself out of the chair and followed Marie Louise into the kitchen. A hot cup of coffee sounded good to me. It was crowded this morning and we worked our way over to the corner next to Paul. We discussed the Ralston case and what seemed to be a right-sided hemiparesis. They had already contacted the American Embassy and put in a call to her husband in Rockland County, New York. He was on his way. We wondered if she was a known hypertensive and on any medication. I couldn't understand why they didn't simply ask these questions when they telephoned. My guess was that she didn't take medications at all. American women tend to carry their medications in their handbags when they travel, and there were none in hers.

Willie stopped me later in the hallway. "Bad news, Catleen. Your blood urea nitrogen is high, fifty-three." Jesus. My brain ran the numbers through. If it's that high I should exhibit signs of forgetfulness, then mental clouding, then death. I asked him about the creatinine and he assured me it was normal. It was possible to have one test normal and the other not, but not probable. "Why don't we do the tests over?"

"It is not necessary. We have computers. They are programmed against human error."

Yeah, programmed by humans, I thought.

"You must come in for an IVP."

"I'll have to think about it, *merci beaucoup*."

We started to walk in opposite directions. I stopped, turned and caught up with him. "Willie," I touched his sleeved arm lightly, "I'm going to New York, to my doctor. No hard feelings." He looked surprised. I stuck out my hand. As we shook hands, I was sure that Willie thought it an impetuous decision. It wasn't. It only appeared to be. I made the decision based on all the information I had.

George Ralston arrived in Brussels. He was sick with anguish and didn't know where to turn. All he knew was that his wife went on her first European holiday with an American women's group and somewhere on the train between Paris and Brussels she had a stroke.

"Gosh darn." George Ralston paced the hall outside Debbie's room. "I don't understand the language...anyone."

He stopped abruptly. "I don't know what to do."

Usually, I don't get personally involved with patients or their families, but Frank and I asked George Ralston to dinner that night. He was so alone. I thought about my role as a nurse advocate and I remembered my promise to the comatose Debbie.

"Take her home. Back to the States...as soon as possible." He put down his knife and fork and blinked. "It can be arranged easily enough," I continued. "Special equipment on the plane...a nurse..."

"Will you take her back? Take care of her on the plane and get her to Kennedy?"

"Sure, if that's what you want."

"Good gosh, I don't know how to thank you."

"Don't thank me, I was planning on going to New York anyway. Beside, I owe Debbie. I made her a promise." Or maybe I owe Sheila McCarthy. Frank never would have noticed me if it hadn't been for her.

Frank drove me to *Ste. Gudule*. He pulled up to the ambulance zone. The whole area was empty. I looked at my watch. Early. I was anxious to get started. I wanted Debbie in New York. I wanted me in New York.

Frank looked concerned. He narrowed his blue eyes and asked, "You sure you're okay?" I nodded. "Kate, take care of yourself. Do whatever Bob Jorgensen tells you to do. I don't want to break in a new wife. I've put in too many years training you." I smiled. "Kate, I love you and I couldn't survive without you."

"Yes, you could."

"No, I'd crack..."

"Uh, uh. You're not the type. You're not a cracker, you're really more of a cookie." The ambulance pulled up. I gave him a quick kiss and ran toward the hospital.

The trip to New York went without a hitch. George was

on the same flight and visited Debbie frequently. Debbie and I were at the back of the plane. Two of the seats were replaced by a gurney. I had enough room to comfortably take care of my patient, and I had enough equipment to take care of the entire planeload of passengers. About two hours out of *Zaventem*, the IV infiltrated so I just started a new one. The oxygen had a foot pedal pump and the hydraulics functioned until we were over Kennedy. If it had to happen, it was good timing. A private ambulance met our flight. George Ralston gave me an emotional "good gosh" hug and I sighed with relief as the ambulance sped away towards Manhattan.

4

I rented a car and headed in the opposite direction, eastward to Long Island. I would be staying with Jenny since Gina and Alex had a very small apartment. I couldn't wait to see everyone. I knew that I looked different. I had been very much influenced by French clothes and makeup. Following the latest vogue, my face and chest were streaked with carotene, and my blouse unbuttoned over my braless breasts. I also wore four-inch platform shoes that pushed me up to five foot nine.

I pulled up into the long, winding driveway and blared the horn. Jenny's dogs were all barking at once and chasing the car. By the time I opened the door, Jenny was already running across the lawn through the large oaks. I slipped off my British driving loafers and slid into my platform shoes. We threw ourselves into each other's arms. "I can't believe it," she screamed, "It's been so long." We jumped up and down in unison without loosing our grip on each other.

"You look fantastic."

"No, you look fantastic."

"No I mean it. You look fantastic and so French."

"You're the one who looks fantastic."

"Oh shit Kate, we both look fantastic. But how did you

get so tall?" I pointed to my shoes and she grimaced.

Jenny had always been difficult to describe physically. She changed the style and color of her hair frequently. When I left New York, she had long blond hair and a full-blown figure–the kind of woman that immediately appeals to men. Now her hair was short, jet-black, and her hazel eyes blinked through her long spiked bangs. She had lost a great deal of weight and taken on a fragile Asian posture.

"Come on, the group's all here. We waited for you for dinner, and we even have champagne in your honor." Jenny picked up my suitcase and I stopped to pet Six, her big, old bloodhound. Jenny never had the time or the inclination to name her animals so they were named numerically in the order that she acquired them.

"Hey, he remembers me."

"Really, Kate, you're the only woman I know who cares whether or not a critter remembers her."

The door flung open and the rest of my gang appeared–Janet, Moira and Libby. We were all hugging each other. Our greetings were high-pitched and enthusiastic.

My girlfriends were really great, very attractive, bright and each in her own way–outspoken. As a group, they were into things such as "consciousness raising," and "weekend marriage encounters." They were "vintage '70s American women." That was probably Jenny's influence. Jenny was street smart and funny. She lived her life running from one cause to another, one goal to another. Whatever was the latest, whatever needed fixing, Jenny was there. Janet was the most sophisticated. She was honest and she had style. She was the Perle Mesta of the group. She had no goals, other than polishing her nails. Libby probed, but she was logical and analytical. The trouble was she thought that she was smarter than the rest of us. She was wrong. It was Moira who was academically the smartest, the one with the 4.0 grade point average. Moira didn't have a mean bone in her body. She was quiet and naïve but she was still locked somewhere in the fifties.

Were they perfect? No. But that's what friendship was all about. Friends put up with you, warts and all.

Once, after having dinner in New York, the five of us got back to the car and found that one of the tires was flat. Unhesitatingly, Jenny and Janet hailed a police car, put on their charming, helpless female act and in five minutes had the officers changing the tire. All the while, Libby was tossing out clever witticisms and Moira was smiling and leaning her broad hips on the car. I remained in the background. I wasn't like any of them. I was like all of them.

The loud pop of the champagne cork snapped us to attention. Jenny was pouring and lapping up the spillage fingers-to-mouth. "Here's to you, Kate. Welcome home. I wish it was for good."

"Soon, maybe."

"You don't sound convinced." Libby sipped her champagne.

"I love the life-style but I hate working over there. My dream would be to work in New York and live in Brussels. That would be the best of both worlds, that is, if you'll all come with me. Hey, aren't the guys joining us?" I looked around the table. No one looked back.

"*Bon appètit*, Kate," they chorused. Something was wrong. I caught Jenny's eye and I knew enough not to ask.

After dinner, I used my credit card to call Gina, Mark and my mother. They were all content with their lives. After two years in the NYU Veterinarian Program, Gina decided to apply to some other schools. She and Alex were trying to coordinate where they lived, where they worked and where they went to school. Mary Ellen was taking bridge a bit more seriously. She was now in pursuit of Master Points. I made plans to visit Gina and Mary Ellen, and I coaxed Mark into spending some of his summer break with us in Brussels. Mark had been enrolled part-time in the MBA program at Berkeley. Although both he and Gina supported themselves, Frank made sure that their tuition was taken care of. He had promised himself long ago that he'd pay for their education for as long as they were in school.

It was close to midnight when Jenny began to fill me in on the events I'd missed while I was away. Moira had finally walked out on Dan. Dear, sweet Moira. Whoever would have thought she'd do that. Ever since I'd known her, she complained year after year about his drinking. At one point in time, she had us all going to Al Anon. It didn't help because he didn't go to Alcoholics Anonymous. The culminating blow, according to Jenny, was when Dan fell down the stairs, dead-drunk, at the Simons' New Years Eve party.

Right after that, Jim walked out on Libby. He said he'd had it, whatever that meant. Libby said that she never saw it coming, never had an inkling–she was the last to know.

"That's hard to believe," I commented, "since Libby is the most secure, the most buttoned-up conservative, the most authoritative of all of us. Besides, she looks great."

"That's new. Since Jim left she's dropped twenty pounds, and had her hair styled. Jenny hesitated as if she was deciding whether or not to say more. "I dropped some weight too, you know."

"Oh yes, and you look smashing."

"But I paid a high price, Kate, I lost my big boobs."

"Does it bother you?"

"Yes it does, but...I had to make a decision, and opted for looking great in clothes. I was tired of looking as if I had two decorator pillows under my blouse and one under my skirt like you know who."

"Oh, really?"

"Not you dummy. You're built like a boy with breasts."
Jenny took a deep breath, "Janet told Libby that she thinks Jim
has a bimbo in the office. Now they're in the middle of a
divorce and she's got three kids to worry about...and Moira
has two."

I reminded Jenny of the day we burned our bras. It was
the same day that Jim admonished us for our offensive
language, which he believed to be a direct result of the
women's movement. He said that Libby would never dream
of using such words, and that her behavior as a woman and a
wife was exemplary. So why did he leave her? Jenny and I
concluded that there was no justice in this world.

I was stunned with the news. We were all so close. The
guys were all smart, funny, educated and had top of the line
jobs. I used to jokingly call the four of them Doctor, Lawyer,
Indian, Chief. David was a dentist, Jeff a lawyer, Dan once
pitched for the Cleveland Indians' farm team and Jim was a
chief engineer.

The women had good protoplasm. We were good-
looking, industrious and educated. But more important, we
were the sisters we never had when we were growing up.

"It's been unbelievable around here. I'll tell you Kate, it
has me unnerved."

"Why didn't you write and tell me?"

"I couldn't. This needed to be done face to face. I wanted
to pick you up at the airport so that I could let you know
before we had dinner. I called you in Brussels this morning,
but there was no answer."

"Oh, I left really early. I had to get to the hospital...but
that's another story. What about you, Jenny? You're not
letting this all get to you, are you? Where are Jeff and the
kids?"

"The kids are up on the Cape with my mother. You know
how much they love going there. Jeff is...who the hell knows
after twenty-five years...he comes and goes...and besides he's
married to that God damn job."

"You still love him, don't you?"

"I guess so. I just feel so angry."

"Want to talk about it?"

"No."

"Jenny, you know that I never give advice but I'd think twice before doing anything rash. It's tough out there for forty-year-old women. Most of Frank's colleagues have twenty-two-year-old girlfriends."

Of our five-some, two of us had married very young. Jenny was eighteen and pregnant. She did it on purpose so that her parents would have no choice but to allow them to be married. I was seventeen and a virgin. I guess my parents wanted to preserve my virginity so they gave their permission when Frank asked my dad for my hand in marriage. Frank was twenty-one, had a job, his own apartment and was working on his degree at Columbia. I graduated from St. Margaret's Academy with honors. The only one in the family who believed in higher education for women was my grandmother Margaret Mullin. I sobbed on her shoulder and begged her to stop pushing education. I wanted to marry Frank. I gave her my promise that one day I would finish my education.

The others married later. Libby, Moira, and Janet all finished college, had jobs and married at twenty-five, twenty-six and twenty-eight, respectively. They got to live a little, and admitted to having had sex before they were married; that is, all except Libby. She was still a virgin in her head, and we just went along with her.

"How are you and Frank?" asked Jenny.

"We're okay." I nodded my head.

"Just okay?" She looked in my eyes.

"Actually, better than ever." I felt guilty for not having a problem and shifted in my chair.

"Tell me something, Kate. Frank was one of the biggest male chauvinist types in the group. How come he let you hang in here by yourself for almost a year?"

"I'm not sure I know exactly why, but I actually do think he's mellowed."

"You want to know what I think?" Without waiting for a reply, she opined, "He had something going for him in Europe." I let it slide. It was not the time to get into it. We said goodnight and I finally settled myself into Jenny's guestroom bed. I tossed and turned. All of my friends were in some state of separation, divorce, or denial. My mind wouldn't shut off. It was churning with the input of the day.

"Kate, are you asleep?" Jenny cracked the door and the light from the hall fell on my face. "I can't sleep. I feel awful. I'd like to talk." She was at the edge of the bed. I had an uneasy feeling. I made room for her as she crawled into bed with me. We positioned ourselves on our backs looking up at the ceiling. Our fingers touched.

"Kate, I've gotten myself involved with some guy. He's married...with a two-year-old kid. And...he's seventeen years younger that I am. And...it gets worse."

With a sinking heart, I braced myself.

"He wants to marry me." Jenny talked for the next two hours. She'd obviously saved it all up and now it couldn't be stopped from spewing out. She wouldn't tell me his name but she did say that he was one of her professors where she was earning her bachelor's in social work. She talked about his sensitivity, his caring, and the fantastic sex in great detail.

"What am I going to do, Kate? I'm really confused."

"What do you want to do, Jenny?"

"I don't know. I thought if I could talk about it, I could clarify my feelings."

There wasn't much that I could do or say to comfort Jenny. I told her that it has to be flattering to have the attention of a twenty-four year old, and I didn't doubt for one minute that the sex was fantastic. "But getting married, I don't know, you have to be awfully sure. Just don't jump from the frying pan..." (My God, I'm beginning to sound just like my mother.)

"No more. Not tonight, Jenny. I can't process it all. I'm exhausted. We'll talk tomorrow."

I lay there like rumpled bedclothes on laundry day. I could think of nothing else but the topsy-turvy world to which I had returned. It was four in the morning before we began to drift off to sleep. I had an appointment with Bob Jorgenson in six hours and I wondered if all of this could affect on my blood pressure.

"One sixty over ninety-five. How long will you be here, Kate?" I told him seven days including today. "I'm putting you in the hospital for tests..."

"Come on Bob, no fair. I can do it as an outpatient. I only have six days left and I haven't been home in years."

"And I'll never be able to find you."

"Please Bob, I promise I'll do everything you ask. I'll be a model patient but I have to spend some time with my family and friends."

"What about a twenty-four-hour urine, times two?"

"I'll manage it."

"Okay Kate, I'll arrange the schedule. You show up."

On Tuesday evening I met Jenny, Janet, Moira, and Libby at Fox Hollow Inn on Jericho Turnpike for dinner. We listened to Moira and Libby as they discussed the status of their respective separations and divorces. They shared how they felt and we empathized. We were well aware that each of our lives could change in an instant. It took only a moment to track back to the place in our heads and hearts where we were with each other a few years earlier. We talked about everything– no holds barred–feelings surfaced.

Jenny and I argued for the Equal Rights Amendment. We believed that women should have equal opportunity when it came to education and the workplace.

Janet took umbrage, "I did that in my twenties. You're the problem, you and your women's liberation. You want everyone to work because you do." She put her hands under her long dark hair and tossed it back.

"That's not so," I said, "Women don't have to work outside of the home if they don't want to. That's the point. They get to choose. And I chose not to be a housewife."

"But you are. That's really the point. You work and you're a housewife too. Now you have two jobs instead of one."

I'd never heard her take that position before. "Some Perle Mesta you turned out to be. You know, she wasn't only a famous hostess, she lobbied for the ERA."

"Come on, Janet. Not true," said Jenny, waving her hands and signaling that she had something important to say. "First, we all have help now. Second, I work because...hah, I still can't believe it...I make fantastic money. I like having fantastic money. I can't believe what they pay me for selling a stupid house."

"You may be overpaid," I agreed, "but I'm underpaid. I haven't even translated my salary from francs to dollars. I wouldn't want to submit my salary as my life's report card whether in Brussels or New York."

Jenny brushed her bangs aside, "Once I get my degree in social work, I'm sure I'll be in your tax bracket Kate."

Libby was uncharacteristically quiet but she finally sided with us. She was about to land a really good job. We were impressed when we heard the salary she had been offered.

I looked at Libby, "Didn't the idea of being 'kept' ever bother you?" I asked. "Even if you change it to 'being provided for,' it's still kind of like being owned. I wonder how many women are afraid to rock the boat for fear that they'll find themselves out in the street."

"I think you mean in the water," laughed Libby.

"At sea is even more appropriate. These women have no metier. No profession to fall back on. It's sad."

"So they worship at the husbands' shrine," chimed in Jenny, "They vote like him, and have the same opinions. They clone his identity."

Moira rarely entered into a conversation. She spoke only when she had something to say—which was unlike the rest of us. Her words sprung from somewhere beneath a mass of short, red, curly hair. "I guess I'll be the next one to work. I have a bachelor's in liberal arts, but I don't have any marketable skills." She gloomily leaned forward in her chair and looked at Jenny with her lime green eyes. "Maybe you can get me a job in real estate."

"Most probably," nodded Jenny, "But better yet, we can always become daytime suburban hookers. It's good pay and we have the skills." Her earrings danced as she spoke.

"Jenny, you're wearing Lippes loops."

She giggled, "Kate, why did I know that you'd be the only one to know what they were?"

"And why did I know that you would be the only one to wear them." We both laughed. The Lippes loops exchange drew nothing but blank stares from the other three.

"Come on, Kate, tell us about all the penises you encountered in your profession." It was Janet's way of changing the subject when she became bored.

"What do I look like? The penis professor?"

"Is it true what they say about black men?" Janet queried.

I thought for a moment. "Let me tell you my dears, you can't tell a book by its cover."

"And the biggest?" We turned and looked at Moira. Her round face was red as if all of her freckles had melted together and she was actually participating in a discussion about sex.

"There was a man who said he was from the Gambia," I began. "He was slightly built. I was stunned when I saw his penis. It was almost down to his knees and that was in a flaccid state."

"Who would care if it stayed the same size when aroused," laughed Jenny.

"There was another guy in New York. He was Asian. I was prepping him for the O.R. Although his penis didn't come down to his knees, and contrary to folklore, he had the second largest one I have ever seen in my entire life."

"I think 'big' is a visual turn-on," commented Janet.

"Since when have you been making comparisons?" I asked.

"Since we went to 42nd Street," confided Moira in a hushed tone.

"You guys went to see a porno flick?"

Libby gasped audibly. I knew that she didn't go, and I was surprised that Moira did. I sat back in my chair. "Well, too bad I wasn't in the country, I would have gone with you."

"Yeah, right," Jenny snickered.

"Oh yes, I would have…Hey, I've been to Amsterdam."

"Oh, come on girls, is sex all you can talk about," admonished Libby, "Besides, everyone knows that size doesn't matter."

Jenny spun around in her seat, "So what are you doing for sex now-a-days, Libby?"

"None of your business, Jenny," Libby snapped back as her brown eyes flashed and her styled blond hair fell over one eye.

Four of us continued talking about penis lengths and we concluded that width was even more important than length. We agreed that a very large penis was a visual turn-on, but when they're too long they hurt because they bang against the cervix uteri or the larynx/pharynx. One that's too small may just as well not be there at all—probably better suited for oral sex. Moira grimaced. We based our conclusions on an old "looks and feels" dirty joke classification. A small penis "looks bad—feels bad." A very long penis "looks good—feels bad." A short, fat penis "looks bad—feels good." We were into our routine. And a large, wide penis—we chimed "looks good—feels good."

"Hush up," scolded Libby.

She was right. I think that we were talking a little too loudly. The woman at the next table looked as if she couldn't decide whether she was being offended or informed.

5

Sally and I planned to play catch-up with hospital news from both sides of the ocean. When I met her in the crowded coffee shop, she waved her hand under my nose. Sally was engaged to Tom and was planning a small wedding. I wished her happiness. I told her that I couldn't be here for the wedding, but I would drink a champagne toast to both of them on the day and the minute she and Tom were wed.

"Thanks, Kate." She kissed me on the cheek. "Now wouldn't you like to know what's going on around here?"

I casually asked her about Dr. Hakim and she gave me that "stay out of trouble" look. She picked up her train of thought and told me that Jimmy Galletta joined the Air Force because the premiums on malpractice had reached a new high and he didn't think it was ethical to pass the rates on to his patients. He reasoned that he would be able to practice quality medicine in the service without hospital politics. Sally caught her breath and went on to say that, happily, Peter Rizzo was appointed Chief of Oncology two years ago. Unhappily, he was not doing well psychologically.

"They lose so many patients down there, Kate, and you know Peter, he takes it all personally–as his failure. He doesn't look well, lately. Everyone's concerned. I know it's a clinical term and we're not supposed to use it, but the guy is depressed–any fool can see that. And speaking of depression, we finally got our psych wing and guess who…"

A volunteer, distinguished by her salmon-colored apron, walked over to our table and said hello to Sally. "Would you mind if we shared? We don't have much time today." She waved her friend over without waiting for a reply. Sally made the introductions, and the four of us were reduced to chitchat.

"Oh, you live in Brussels," said Cheryl, the prettier of the two. "Do you know where Louvan is? My husband had been working there for a few months. Perhaps you know him? Dr. Sternberg? He's a psychiatrist."

Before I could answer, Sally said, "Dr. Sternberg, oh yeah, we know him. Good Doc. By the way, Kate, did you ever run into him over there?"

"No, I didn't. Belgium may be a small country, but it's not that small."

Sally stood up to leave and I quickly joined her. "Nice meeting you, Cheryl." I didn't ever want to know what she looked like. I didn't even want to know her name. Now that I'd seen her, living and breathing, it validated my guilt.

On our way to Four West, Sally casually commented that Dr. Sternberg had asked for my telephone number before leaving. "I'm surprised that he didn't call you."

"I'm sure he had a million other things to do." I stared straight ahead.

The lazy elevator yawned on the fourth floor. Taf was writing orders at the physicians' desk. He smiled broadly and extended his arms in a greeting, "Kate, how are you?" There was genuine warmth in his voice and it touched me. "Sit down and tell me what you've been doing."

I collapsed into the chair and smiled back. Grant Owens, Chief of Orthopedics, came out of room 420 and joined us.

"What's there to tell? I work full-time in ICU, buy my clothes in London and Paris, drink Dom Perignon and travel all over Europe," I said, all in one breath. "See, nothing special." I laughed.

"You're right, it is nothing special. That's because you're not working in orthopedics," chided Grant.

"If I wanted to lift weights, I'd go to a gym."

"I didn't think it possible, but she's gotten a lot more sassy than she used to be. Must be because she has her research articles published by The New England Journal of Medicine and JAMA," he commented to Sally as he hurried back toward room 420.

"And a pick-up of her cover story from the American Journal of Nursing, and I emphasize nursing, as part of a larger New York Times story on older adults," Sally called back.

Taf put out his hand, "Congratulations. You've gotten a lot of ink lately. And you do look marvelous, Kate."

"So do you. Where'd you get that tan?"

"In the good old U.S.A. I don't ever want to leave the security of its shores. I have been over there...remember? How about dinner?"

"No, I can't."

"Why not?"

"I don't know, but it's just not a good idea."

"And I thought we were friends?"

Peter Rizzo came through the double doors and stopped momentarily in mock surprise. "What's going on here? Looks like a party." He turned to me and smiled, "Hi Kate, heard you were here. How's it going?"

Grant rejoined us just as Peter began talking about his new plans for the oncology unit. Sally's voice interrupted, "Kate, you have a call on 29."

I walked over to the desk and picked up the call. "I can't imagine who's calling me here," I apologized. Sally shrugged, "Don't know. Didn't ask. Guy's voice." She walked over to join Taf, Grant and Peter at the physicians' desk—out of earshot.

"Hello, Dr. deMeo here."

"Kate, why the hell didn't you let me know that you were coming or at least let me know that you were here?" Aaron barked, "I had to find out through the hospital grapevine."

"I didn't think it wise, I..." I watched Sally, Taf, Grant and Peter interact. The tone of the conversation certainly seemed upbeat.

"Kate, I've got to see you."

"I can't talk now." Taf left the group and was walking toward me.

"Meet me later, meet me, or I'm coming up there right now."

"Will you hold for a moment?" I smiled at Taf. "I'll be off the phone in a second, Dr. Hakim."

"Listen Kate, I'll pick you up at two-thirty, on Archer and Second, in front of the bank."

I hung up without responding. I couldn't think of anything to say. Peter and Grant, engrossed in conversation, waved an automatic goodbye and headed for the elevator. Sally was coming to reclaim her desk.

Taf was still standing there. "Dinner?"

"Huh?"

"Dinner? Where do I pick you up?"

I looked at him blankly, "Wait a minute. How is Peter? I didn't have a chance to talk to him. I heard he was depressed..."

"No, no, he is fine. He is all excited about buying one of those European sports cars." My eyes met Sally's. Neither of us seemed convinced. When a patient moves from depression to "happy plans," it's usually a prelude to suicide.

"Dinner," he repeated, "the address? Where are you staying?"

"I thought I said no. Oh, I don't know. Maybe, I'll call you later." Sally shook her head and walked away.

I stood in front of the bank on Archer Avenue. Aaron's car pulled up. He leaned over and opened the door. "What the hell were you doing with Hakim?"

"None of your business, Aaron."

"After all we had together, I don't understand you."

"What did we have? Tell me so I know. What is it? Are you in love with me? Say it, come on, say it."

"Yes, I love you."

"Aaron, let's be honest, it's not love, it never was; it was sex, period. You wanted sex...you got sex. I wanted to experiment...to experience. We both got what we wanted. It was a fling, Aaron, nothing more."

"Jesus, we had such a nice ten percent arrangement."

"I thought ten percent had something to do with ether or cocaine. And by the way, I met your ninety percent today."

He pulled over and stopped the car. "Cheryl? You saw Cheryl? Okay, okay, I see."

"Do you? I don't think so."

"Kate listen...you knew I had a wife. Jeeze, all this because you happened to meet her? Did she look deprived?" I opened the door and got out. "Wait, wait, you're upset now, I'll call you later. Where are you staying?"

"Aaron, face it, it's over. It's been over since Greece. Let it die a peaceful death." I slammed the car door.

6

I thought about all of the affairs that went on in Frank's office and in the hospitals where I had worked. There were marked differences in the behavior of most of the men and women. Men fully understand that a sexual relationship can have a positive side. It can alleviate boredom, prove something about one's sexuality, present a new challenge, and of course—it simply feels good. You can usually tell when a man is having an affair. He suddenly begins to scrutinize his appearance. He may start going to the gym, invest in a new designer wardrobe, or simply look more charged up than usual. I think that Aaron's outward sign was growing his beard. The changes in a woman are subtler. A woman feels more desirable. She exudes something mysterious—something that causes men to look at her.

When married men have affairs, they seem to be attracted to younger, prettier women. It's as if they need good-looking accessories on their arms. Women, with the exception of Jenny, seem to choose men that are less good-looking than their husbands and not necessarily younger. More than likely, men view having a younger woman as sign of virility and power.

A couple of Frank's colleagues had introduced their dates by saying, "This is Michelle, my twenty-two-year-old girlfriend," or, "Have you met my twenty-six-year-old fiancée?" Frank never once said, "Let me introduce my forty-three-year-old wife, Kate." Under similar circumstances, a woman wouldn't introduce a younger boyfriend by stating his age. I can't imagine Jenny saying, "Have you met my twenty-six year-old boyfriend?"

Another variable is that a new girlfriend (no matter what age) is a brand new audience. The stories, jokes, quips, and repartee that bored his wife after hearing the same routine through the years are now fascinating to someone who hasn't heard it all before.

Men have the unique ability to compartmentalize. They can have a sexual relationship without an emotional involvement, whereas most women can have an emotional relationship without sex. It's the differences in these attitudes that enable men to function at full capacity, and sometimes render a woman helpless.

I'd met a lot of women who had fallen apart because they didn't face reality from the beginning. If a woman wanted the man to leave his wife, all she had to do was ask and he would leave his wife in an instant—that is, right after the holidays, or someone's birthday, anniversary or graduation.

Of all of the extra-marital happenings in this world, how many men ever leave their wives? Most men are not really unhappy. They're basically satisfied and "time in" does seem to count for something. For the most part, it's economically and socially sound to stay married to the same person. Most men just want to play around. They want to push some tired blood through their circulatory system, feel the surge, taste the adrenaline. Women ought to do the same—approach an affair with a man's point of view. Unfortunately, they fall into an emotional trap. They fall because they're vulnerable, and they're vulnerable because of the basic inequality of the sexes. The one thing I knew was that I was not like most women. I told myself that I was in it for the same reason as a man. I was playing around.

7

Taf and I were playing a game and we both knew how it would come out. He slowed up as he drove down the ramp to his garage.

"Hey, you passed my car."

"Really? In that case, you must come up for a drink."

"Forget it," I said. "We did that once before."

"If at first you do not succeed…"

"I did have a great evening," I said as we got out of his car.

He stood in front of me and playfully pinned me against his racing green MGB. "You're not getting away this time."

I ran my finger over the cleft in his chin, and felt the heavy stubble on his face. Maybe I did owe him something after all. "I can't, the meter has run out on my car."

"I put it in the 24-hour parking zone." He took my arm and headed for the lift.

"Oh, I almost forgot, I can't, I'm no longer on the pill."

"No problem, I have a good supply of condoms."

"Look Taf, this isn't going to work, I think I'm getting my period."

He smiled as we exited the elevator, "That's fine with me. A woman is even warmer when she has her period." He had an answer for everything.

"Yeah, but I'm staying with one of my girlfriends. She'll worry if I'm late."

He unlatched his door. "You had better call her, because I

do not think you are going home tonight." He handed me the phone.

"What will I say?"

He shrugged, "You will think of something,"

"Hi Jen. Oh God, I hope I didn't wake you. I'm at the Maine Maid with some friends from the hospital and we haven't even had coffee or dessert yet. Yeah, you know how slow they are. Anyway, we'll probably be up half the night reminiscing, so Sally suggested that I spend the night at her place...okay, I'll say hello...see you tomorrow."

He handed me a drink. We stood there facing each other, then awkwardly kissed. Our glasses clinked. He took the drinks in one hand and me in the other and walked me into the dimly lit bedroom. He put the drinks on the bedside table and kissed me again. He took off his clothes except for his briefs and socks. I started to strip, but he stopped me. He wanted to undress me. He was deliberate in his actions, carefully folding each article of clothing. Next, he took off his briefs just before he removed my bikinis. I looked at him—the socks, the socks—not until you take off those socks, I thought. He kissed, touched and did all of the expected foreplay. His penis wasn't very large, but someone once said that size didn't matter. Now I remembered who said it. It was Libby. As he penetrated me, I wrapped my legs around his back.

"You make love like a twenty-year old," he said.

What did he think? Only guys can be physical after forty? "I'll take that as a compliment," I said.

Taf grabbed my legs and pulled them down so that I was flat on the bed and he was flat on top of me. Taf continued thrusting until he climaxed. I didn't. He was still looking into my face. "Beautiful, wasn't it?"

"It was no big deal," I laughed. He laughed too. He remembered telling me that one day I would learn that screwing was no big deal.

We began making love for the second time. Taf had good recovery power, but I guess that's par for the course when you're a thirty-five year old bachelor. Recovery power is one thing, but he used the same boring flat on top of me position.

As Taf was climaxing a car muffler backfired, disturbing the predawn stillness. Minutes later, the telephone jangled. I jumped out of my skin.

"Do not worry, it is only my answering service." At the same time, there was a loud banging on the door, and a man's voice shouting, "Dr. Hakim, Dr. Hakim." Taf wrapped a towel around his waist and ran to the door, ignoring the phone.

He was back in an instant, pulling on his trousers. "It's Peter Rizzo, I think he shot himself. A neighbor heard the gunshot and got the superintendent to open the door. He's already called the hospital. You stay here. I'll be back."

"No, I can help," I quickly slipped into his shirt, fastened the buttons and rolled up the sleeves.

"Kate, many hospital staff live in this complex. I do not like my private life made public."

"Neither do I, but this is Peter." We raced barefooted up a flight of stairs and into the open door of the apartment. The neighbor pointed, "In there."

"Jesus, Mary and Joseph." The back of his head was gone and Taf was kneeling beside him. There was blood and brain tissue splattered about. Suddenly I was aware that I was standing on parts of Peter Rizzo's brain, pia mata and dura mata between my toes. I shook off the thought and pulled a sheet off the bed to cover him. In life, professionals surrounded Peter, and not one of them saw it coming because they were so involved with their own problems. Now, in death, everyone would reflect and recognize the clues he gave to us. Had I been so preoccupied with my own life that I didn't notice? I did notice, I just didn't follow through. Peter was a colleague and I should have.

A member of the Emergency Room Ambulance Squad came through the door with the equipment. "Never mind," Taf put his hand up. "Better call the police."

"What happened, Dr. Hakim?"

"It looks as if he put a pistol into his mouth, bit down hard, and pulled the trigger. I will be over later to make my report."

We were leaving when the driver arrived with the stretcher. "Hi, Dr. Hakim. Hi, Dr. deMeo." He looked puzzled. "Hey, aren't you living in France or some place like that?"

8

I got back to Jenny's at about ten a.m. She was sitting cross-legged on the floor in front of the TV drinking coffee. "Well, well, hello, night owl. When the hell did you learn to fly?"

"Got some coffee?"

Jenny thumbed at the pot on the table behind her and I poured myself a cup.

"I thought you didn't drink coffee?"

No answer.

"Where have you been," she persisted.

"I told you when I phoned."

"Bullshit. Kate, I wasn't born yesterday...and do I see whisker burns on your face?" I jumped to my feet and ran to the bathroom. I could still feel the brain cells being crushed under my feet and oozing up between my toes. Jenny was right behind me. She held me as if I were a child, one hand holding my forehead, the other around my waist as I gagged and retched into the toilet bowl. She filled the basin with water and I put my face in. "Sorry sweetie, I didn't mean to upset you. We've always been pretty honest with each other and I thought..."

"It wasn't you Jenny. I'm okay." We walked back to the living room and sat on opposite ends of the couch, facing each other, feet overlapping. These were our assigned positions for serious talks. We'd faced each other like this for many years forcing each other to face the facts.

"I was out with some guy last night."

"Welcome to the wonderful world of grown-ups."

"What does that mean?" I asked.

"It means, dear heart, that you were the only angel in the group who had not fallen...the only real virgin. Well, except for Libby, and the jury's still out on her. But in her defense, she'd at least share a joint. That's more than you ever did."

"So what? Dan never shared a joint either."

"That's for sure," said Jenny, "His drug of choice was alcohol. Made it hard on Moira and the kids."

"How come you never told me about this?"

"Well, you were always kind of prissy."

I was shocked. "Prissy? Me?"

"Face it, 'Miss Goody Two Shoes,' would you have understood?"

"Yeah, maybe, I guess not."

Jenny repositioned herself, "Anyway, tell me all about this guy."

I told her that he was just a friend and I was very sure that I'd never see him again–that is, sexually. I just felt that I owed him. But I couldn't tell her about Peter. It was too painful.

The phone rang and Jenny grumbled as she tugged at the cord and pulled the phone to her. "Hello, oh yes, she is," she sing-songed. "It's for you." She tossed the long corded receiver at me.

"Hell...oh...uhm, I can't." I threw a pleading look at Jenny. She folded her arms and shook her head. There was no way she was leaving. "No, I can't, I won't. It is over." I tossed the phone back to her and she placed it in the cradle.

"Was that your friend from last night, as if I didn't know?"

"No, smart ass, that wasn't my friend from last night, that was another one."

It was the first time I could remember that Jenny didn't

have a comeback.

"The sad thing about all of this infidelity business is that we view it strangely. Men have sexual rather than emotional relationships. But if men were forced to vote on the type of relationship they'd want for their wives, I think they'd prefer it to be sexual."

Jenny shook her head, "I disagree. A man can close his eyes far easier to an emotional relationship than to a sexual one."

I thought about that for a few moments.

"You're probably right," I finally said.

"Yeah? Well, it's the first time in my life that I got to be right with you."

"Listen, Jenny. My pursuit has always been equality. I looked for it in the work place, at home, and in relationships. Equality."

Jenny sat silent for a fleeting second, then asked, "Did you ever find out who Frank's girlfriend was in Europe?" I didn't answer. "Libby said she heard Frank tell Jim about some woman." I still didn't respond. "Aren't you angry at him? Isn't that really why you got even?"

"I'm not angry...just a little hurt. You shouldn't have told me. I didn't want to know, and I don't want to know now. I never did what I did to get even. I just wanted to be a part of the sexual revolution. I wanted to know what it was all about. Find out if I'd missed anything. That's all it was, Jenny...that's all it was."

"Well, I thought that since you were always expounding your equality ideas you'd want to know." She asked, "What are you going to do?"

"Do?"

"About Frank?"

"What do you want me to do?"

"Confront him."

I looked into Jenny's eyes, but I couldn't find her there. This was the first time in all the years I'd known her that she wasn't really listening.

"Confront him like Moira? Drive him away like Libby? Have a serious relationship with another man like you? Uh, uh, I'll do whatever it takes to make Frank happy," I lashed out, "Jenny, you didn't tell me about Frank because you're my friend. You told me because misery loves company. You just want me to fit in better with the group. Well, I don't fit." I ran into the guestroom with Jenny at my heels, and I started to throw my things into my suitcase.

"What are you doing?"

"I'm going to a motel. I'm sorry, Jenny, but I've listened to about all I can at the moment."

"You're leaving because you want a motel room to screw around in."

"No, I'm leaving because I'm stressed out. First of all, I brought a stroke patient over here on the plane with me on Sunday. I was solely responsible for her. Second, I came here for tests because I think I might have something seriously wrong with me. Third, I've been sleep deprived from day one. And last, but certainly not least, I saw the back of a colleague's head blown off this morning."

Jenny moved toward me and started to say something.

"Don't say any more. I'll call you when I find a motel. Okay?"

"Don't leave, Kate. I didn't know. The house is so empty. You won't be safe in a motel. That singing star, Connie Francis, she was raped in one of those places." Her lashes were fluttering valiantly to keep the spikes of her bangs from attacking her eyes. "Please don't leave. I don't know what came over me."

"I know, Jen, I'm edgy too." I felt sad, and I hoped that what Jenny had heard was untrue. Not that Libby would lie, but perhaps she misheard.

"You know, Kate, I can't figure out if you're the strongest woman in the world, or the weakest."

I kissed her on the cheek, and whispered, "I'm neither."

Twenty minutes later I checked into a motel. I called Jenny to let her know where I was and that I was safe. She sounded as if she'd been crying.

Later that day, Bob had the results of my tests. He stood there, leaning his lanky frame against the wall, his hands thrust in his pockets. Okay, tell me. What is it, I thought. I'm ready.

"Kate, we've gone over you with every test we can think of and nothing shows."

"Wait a minute. What about those test results I gave you from Brussels. According to those numbers, I should be in a coma."

"I can't explain it. Maybe someone dropped your blood on the floor, mixed it up with someone else's. It happens here too."

"What about that 'rule-out Green Tumor' thing that was on the report? You think maybe something was lost in the translation?"

"Kate, I haven't a clue. What I do know for sure is that the Europeans have different methods of measurement. More important, you're okay. Now it may be essential hypertension, it may be a transient thing or it may be the pill. I suspect it's the pill. However, I'd like you to get on a medication to lower your blood pressure. It would be better if you had a doctor over there. Isn't there someone you can go to?"

"I wouldn't be here if there was." I was trying to process everything that he said.

"Okay, I'll prescribe something for you." He began writing.

"While you're at it, I need a prescription for a diaphragm. I got one in Brussels but I couldn't insert it." I rummaged through my tote bag, fished out the compact, flipped it open and showed it to him. "It looks like a yarmulke, for heaven's sake."

Bob cleared his throat, "Yes, I see. It is the wrong size."

"Well, no wonder, all I did was walk into a pharmacy, ask for a diaphragm, and the size was determined by how many children I had. I said two or four. I wasn't sure how they counted so I included my two miscarriages."

When I stopped at the local drug store to pick up my new diaphragm, it looked like a microdot by comparison.

9

On Saturday morning, I stretched out on the bed and watched television. It was a treat. We didn't watch television in Brussels except for the BBC, since most of the programming was in French or Flemish. This year, we expected to have the privilege of voting in the presidential election. It would be a first for expatriates. Until now, I hadn't heard any of the politicians' voices. They were always voiced over in French or Flemish, depending on the station. When you don't have the experience of hearing a voice, your mind selects one and puts it to the face. The voices were nowhere near what I had imagined.

I thought about all of the things Bob had said yesterday and that I was okay. I think it's easier to be frightened in another language. Part of my problem was that the hospital personnel thought I knew French better than I did. So the parts I didn't understand, I filled in from the expression of their faces, their tone, and posturing. My interpretations were not always accurate.

I thought about Frank. I missed him. I put in a call to him and gave him the good news. He sounded relieved. I told him of my visits with Gina and with Mary Ellen and that I'd even managed to have David clean my teeth. I casually mentioned that I moved to a motel because Jenny's dad was spending the weekend. I also said that I should have called him yesterday. I was sorry that I hadn't.

That night Jenny called. She had another row with Jeff and was very upset. I tried to console her. We talked for a few minutes. She said she needed to stay with me.

It was almost midnight when Jenny arrived. She was visibly on edge. I listened, but nothing had changed. She talked about her relationship with Jeff and her relationship with the professor, again in graphic detail. She said that this relationship bore no resemblance to an earlier indiscretion. Jeff had been the best and their marriage was good until she met this young guy. A rhythmic banging coming from the adjacent room interrupted Jenny's discourse. She pounded her fist on the wall and yelled, "Shut up."

Listening to Jenny made me realize what I'd been searching for, and what I had found. I told her how I felt about Frank–how much I loved him.

"He was better looking, had a better body, and he was better in bed than anyone else," I paused, "Well, maybe not everyone…Italy was pretty good," I quipped.

She laughed for the first time since we quarreled.

"And most important of all, Jen, I orgasm with him."

"Do you think it has to do with the size of his penis?"

"Jenny, I don't know."

"I always knew that Frank was hung. I could tell by his hands…big, meaty hands."

I laughed loudly, "Janet told me you could tell by the size of the nose."

Now it was Jenny's turn to laugh, "Yeah, and Libby said that size doesn't matter. I can tell you with certainty, Kate, neither is true."

We were convinced that women talk about intimate things more than men do.

"I don't know how my life will work out…whether or not I'll end up divorcing Jeff, but I do know that I'll never divorce you, Kate."

Jenny and I slept like spoons that night.

Chapter Twelve

"...joy and sorrow are inseparable...when one
sits on your board...the other is asleep in your bed."
Kahlil Gibran

1

Frank met me at the airport driving his Jaguar, music blasting. "That was good news, Kate. I'm relieved that you're okay. I was worried."

"Me, too."

When we reached the apartment, I asked if he had to go back to work.

"Why, what did you have in mind?" We spent the entire day making love. I didn't bother breaking in the diaphragm. It would have ruined the spontaneity.

2

It was six fifty-five in the evening, almost the end of the shift, and it had been a good day until *Monsieur* Anton called me into the Doctors' Room.

"*Madame*, you will kindly extend your day."

"Why? Marie Louise and Paul are on from seven to seven."

"We have a special patient, an American V.I.P. Gentleman. Your services may be required."

"But of course, *Monsieur*."

The noisy elevator announced the patient's arrival. There were a lot of people around the gurney, but the orderly pushing it rattled out, "Tension high, all tests done, negative, no brain bleed, diagnosis Cerebral Vascular Accident."

"No IV? No heparin drip? No KVO?" I asked, as we transferred the patient from the gurney to the bed in *Chambre* 1, our prepared private room. "How long has he been here?" The orderly didn't answer, and then he was out of earshot.

Anton appeared, carrying the dossier. He looked over my shoulder saying, "I see no urgency here."

I lowered my voice and said, "This is urg..."

He turned and walked out of the door.

I turned my attention to my patient, "Sir. Sir. Excuse me. My name is Kate deMeo. I'm a New York State Registered Nurse. I'm going to start an IV with a heparin drip." I was concerned that too much time had elapsed. "I'm going to be monitoring your blood pressure and taking blood samples."

I looked at the patient's face. It was a nice face, handsome in fact. He looked familiar. I just couldn't place where I might have seen him.

"Sir, can you talk to me? I need you to tell me your name. Can you tell me your name?"

"Em...Emerson...Charl...," he struggled, mouthing his answer.

Oh my God. All at once, I knew who he was–the Vice President of the United States. Holy mother of God. I took a deep breath before I continued. "That's good. That's good. Can you tell me what happened?"

"I was...we were...you know...go dinner...my." He

pointed to his right hand, "It didn't...wave." He was searching
for words as he spoke.

An authoritative voice behind me filled in the blanks. "We
were leaving the Hilton to go to the EEC dinner. Suddenly, as
we were getting into the Limo, the Vice President seemed to
lose control of his right side. We came here right away."

"Sir, squeeze my hand." There was a very weak response.
I went through the standard neurological exam. He had right-
sided weakness.

"How... bad?"

"Sir, Mr. Emerson, you're going to be just fine."

I looked deep into his eyes and I saw fear. Anyone who
ever experienced the inability to find words that made sense,
or a hand, arm, or leg that didn't function, had to be
frightened out of his mind.

"Kate? Right? Stay...you know." He patted the bed with
his left hand, making an effort to control the timbre of his
voice. He was fighting.

"Yes, sir. I'll stay. I won't leave you. That's a promise."

I was so focused on my patient that it took me a while to
notice the two Secret Service men standing at the doorway
like pillars of stone. Their faces never softened. They were
always in an alert posture.

"*Merci, Madame.* You may leave. I will take over," Anton
called from the doorway. "And when you leave, take that
heparin drip with you. It's not necessary as yet."

"No, *Monsieur*, I'm staying with my patient."

"You forget your place, *Madame*. You are practicing
medicine. I am in charge and you may leave."

"I'm not leaving my patient. It's against the law. I'm a
New York State Registered Nurse. The moment I began
taking care of this patient, an 'implied contract' was legally
formed. To leave him now would constitute abandonment." It
was only a half-truth but it was all that I could think of.

It was seven p.m. I knew that Karambuku would be here
in a matter of seconds and I trusted his judgment over Anton's.

Besides, Anton had been acting really strange lately–actually weird.

He walked menacingly toward me but I held my ground. I hadn't realized the pillars of stone were quietly menacing him.

"She…stays," said Emerson.

"She stays," echoed the authoritative voice. There was absolutely no question as to who was in charge.

Karambuku arrived and confirmed the rule out diagnoses. It was either a CVA (Cerebral Vascular Accident), or a TIA (Transient Ischemic Attack). Only time would tell.

Arrangements were underway to fly the Vice President home to Bethesda Naval Hospital. They were also trying to get an American doctor from SHAPE (Supreme Headquarters Allied Powers Europe) to accompany him.

"In the meantime, Mr. Vice President, you need to rest, and that's an order."

"I'll rest…if you…eh…tell me what you…think."

"I'm not supposed to diagnose medical issues."

"I want…your, you know, think…opinion. It's, it's special. No…it is important to me."

"Okay, sir. But this is only what I think. Just remember, I'm not a physician. Okay?" I paused, "I think you shot a clot and it interfered with the blood supply to your brain. I think it's a TIA, based on the fact that your speech has improved in the last hour. Your hand and your leg show some minor improvement. The good news is that you have time on your side. By definition, a TIA is asymptomatic within twenty-four hours. The heparin is an anticoagulant. It makes your blood take longer to clot. The trick is to find the origin of the clot. It could have come from the aortic arch, the mitral valve, the carotid artery…" My voice trailed off.

"Thank…you, Kate." He was trying to be charming, still fighting his fear. "Tell me…uh…your…your…story."

"My story? That would really put you to sleep. Now close your eyes. I know you were a running back at Ohio State. So go Buckeyes. That means go to sleep. I'll be here for as long as it takes."

Less than one hour later, the doctor from SHAPE arrived. We spoke in hushed tones. I reported every detail to him, then handed him the dossier. He was young, but he was knowledgeable and smart. The Vice President was in good hands. The sun was beginning to rise and my patient was still sleeping.

At the airport, the ambulance pulled up to the plane. The doctor and I helped the Vice President to his feet. Before boarding the steps, he took my hand and held it. He took a long time to let go. He was showing me that he could use it. I followed the Vice President and the doctor up the steps. The plane was much better equipped than the one I had recently taken Debbie Ralston home on. The Chief of Staff was signaling orders as the small entourage boarded.

I wished the Vice President Godspeed. "Kate deMeo," he looked at me and smiled, "You're my nurse for life." I turned quickly and descended the steps. The two pillars of stone offered their hands on the last step and they almost smiled when they said, "Thank you, Ma'am."

3

Marie Louise looked down as she spoke. "I didn't know anything, but you're right...I wouldn't have told you about the diagnosis and the surgery even if I knew, Catleen. You would have had an opinion, made a big fuss. The truth is, I didn't believe that Simone would die. Anton said it was just a little something that she should have taken care of. There was no hurry. It was not an emergency. There was nothing to worry about. Simone didn't want it preying on her mind so she went right into the surgery. It was three or four days before you left for the United States."

"You could have told me then."

"Weelie Goosens said not to tell you because you had enough on your mind," she sucked in her breath, "I don't know the details. I saw her only once after the surgery. I bought her a book written in English. She loved to read in English. Then suddenly, she decided to recuperate in the south of France with her family. We didn't hear anything until after she had been buried. It happened so quickly. I can't believe she's gone."

Marie Louise was crying. She had just lost her best friend. I held her close as much to comfort myself as to comfort her.

Later, Marie Louise and I were assigned to do all of the Sed rates. Martine was excused because she was pregnant with Willie's baby. These tests measured the rate at which RBC's settle out in unclotted blood. We used pipettes to draw up the blood from the test tube. Pipettes were long, thin glass straws with a mark designating where the blood should be drawn. Above the line was a small piece of cotton wedged in to prevent sucking the patient's blood into your mouth. The problem was that we treated the pipettes as reusable. That meant that the cotton barrier had long since been washed away, so we'd cross our eyes trying to see how far the blood was coming up the pipette. Once we had the correct amount we'd use our tongues as stopcocks and jam the other end into a tray filled with a bed of clay. This prevented the blood from leaking out and held the pipette perpendicular.

Most of the time we were pretty good at judging how high we'd siphoned the viscous fluid, but it was horrible when any of us missed. We were down to the last two when Marie Louise spit loudly and jumped out of her seat. I looked up at her, her mouth open, blood dripping from her teeth. She bent forward to facilitate the expulsion of the blood and to prevent it from dripping on her uniform. Martine came in to see what the commotion was about and threw up on her red shoes. We had no mouthwash on the service, so I ran to get a bottle of whiskey. They had a stash on the top of the kitchen cabinets.

4

La Douze was the last on my list of patients. *Tentative Suicidé*. Another barbiturate overdose. It was her fifth attempt and she was only twenty-one. She had been *lavaged* with ten liters of normal saline. The blood and first 1000cc's of the *lavage* had been sent to *Poison Contrôle*. She was unconscious and on a respirator.

I'd seen more attempted suicides here in a few months than I saw in New York in a year. I had no idea as to what the official statistics were, but I had observed a remarkable contrast between two major cities of the world, at least within the hospitals in which I'd worked. Although the majority seemed to be female and the methodology relatively the same, the similarity ended there. In New York I had patients who ingested as much as sixty Quaalude, eighty-five Darvon, or forty Phenobarbital. These were planned, serious attempts and unless those patients received immediate medical intervention, they would die or become vegetables, spending their remaining days on a respirator. Few patients in Brussels resorted to drugs in such proportions. They would swallow a few Valium, a few Aspirin, whatever they happened to have on hand and wash it all down with alcohol. Usually, it would be just enough for a stomach wash and occasionally a respirator, but generally a good prognosis. It had little to do with the accessibility of drugs from one city to the other. Drugs were readily available in Brussels. Most medications, including syringes, could be obtained in many pharmacies without a prescription. They hadn't experienced the drug problem that existed in New York, so they saw no reason to form additional safeguards against drug abuse.

In Brussels the only age group I had were the young, in their twenties, some in their teens, even as young as twelve. The reasons varied. "My boyfriend or husband or someone significant doesn't love me," was the number one reason. It was followed by unhappiness over physical attributes. "I'm too fat, too thin," and went as far afield as "my husband wanted us to engage in multiple sex." There were many four, five and six time repeaters. There were those who died without intending to commit suicide—simple acts of stupidity. A young man in his late teens downed an entire quart of whiskey at lunch on a dare from his buddies. We did everything humanly possible, but we couldn't save him.

One of our patients jumped from the first floor, which is the equivalent of the second floor in the States. All she managed to do was to break many bones and end up tucked away in the corner of orthopedics in a double hip spica cast. A pitiful way to cry for help. Especially when no one is listening.

When a New Yorker decides to jump, it's usually high and hard. And all that I really know for sure is that the blanket covering the suicide jumper in New York appears too flat to believe that there's a body under it. I can only conclude that New Yorkers are better at suicide than Belgians.

That's not to say that all Belgian attempts were unsuccessful. On my first day of ambulance duty, I was with Jacques Hubert, the medical student on our service. We arrived at the scene and saw a young man hanging from a beam in the basement of his home.

"You cut, I'll catch," Jacques instructed as he picked up the overturned chair for me to stand on and handed me a scalpel. As I reached up and began to cut through the rope, he and the ambulance driver steadied the body and braced themselves to catch it. I tried to concentrate on the task at hand so I wouldn't see the bulging eyes staring out of the blue face. The scalpel was sharp and cut quickly through the rope.

Jacques and the ambulance driver lay the body on the floor and the driver immediately began to give oxygen. I started to protest, but Jacques stopped me by whispering, "We're supposed to give him a few minutes to practice. He hasn't done this too often."

Monsieur Hubert finally went through the official processes of testing a body for signs of life. Finding none, he pronounced the man dead. Then he and the ambulance driver rolled the body in a blanket and carried it upstairs. I was struggling with our two suitcases filled with medications and equipment when I became aware of a soft moaning cry. It was a young woman, now widowed.

"*Pourquoi, Maman?*" She kept asking of the older woman who had her enfolded in her arms. "*Pourquoi?*"

I couldn't have answered her question even if I had been fluent in her language. I left the suitcases and walked to the two women. "*Je le regrette.*" I put my arms about them and walked them upstairs to the kitchen.

On our return ride to *Ste. Gudule*, Jacques said, "Your first time?"

I nodded.

"Me too."

5

It was ten-thirty and most of the nurses had already finished their morning care. They were converging in the hallway and heading toward their coffee break. I decided to sit with *La Douze* for a while, but I wanted to ask Marie Louise to have coffee with me a bit later. I stepped through the doorway in the midst of the nurses. *Monsieur* Hubert walked toward us with a pail in his hand. He stopped and made a tossing gesture aimed right at us. The nurses shrieked and scattered. I stood there. I couldn't believe that he'd do anything so childish. He looked at me with open-mouthed surprise, waiting for me to say something—so I did.

"Americans stand their ground."

"I noticed that in Southeast Asia, *Madame*," commented Anton as he skirted past us."

"And how do you justify Zaire?" I called after him. Our cold war had turned into a heated one.

Marie Louise put her arm through mine and called out in English, "Break time."

Paul laughed and put his arm around my shoulder and we headed toward the kitchen.

6

I didn't quite realize it, but I was about to come precipitously close to the edge of reason. That afternoon I watched as *Monsieur* Anton pulled the plug on a hopeless patient. It was medically indicated. I felt relieved and I experienced my first feeling of warmth toward him. I remembered in New York that patients were kept alive on and on, week in week out, because the physicians were reluctant to take the final step. Even when "no heroic measures" or "DNR" were penciled in on the Kardex, most of the time extreme measures were taken anyway. No one considered the emotional anguish that was fostered on the family, not to mention the expense. In the States, resuscitation was billed at over nine hundred dollars. No one wanted to play God by pulling the plug, but I suppose one played the same role by not pulling the plug. Either way, someone was making a judgment. Nurses usually had different feelings about arrests and plug-pulling than the doctors. They were less reluctant. It had to do with spending eight hours a day with patients and watching their decline. Now I was able to understand my patients when they asked to be allowed to die, in three languages.

Anton pulled the plug and for once we were in total agreement. I extubated the patient and took her radial pulse. It was palpable and regular. I discontinued the IV, bathed her, and changed the linens. She was still breathing on her own and in the event that there was still feeling on this side of death, I wanted to make her last moments, minutes, hours comfortable. *Mademoiselle* Follet came in and threw a morgue pack on the bed.

"What's this for," I asked.

"For her, of course."

"Oh no," I smiled and shook my head at what could have been a terrible error. "She's quite alive, a normal pulse." I offered her the patient's wrist for proof.

"Cessez de coupe les cheveux. You're splitting hairs again, *Madame*, and we need the bed."

It took a split second to sink in. Wait a minute. I am in favor of plug-pulling but I am not in favor of deliberately killing someone. Jesus, Mary and Joseph, this is even worse than injecting potassium chloride into the vein. When a morgue pack is utilized, huge amounts of cotton batting are stuffed into all of the patient's orifices. That's fine with me as long as the patient is dead.

"*Mademoiselle* Follet, I refuse. I will not use the morgue pack until she is dead and has been pronounced by a physician."

"Americans," she spat. She tore open the morgue pack and I stood there watching her stuff the woman's nares and mouth full of cotton. I stood by and watched her being suffocated and I did nothing. *"Ca va,* now she's dead, perhaps now you can finish this simple task as ordered."

I ran past her out of the door and down the hall to *la toilette*. I was an accessory to murder. I was sick. I threw up until my stomach had emptied all of its contents, and then I retched for another ten minutes. *Madame* Descamps was so concerned and because it was the influenza season, she assumed that I had *La Grippe*. She gave me some *medicament* to calm my upset stomach. Then she sent me home with the bottle of Premparin with instructions as to the dosage and told me to get some sleep. "*Dormez-bien*," she cooed. I couldn't tell her how I felt or what made me vomit. That was the whole point. I was challenging still another of the practices in *Ste. Gudule*. And yet there was a scary part of me that still wanted to please.

I called Frank and asked him to meet me in our favorite Spanish restaurant, near the hospital. I went to the vestiere to change. I realized that I had worn the same uniform for the last six days. The laundry service said they were out of clean uniforms and I should try again next week. Wearing a dirty uniform—just another thing I thought I'd never do. Two or three clean uniforms per week was considered very good. Now I thought so too. I had given up. They had won.

By the time I got to *El Savilla,* Frank was already there. I must have looked like judgment day.

"Have a drink," he offered, "You look as if you need one. I've already ordered sangria...want something stronger?"

The waiter put the pitcher on the table.

"No, sangria is fine."

The waiter poured the fruit-laden mixture.

"Frank, I don't know how to tell you this but it's been on my mind and steadily growing...worse."

His frame seemed to stiffen and his blue eyes engaged mine.

"One of my patients died today...and I guess I was responsible." Sins of omission are as bad as sins of commission, Kathleen Mary. I looked down at the table and related the entire story. "If a lawyer asked me, in a court of law, is that what a reasonable, prudent nurse would have done under similar circumstances, I couldn't answer 'yes.' I'd be guilty of malpractice or negligence, at the least. I'd fail the first element of Tort Law. I thought about Sally, Patti, and Mary.

They wouldn't have stood by and let it happen. It's not even civil law—it's criminal law. It's accessory to murder."

"It's not accessory to murder, Kate. It's…" He tensed his mandible and asked, "Is that it? Is that what you came here to tell me?"

I nodded.

"Jesus, I thought that you were going to tell me that you were leaving me."

"Leaving you?" I asked incredulously, "If I were the type to have a nervous breakdown, I'd have one…right now…before your very eyes." I put my glass out for more sangria. "Jesus, Mary and Joseph, I'm about ready for the loony bin."

"Well, let me tell you how I feel. You called me and said that you had something to tell me that couldn't wait. You picked a crowded restaurant in which to meet. Then you walked in here with doomsday written on your face. What was I supposed to think?"

I was taken aback by what he said. This was a side of Frank that I had never seen before. It was the first time that he showed his feelings. I was behaving as if I was the only one with problems. I had no answer except to tell him that never in my entire life had I thought of leaving him.

Frank ordered for the both of us. I couldn't eat. We talked for a long time. He was patient and empathetic. He allowed me to wander about in my circular articulations and somehow his calm logic entered my mind and made things seem better.

7

I was alone in the hospital kitchen having a non-alcoholic beer when the door opened and Anton came halfway through it. He hesitated as if trying to figure out if a cup of coffee was worth being in the same room with me. He walked straight to the coffee urn and poured himself a cup.

"Was it necessary?"

He studied the urn in between sips of coffee.

"Was the surgery necessary, *Monsieur?*"

He continued to sip his coffee.

"That whole big surgery? Why the hell did you do it?"

He turned and raised his eyebrows, "*Madame?*"

"I don't understand. You wouldn't do surgery on *Madame* Gaspar when there was a chance to save her, and then you practice on Simone and kill her." I had no right to accuse Anton, since I was the proverbial pot calling the kettle black. It could very well have been projection on my part.

"*Madame*, you know nothing of surgery, and I advise you to be careful with your accusations."

"There's talk all over the hospital." I spoke slowly and softly, "I'm just saying it to your face. Everyone says that she didn't need the surgery. What were you doing? Practicing? Was it the money? Did you make a lot? Did you put her through additional agony or did you just open and close. I know that you can make the O.R. records read any way that you wish."

He turned back and gave his full attention to the coffee urn.

"Can you please answer me? Why did she die?" Answer me you little...weasel. Tell me why? Why? Why? "All I can hope and pray for is that you have a doctor just like you, when your time comes." I slid off the stool and left him still in communion with the coffee urn.

8

Someone else was in Simone's chair. The desk wasn't as neat and somehow, it looked wrong. I told this unfamiliar person that I wanted to review my contract. She searched the file and handed it to me. I started to walk toward the door.

"*Madame*," she trilled, "that is not possible."

"What's not possible? You mean I can't take this with me?" I asked.

"*Non, Madame.*"

I walked back to her desk and said, "Anything is possible, but I'll leave it here anyway." I tore the contract in half, and in half again. I crumpled it and dropped the pieces on her desk. "Consider this my two weeks notice."

Illegal? Probably. I may as well add that to my repertoire. The contract called for one month's notice, but I'd been working at *Ste. Gudule* long enough to know that I could claim that I was depressed or any one of a dozen excuses that were commonly used to avoid working. Besides, they'd accept my resignation with pleasure for many reasons. The only reason that administration might want me to stay would be based on economics.

I knew that I would miss *Madame* Descamps, Marie Louise, Martine, Paul and Willie, even Jacques. But most of all I would miss nursing. I decided to write them an upbeat "goodbye thank you note." I'd say that I had an emergency in the States.

I came to *Ste. Gudule* with a passion for nursing. It was difficult bucking the system in inadequate French. But with all of my education and experience, I still thought I could make a contribution. I had many good days and made many friends, but I couldn't handle the Antons and Follets of the world. Most people resist change. They know what they have and are never sure of what they might get. In the States, the nurse-doctor relationship was grounded in mutual respect. In Brussels the nurses were still handmaidens. Most of what I tried to do was simple stuff–having clean thermometers and using aseptic technique. Anton, his doctors and Follet thwarted many of my efforts. They had us using an open communal pot of gel as a lubricant for urinary catheterizations, oil-based

lubricants for suctioning tracheotomies and transfused blood
with D5W. What frightened me most was that I witnessed
iatrogenic deaths and I did nothing.

I stood by and did nothing.

Sometimes our failures are remembered more vividly
than our successes. But Marie Louise, Martine and Paul, one
by one, saw the logic of my practices of patient care and
adopted many of my nursing standards. They were my
successes. Although some protocols will probably be lost along
the way, these nurses will pass the methods on to others.

If I stayed, I was afraid I'd begin to accept practices that I
never would have tolerated in the States. I couldn't change
the system, nor could I allow the system to change me. I had
worked too hard to become the nurse that I was. And the
death of Simone put me over the top. I drew comfort from
knowing that sooner or later, I'd go back to the States, where
my nursing skills would be recognized and my research and
articles accepted by the health care community.

Now I had to tell Frank that I'd quit.

9

"Good news, Kate," said Frank, "I just got a call from
New York. My replacement has been selected. A few weeks
or so, maybe a month, and we're on our way home."

I knew that time sequences were never absolute. Rather
than noisily mark time, I decided to finish the book I had been
working on. It was based on my research on aging. I thought
that since the older population was increasing twice as fast as
the rest of the population, one of nursing's missions would be
the promotion and maintenance of the health and well-being of
this age group. Even though the book would be theory-driven
and statistical, it would be written in a way that anyone could
relate to. The working title was "Successful Aging," and I
think anyone could relate to that too.

Chapter Thirteen

"The righteous is not innocent
of the deeds of the wicked."
Kahlil Gibran

1

Drinking at *Ste. Gudule* was not unusual, especially during the night shift. I was horrified the first time I discovered wines and spirits on the top of the shelf while searching for tea. I was acclimated to the unending celebrations: birthday, promotion, departure, marriage, or a Thursday. Not that Thursday in itself was particularly significant. We could just as easily have celebrated any day of the week.

I had not been able to shake that basic American nurse reaction to drinking on duty, and I never could bring myself to have more than a sip of anything.

I knew without looking at the clock that it was close to seven. The other nurses were shuffling about in their clogs doing a last minute check on infusions in preparation of giving the data to the next shift's charge nurse. The day shift doctors had already disappeared. Only ten more minutes to go. Only one week to go. The two weeks I had promised seemed like two years. This had not been one of my fun and frolic days at the hospital. Everything that could have happened–did. I sighed aloud. Frank must be in London by now.

I was outside *le bureau* when the phone rang. I hurried to answer it. "*Allo, Réanamation, Madame* deMeo."

"Ah, *bonjour Madame. C'est moi*. It is I, Marie Louise," she identified herself, speaking very slowly and clearly. "I have a very special favor to ask of you. I am having a personal problem. Would you be so kind as to work for me this evening until twenty-three hours?"

Cover for her until eleven, I quickly translated. Oh shit, I'm really beat and I don't want to do it. "Uhm," I stalled.

"Please, Catleen," she entreated, " It is important to me."

It seems that young women have personal problems, and I was a soft touch for their pleadings. Oh well, what the hey? Frank's not home anyway. All I need is a hot cup of coffee or tea to put me back in fighting form, rev me up, or whatever. "*Oui, ça va,* Marie Louise. *Pas de problem.*"

"*Merci. Merci bien*, Catleen, *vous êtes très gentile.*" She hung up quickly before I had a chance to change my mind.

Yes, I really am a nice person, I agreed, trying hard to cheer myself up. At least I will be after a nice cup of hot tea. "*Après une bonne tasse de thé, bien chaud,*" I repeated, practicing my French as I headed toward the kitchen.

I hadn't checked the night schedule to see who was working and I was delighted when Lepage arrived on the scene. We warmly exchanged greetings in French, although her English was far better than mine. She had left her native London years before after marrying a Belgian national. She became so very Belge in her attitudes, demeanor, and accent, even the Belgians thought of her as a native daughter.

I told her that I would be filling in for Marie Louise until eleven. She looked at me incredulously. "You're bloody crazy, deMeo," slipped out. "Always working in place of someone. That's the way to an early grave."

"It's already too late for that," I laughed, "I'm almost as old as you, Lepage, and my God, is that ever old."

Her voice became serious, "Heard you quit. Is it true?"

I nodded.

"That's why I work nights. I don't have to deal with Anton and his indulgences."

"What do you mean?"

She put her hand on my shoulder and said, "deMeo, be careful of Anton. I think he's using. He could be dangerous...maybe try to hurt you in some way. "

"Anton is odd to begin with, Lepage...but now that you mention it...he's been even stranger lately."

She nodded and turned away. "Be forewarned," she said into the empty corridor.

Working with Lepage was a pleasure. She had been in the business over thirty years, same hospital, and same shift. Occasionally we would speak in English, but only when we were alone. The rationale was that speaking French would improve mine, and the other members of the staff would not feel left out of the conversation. I understood. I knew that left out feeling.

Moments later, quiet little Henin walked in. Lepage and Henin frequently worked together. They physically resembled Don Quixote and Sancho Panza. Henin performed like a robot. She rarely spoke, never seemed to make a move on her own, and Lepage would somehow wind her up, aim her and off she'd go.

We were a good night shift team and we worked well together. A one to four nurse-patient ratio was considered the norm at *Ste. Gudule*. It was hard work, not unlike most intensive care units; it could certainly be unnerving at times, but all in all it wasn't bad. We always had one of our doctors on the premises. His office-sleeping quarters were at the end of the hall, making him instantly available in case of any

emergencies. A comforting thought for us. Of course we had
to be damn sure it was a bona fide emergency before daring to
awaken one of the sleeping lions in his lair. Some of the nurses
waited too long before calling for help. Lepage and I were not
in the least intimidated. We were far too experienced, and
would not hesitate to rouse a doctor at the first sign of what
might be trouble. A comforting thought for the patients.

Some two hours later, we had just about finished our
preliminary rounds. In addition to the nursing care, we
checked the equipment and made simple repairs. It was not
unusual to have a screwdriver and a pair of pliers as part of the
tools of our trade.

Lepage and I were in the *Cardiac Chambre* changing leads
and connections at Bed 2. We were in hope of getting sharp
electrocardiographic information on the oscilloscope of a
particular monitor that was out of date and should have been
sold at the flea market long ago.

The unmistakable bass voice greeted us with, "*Bonsoir,
Mesdames.*" Karambuku's frame filled the doorway. "*Tout va
bien?*"

Lepage assured him that all of the patients were doing as
well as expected, and no crisis seemed imminent.

"*Bon,*" he nodded, surveying the monitors. He winked at
me and I smiled back. He turned and walked with giant steps
toward *Respiratoire*.

"*Voilà*, Lepage," I smiled triumphantly, "I'm the best
damned electrician on this service. Just look at that heartbeat.
It's good enough to be put on your BBC telly."

We found Henin judiciously recording the blood
pressures, pulses and temperatures into the night log. She
handed me the results of the "S & A" tests she'd done. All
negative. Good, there's no sugar or acetone in anyone's urine.
Things were looking up and the three of us retired to the
kitchen for a coffee break. That is, mint tea for me and coffee
and cigarettes for them.

I really disliked the smell of burning tobacco. Until

recently, I had worn an American Lung Association pin announcing, "Your smoking HURTS my lungs." Even if my co-workers understood the meaning, they enjoyed their smoking far too much to care about their own lungs, much less mine. My Belgian colleagues were heavy smokers or as they said in French, "*fumer comme Turc*." Smoke like a Turk. My God, if Turks smoke more than Belgians, I'm glad I'm not working in Turkey. I finally gave up wearing my anti-smoking button when a surgeon, educated at the NYU School of Medicine, commented, "Nothing, but nothing could ever hurt your lungs, honey." I suppose it was well timed. Frank's clients took a dim view of that button, especially his cigarette account.

The three of us sat on the high stools at the counter. Lepage poured coffee for Henin and herself. I prepared some mint tea. It was hot but not too strong. Grandmother Margaret Mullin never liked strong tea. Grandmother Kate O'Reilly couldn't understand how a true Irish woman could drink insipid tea. She often said of Margaret, "She buys tea that comes in those little bags, and then only those brands that take a firm grip of the third water." I liked thinking about my grandmothers. I brought the mug up to my lips and inhaled the fragrant aroma. The steam under my nose helped to mask the billowing clouds of cigarette smoke. My eyes were closed in protest, and I was cautiously attempting the first burning sip when something stopped me. I opened my eyes and saw a large black hand surround the mug and gently pull it away.

"Oh, *Monsieur* Karambuku, I didn't hear you come in."

His other hand held, with a finger in each, four tumblers filled with what appeared to be whiskey.

"*Boire, Madame* deMeo. *C'est obligatoire,*" he firmly stated as he planted one of the tumblers in my hand. Without looking around, he put two of the others on the counter to his right for Lepage and Henin. They looked pleased as I watched them sipping away at what was indeed whiskey. No one could possibly drink all of that whiskey, especially if that someone happens to be me.

He was serious. Karambuku's muscular body hadn't moved. He stood there, staring hard at the glass in my hand as if willing me to drink it, making me feel more than a little uncomfortable. He spoke not one word of English and my French wasn't good enough to refuse his drink politely. I started to protest but he wasn't taking no for an answer. I took a sip. Jesus Christ, it's warm whiskey. Scotch. It tasted terrible when served warm.

"Okay Doc, since you insist on throwing this party, where the hell are the ice cubes and water?"

He looked blank at my English. Lepage raised a disapproving eyebrow. Henin didn't react at all. They were both enjoying their drinks. Oh well, I rationalized, if I take a sip now and then for the next two hours, maybe he'll be satisfied and I can go home sober. With a little luck, I might even be able to pour it down the drain when no one's looking. Good Lord, there had to be ninety cubic centimeters in that tumbler.

I swallowed another small sip, slid off the stool and said, "I'll do the patient check now." Before anyone could answer, I was out of the door.

The lights had been turned off, except for the few scattered dim night-lights. It gave an eerie look to the service and made it hard to believe the amount of activity that went on during the day. It was unusually calm, too calm. No patient crisis. No equipment crisis. Unusual. It made the night seem longer. The alarms of the cardiac monitors and the IVAC infusion pumps were quiet. Only the steady mechanical swoosh of the respirators could be heard through the darkness.

A patient's buzzer jarred the silence. I could see the red glow over the door. I entered the darkened room and approached Bed 12, *La Douze,* the young woman who had attempted suicide. I averted the bed light from her face before turning it on. She was restrained, regaining consciousness, and still had the call button in her fist where I had taped it earlier. I searched her face carefully, while explaining to her that she was in *Hôpital Ste. Gudule*, I was a nurse and that we were taking good care of her. I continued to explain that the tubes and the respirator were all necessary. I couldn't tell whether or not she understood. It was always difficult to assess how a patient who had attempted suicide might respond. Most of the time they're furious at finding themselves alive and strike out at whomever happens to be there. Frequently it's the nurse who bears the brunt of their anger.

The young *La Douze* seemed frightened rather than angry. I released one of her hands and held on to it while she ran her fingers over the tubing that went into her nostril, and then the larger tube that went into her mouth. I explained what they were and why they were needed. She relaxed and returned her hand to her side. I held it and told her that I'd stay if she wanted me to. She blinked her sad eyes and squeezed my hand. This was her fifth attempt. I wanted her to know that some one cared about her, cared whether she lived or died. She lapsed back to a deep sleep in a matter of seconds. I restrained her hand before leaving.

I returned to the kitchen. Karambuku and Lepage were absorbed with a patient's dossier and discussing transfusions. Henin was contentedly knitting. After making her point, Lepage looked up at me.

"It was *La Douze*," I reported, "She's okay, sleeping. Should be off the respirator tomorrow."

"*Bon,*" replied Lepage, slapping her leg, "I'll check the medication list and make out the assignment sheet for tomorrow."

"I'll go with you," I volunteered.

"It's not necessary, deMeo. Sit."

I sat.

Henin sat.

Karambuku sat, and so did my whiskey. The more I

sipped, the more filled it appeared. It reminded me of the times my mother would pile the mashed potatoes on my plate. Her intention was to fatten me up, but my mind couldn't accept such a huge portion and I'd gag at every mouthful. No matter how much I pushed the food around the plate, no matter how many little mouthfuls I swallowed, the pile never seemed to diminish. And neither did my whiskey. It had become a *cause célèbre* on his part and by eleven o'clock I realized that I had downed half of it.

Come on, Marie Louise, I groaned to myself. It's five minutes past eleven and I want to go home. I'm tired. I want to go to bed. Why don't you go to bed, Karambuku? Your bed is just down the hall. There's no reason for you to stay up. Go get some sleep. You've had a busy shift. You'll be sorry if you have an emergency at four in the morning. Oh God, I'm getting punchy and damned irritated with Karambuku. Why should I be annoyed? That's not fair. He's a good doctor. He's worked hard since he's been at *Ste. Gudule*. When he inserted *Madame* Gaspar's esophageal tampanade, he demonstrated good technique, good judgment and most of all, he really cared about his patients. I have respect for him as a doctor, and I like him as a person.

Then why am I so ticked off?

It's this drink thing. Damn. Is it? Or is it because I find him physically attractive? Am I really angry at him, or at my own feelings? Please, Marie Louise, I am really tired. I'm tired of the steady swoosh of the respirators, tired of watching wavy green lined monitors, tired of Karambuku staring at me, and tired of him trying to turn me into an alcoholic, all in one night.

I could feel him looking at me. He tried to engage me in some small talk. I returned polite short answers without turning around from the counter to face him, then returned my attention to reading the dossier of *La Sept*. Henin's knitting needles clicked away at the silence. I poured over the dossier longer than reasonably possible. When I finally turned around on the stool, his face broke out into a big, good-natured smile. Even his smile was big.

I smiled back my friendly "I'm just one of the boys" smile, but I retrieved it quickly as I remembered Lepage's recent admonition. It had been only a few short weeks ago, as we'd been walking through the hospital courtyard toward the gates.

"Women who speak out on racial equality are believed to be easy lays for black men. In particular," she emphasized, "American New York Jewish liberated women."

"What are you talking about, Lepage? I'm not Jewish," I protested, "I'm Catholic and I've never even lived in New York City. But I am liber..."

"Catholic, Jewish, that's not the point. You cannot continue to defend Karambuku and his colour in front of *Monsieur* Anton. You'll end up on Anton's fecal roster and far worse, Karambuku may get some ideas you hadn't bargained for."

"Come on, Lepage, that's ridiculous. Besides," I reasoned, "there's less racial bigotry here than in New York."

Anton may have been *Chef de Service*, but he was a *trou de balle* as far as I was concerned. He considered persons from the African nations and even his own Flemish compatriots as inferior and he certainly wasn't all that fond of Americans either. I had let it be known on more than one occasion how I felt about his racism. What amazed me was how my inadequate French came through so clearly.

"I don't care a thing about being on Anton's shit list. As a matter of fact, I'd consider it a privilege. And as for Karambuku, that's all sheer nonsense."

Lepage shrugged, then hunched her shoulders against the damp air and queued up for the *autobus*.

I stood for a moment feeling that there was more to be said, then turned and walked past the casket shops that lined both sides of the hospital street.

2

The clack–clack of scurrying clogs disturbed the silent corridor. Marie Louise, like Cinderella, arrived at the stroke of midnight. Normally I would have behaved like her mean old stepmother, but because I'd downed the remainder of my drink in the last forty minutes, I felt more like her benevolent fairy Godmother. I waved away her *"Excuzez-moi,"* gave her a report and whispered out a general *"Bonsoir."*

I took the lift down and walked across to the nurse's building. Jesus, it was cold. The air was heavily laden with a rawness that turned it into another wet, bone-chilling spring. I should have used the underground tunnel. Funny, I never used them in New York either. I have an aversion to tunnels. I think they've always given me a trapped feeling, like being in a tomb or a grave.

I rolled up my bloodstained uniform and put it on the floor of my *vestiere*. I quickly changed into my sweater, skirt, boots and coat. Then I pulled my woolen cap over my ears and down to my eyes. I wound five feet of matching muffler around my neck, put on my mittens and was ready to meet the cold.

It wasn't the cold I met but a warm-looking *Monsieur* Karambuku leaning against the entrance on the outside of the windowed door. How come he looks so warm? He should have been freezing in his white coat. I wondered what he was doing here? I had left everything in order. I knew I had finished my whiskey. Now what could he want? Uh, uh. No, he couldn't. That's not possible. I hardly knew him. He didn't even know my first name and I couldn't pronounce his. Slow down Kate. You're tired, you've been drinking and now you're letting your imagination run wild. Damn you, Lepage, it's your fault. You put these ideas into my head. My God, you couldn't convict a doctor for leaning against a building on hospital property even if it was twenty minutes past midnight in the middle of March.

As soon as he saw me, he pulled the door open and came at me in rapid French. I had to slow him down a little in order to understand what he was saying.

"You have not given a proper report before leaving, *Madame*, and..."

"I gave a report to Marie Louise before I left," I interrupted, "Anyway, Lepage knows everything that is happening on that service."

"But you did not give me a report." That was technically true but usually the doctors never wanted a report unless there was something out of the ordinary.

He went on saying that he couldn't figure out if I had given blood to *La Sept*. If so, how much, at what time?

I explained that I had given 420cc's of fresh whole blood and that there was another in *le frigo* to be used later if needed. "I don't understand the problem. Everything is charted."

"That is the problem exactly, *Madame*. Your writing is not clear. I am not able to understand."

You have got to be kidding, I thought. He was looking at me, waiting for an answer. True, my handwriting was good in English, but in French—I wasn't sure.

"Allons, Monsieur," I sighed, and followed him back to the hospital building. I almost had to run in order to keep up with his stride. The lift had an *"on panne"* sign on it. Oh shit, wouldn't you know, now we'll have to trudge up the stairs to the third floor. I'm not sure I can make it. Of course, he had no trouble. He got there ahead of me and opened the door of the stairwell adjacent to his room.

The corridor was dark and silent. There was light coming from under the kitchen door at the opposite end. I could picture Lepage and Henin joyfully puffing away on their cigarettes and Marie Louise dozing in a patient lounge chair. The door to the doctors' room was open and the desk light shone on the dossier in question. I walked in and started flipping sheets with my mitten-clad hands. It wasn't easy but I was too cold and tired to take them off. I found the page with the type and cross-match, the sheet that came up with the blood, the transfusion sheet complete with date, time started, time finished, the observations and my signature all over everything–not a requirement at *Ste. Gudule*, I might add. I read aloud as my blue mitten clumsily pointed to each entry.

At last he seemed satisfied, and he smiled, "*Bon. Je vous remercie, Madame* deMeo."

We shook hands. I turned to leave but he held fast. He whispered something that I didn't quite get and just on pure instinct I shook my head no. He relaxed his grip a little. I pulled my hand back quickly and he was left holding my mitten.

"You've pulled off my mitten. Damn it, give me my mitten," I said, irritation filling my voice.

My God, he was good-looking standing there, smiling his big toothpaste ad smile. He almost made me forget how tired I was. I had to smile in spite of myself as he dangled the blue mitten in front of me with two fingers. I reached out for it. He grabbed my right wrist and effortlessly pulled me to him.

"Hey, come on now. What the hell are you doing?"

He was trying to kiss me. He wasn't having a great deal of success since there was only about a six inch circumference of my face exposed, and my head kept turning from left to right, from right to left. He was kissing my wool cap, my muffler, my coat. The whole scene was ludicrous. I couldn't believe it was happening. I hadn't felt so completely foolish, so unable to handle a situation, since the groping high school days.

"Look Karambuku," I said in English, "let go. I don't fool around. I'm going home now. Leaving. That's it, period. Bye-bye."

He cupped his other hand behind my head and neck. He held me steady and started kissing me on the lips. His tongue forced it's way into my mouth. Then he sucked my bottom lip pulling it into his mouth. No one had ever done that before. He held my arms with his large hands. His biceps were as big as my thigh. I don't ever remember feeling so small before.

He was getting carried away and he was carrying me right along with him. I vaguely heard the snap of the door latch behind me.

My body was warming up to the situation independently of my head. I was in the arms of a beautiful six-foot-four black guy, maybe ten years my junior and he was kissing me. Oh God, what am I doing? This is stupid. I've got to get out of here, NOW. Jesus, Mary and Joseph, I had thought about it, about how it might feel. But I didn't really want to do it. Oh God, This is insane. While I was arguing with myself, the question of whether I "wanted to or not" became academic. It was patently obvious that I had no say in the matter. He pushed me down onto the bed and my bottom landed just at the edge. For the first time I was terrified. My boot-clad feet planted themselves unattractively on the floor with his legs between them. He leaned on his left hand, pinning my muffler to the bed. I tried to raise my head and almost strangled myself. I pushed against him with my hands. It was like hitting a stone wall. "No. Please stop. This can't be happening," I gasped. I kept trying to talk my way out of it but he didn't understand my language and I didn't understand his rules. Everything was out of control. I couldn't think in French and I panicked in English. I threatened to scream. I threatened to call Lepage.

Unmoved by my threats, he reached under the back of my skirt and quickly found the waistband of my pantyhose. He pulled them down as far as he could, dragging my bikinis with them. I could hear the snapping of stitches. He pulled them in an upward motion raising my thighs at a right angle to my body. He leaned his body against the bridge of pantyhose between my legs, driving my thighs even closer to my body. I couldn't move. I couldn't scream. I wouldn't scream. If I did, Lepage would know and by tomorrow the whole hospital would know. The next day, the world, and Frank. Oh God, Frank.

How did I get here? I can't think. My head is spinning

with confusion. Drink? Fear? Fatigue? Was this what Lepage had meant? Had he misinterpreted things I'd said. Had I given off warm vibrations? Unintentionally? Intentionally? Does it matter? I don't know. Was it my fault? Please God, make it yesterday. Give me one more chance. I'll be good from now on. I promise. But God wasn't listening.

I was whispering now, terrified of being discovered, *"Non, non. S'il vous plaît, s'il vous plaît,"* searching for lost French, "Wait, *attendez*. Don't. Please don't do it. Let's talk for a minute." Too late. Too late. We had been playing "Hide and Go Seek" and I was it.

"Chérie, chérie," he whispered, as he put more of his weight against my stretched pantyhose.

I saw my expensive French boots looming over me. My right palm was still pushing against him. My other hand clutched my shoulder bag tightly to my body, as if I was afraid of losing it. I couldn't see his face, just the buttons on his white coat and the bulge his pens made in his breast pocket. I never saw him open his fly. I never saw his penis, but I felt it. He rammed home on the first stroke. I felt a searing pain deep inside me. I thought he'd ruptured my uterus. It was agony and I was scared to death that I'd end up in our own intensive care. With each successive thrust, he jarred my insides. He hit bottom and kept going, pounding my cervix. I could see my boots rhythmically moving along his upper arms. It occurred to me that my boots would leave tell tale signs of polish on his white coat. I had to tell him. It seemed so important at the time.

"Chérie, chérie," he whispered, over and over.

My vagina was choking and it wanted to vomit. My back and my legs were breaking. And my eyes were now brimming with liquid pain. Finally, I forced my mind to go to another place. I had to become numb, both physiologically and psychologically, until this nightmare ended.

He finally came to a low grunting climax.

After a few moments, he searched my face, and obviously

mistook pain for pure passion. *"Je t'adore, chérie,"* he kissed me on the nose and pushed up. He stood over me zipping up, very pleased with himself.

I lay there, hurting too much to move, in my hat, coat and muffler. My mitten-clad hand was still clutching my shoulder bag. He never saw or touched my body. He just jerked off inside me. Everything was all wrong. It was upside down and inside out.

I pushed myself into a sitting position and dug into my bag for tissues. God, oh God, how I hurt. I cleaned his semen mixed with my blood off my leg and vulva. I pulled up my bikinis and pantyhose, smoothed my clothes, retrieved my errant mitten and walked wordlessly to the door. It must have been my fault. That's why I was punished. He followed, turned me around by the shoulder and gave me a warm hug. Why not? He got his rocks off for the night, and me—I wanted the earth to open and swallow me up, or God to strike me dead so that I'd never have to face another day. It must have been my fault. That's why I was punished.

"I have to go home." My voice was weak and flat.

He looked puzzled at my flat-affect. Then he decided he must have read it wrong. I'm sure he believed that he had just given me the fuck of my life. He had. He really had. And he sure as hell didn't think he raped me, but he did. He did.

He bent down and kissed me lightly on the lips and in soft French he murmured, "Too bad you are leaving. We could have met like this three, four times a week." He kissed me as if he really meant it. I didn't resist. I couldn't. I was numb.

He checked the corridor to see if it was clear. I glanced at the big clock on the wall. It was forty-five minutes past midnight.

3

The harsh sound of the telephone pierced my sleep. I

groped for it without opening my eyes. As I shifted my body, I felt a stabbing vaginal pain. The horror returned. I died last night.

My first attempt to say hello didn't materialize, so I cleared my throat and tried again.

"Hello." Oh God, Another stabbing pain. I held my breath.

"Kate? Are you alright?'

"Frank?" Oh God, Frank. Oh God, God. God. Pull yourself together. Clear your head. Nothing has happened. It was all a bad dream.

"Hi, honey. I'm fine. I was asleep. You woke me up, that's all."

"Asleep? At noon?"

"Oh, I worked last night until midnight for Marie Louise. I guess I was really tired." I clenched my teeth.

"You sound strange. Are you sure you're okay?"

"Aside from working a thirteen-hour shift, I'm just fine." But I'm not fine. I feel sick. I hurt inside and out. I wanted to cry. I wanted to crawl into Frank's arms. Instead I said, "How did everything go in London? When are you coming home?"

"Not until tomorrow night."

"Oh?" I guess I should be grateful. It will give me time to recuperate. "Okay, honey, I'll see you then."

"Bye."

"Frank, wait, don't hang up. Talk to me."

"What do you want me to say?"

"I don't know. 'I love you,' I guess."

"Come on Kate, you know I love you." His voice was impatient, then it softened, "I'll see you tomorrow...we'll talk then."

I did know that he loved me. I wondered if he would still love me if he knew. I sank back into the pillows and pulled the eiderdown up to my nose.

I hurt with all of the horror of the night before. The minute I had entered the apartment, I had put my underwear and pantyhose into a paper bag and thrown it in with the trash. I spent the next hour and one half doing a full body pre-op scrub in the shower, hoping that some of me and all of Karambuku would eventually spiral down the drain. It didn't make me feel the least bit better. Nothing would make me feel better ever again. I couldn't believe what happened. How could he? Of all people not him. I was vulnerable and stupid, but he betrayed me. He raped me. He brutally raped me. He was supposed to "do no harm" and he brutally raped me.

I was dead. I was cold–so cold that my teeth began to chatter. It was as if I were standing naked in the wind.

If only I had the power to make my life go backwards. Now all I can do is pull the bedcovers over my head and try to shut out the reality of one yesterday and all the tomorrows.

I thought about my girlfriends and all our talks about sex. Jenny continually advised us that if we were ever in a compromising situation we should "Deny, deny, deny."

Janet agreed, her head bobbing. "That's what men do," she added knowingly.

Moira Kelly didn't say anything, but she rarely did when we talked about sex. But we knew that she listened. She always narrowed her eyes when she was making a mental note. Libby didn't say anything either, but that's because we rarely talked about sex in front of her. She said that sex had no right to be included in "girl-talk." The rest of us thought that that's what "girl-talk" was.

Although I was convinced that Jenny gave good advice and that she, Janet, and Moira would stand behind me, I knew what had happened to me was not sex, it was brute force. I stayed in bed, and broke the family rules about crying. I cried the rest of the day and most of the night. But that didn't make me feel any better either. My mother used to say that you can't cry over spilt milk. Well, she was right. You can cry if you want to, it just doesn't do any good. I went into the

kitchen to have a cup of tea. I thought again of Grandmother
Margaret. When I was a little girl, she told me that I must
never feel sorry for myself. Of course it was usually in
reference to a horse that I'd just tumbled off of. She'd grab
the reins, give me a leg up and say, "It's not the first mistake
you've made and it won't be the last. Put it all in the proper
perspective and start again–start from right now." It seemed
like a good philosophy to live by.

Okay, what's done is done. No time to brood. Time to
problem solve. Get your head together. What do you intend
to do? What should I do? I decided that the first thing to do was
to call in and take some sick days.

I took ice cubes out of the freezer, wrapped them in a
tea towel and held them on my eyes. When Frank comes
home, I'll tell him that my allergies have been kicking up and
that I was having my period. And most important, I will not
behave like a rape victim.

4

Marie Louise and Martine were chatting away while we
were dressing in our *vestiaire*. I wasn't trying to follow what
they were saying. My mind was busy, rehearsing what I would
say and do when I faced Karambuku. Two days off had given
me time to prepare. I would be extraordinarily professional
and distant. Language barrier or not, he had to understand
coolness. *Sang froid* was an international communication.
Besides, I had only three more days to go.

The door opened and *Mademoiselle* Follet charged into the
crowded locker room. Martine was spraying aerosol
deodorant under the arms of her uniform, a frequent sight for
those who used deodorant.

"I hate Americans," the voice of Follet came filtering
through, "They live together in the American Ghetto. They
never try to have a Belgian friend. They never bother to learn

the language."

"Which language," asked Martine? "You were born here and you don't speak any Flemish."

Marie Louise was signaling her as to my presence. She didn't have to. Follet knew I was there. I was sure that she felt that this was her last chance to vent her "I hate Americans" speech. Everyone knew that I was leaving. Her performance was clearly for my benefit.

"Americans come to Belgium to make money. They take and take, never giving anything in return," Follet continued ranting.

"That's not true," defended Marie Louise, "*Madame* deMeo is an American. She doesn't live in the American Ghetto. She works here and she has Belgian friends."

"*Madame* deMeo works here because she needs the money."

"But she worked for months without pay."

"That is not important," she shouted in Marie Louise's face before storming out.

Follet never seemed to walk in and out of doors like everyone else. She stormed, thundered and charged. Good Lord, she's back. "Another thing..."

"You know, *Mademoiselle* Follet, Martine, Paul and I learned very much from *Madame* deMeo, and we are her friends."

I walked out of the *vestiaire*, sandwiched between Marie Louise and Martine, who were giggling.

"*Merci*, mes amies. *Bien dit*, well said," I smiled.

My good humor abruptly left when I saw Karambuku in the hall.

"*Mesdames*," he greeted us with his broad smile.

I was enraged at the sight of him, but I nodded and forced a polite smile. You raped me, you son of a bitch. We were colleagues and you betrayed that trust. You're nothing but a bully. It wasn't my fault–not my fault and I'll never rid myself of this anger. It wasn't God who was punishing me, it was you.

I felt my lip twitch, and the beat of my heart was pulsing in my ears. I thought I was going to be sick.

The entire year had been unreal. I must be asleep. The whole damn thing is a nightmare. I wish the alarm would hurry and go off and I'd wake up in my old house in Oyster Bay.

5

The morning before we were leaving Jenny called. She and Jeff had finally called a halt to their marriage. He had hired a lawyer who had the reputation of doing anything and everything to win, while Jenny had hired the guy who handled the closing on their house. I advised her to find a lawyer who believed in nothing less than a scorched earth policy.

"I need you, Kate."

"I know."

"I can't go through this alone. I need my people around me. I desperately need you, Kate."

"I'll be there. "

"Promise."

"I promise."

Chapter Fourteen

"And the buds of your tomorrow
shall blossom in my heart."
    Kahlil Gibran

1

On our last night in Brussels, Frank and I were having dinner at *Au Pou Qui Tousse*. It was a small Sardinian restaurant and it was one of my favorites. Being there was bittersweet. We discussed our "going home" plans. Frank wasn't sure if he was making an upward or a lateral move.

"Reentry back to the States is always a problem, but with my background I'm sure it will be okay," he stated as he sipped his wine.

I gulped mine. I needed to drink a great deal of wine to help me "repress." I had to put up a good front. I had to keep telling myself that it had never happened.

"It's a lot easier for you, Kate," Frank continued, "You have a standing offer from your old hospital, and you have 'Head-Hunters' after you. How many offers now?"

"A few." I told myself, be charming–be funny–be

careful. Don't slip up. Don't trip and fall into the victim's mode. "You should see the one I got today," I pulled out the letter and handed it to him, "University of Tehran. I would only be required to teach in English. I would have an apartment, in a closed compound, rent free and the money is unreal."

Frank looked at me, "You're not?"

"No, oh no, but how tempting." I was hanging on with my fingernails. "Actually I have two offers from Florida–so they're out. I have an interview at Manhattan University Medical Center and, as you said, I can always go back to my old stomping grounds." Suddenly I felt blue. "Frank, I'm really sad about leaving. I love living here. I love the people, the friends we've made." I paused, "But, I'm not sure to what extent I improved the quality of care at the hospital."

"Hey, you did what you could. It's been a good tour. It must have been. We extended it two years."

"Would you do it again, Frank? Would you not change anything?" I asked.

"Pretty much no." He shook his head. "You?"

"Just some minor fuck-ups."

"Like?"

I hesitated and then said, "I should have killed Anton."

Frank smiled. "I'm glad you haven't lost you sense of humor."

"At the moment, I have a bigger worry than Anton. Frank, I told you about Jenny's frantic phone call this morning …nasty divorce…you know, I can't go to Manhattan with you just yet. I promised Jenny I'd stay with her during the divorce."

"Jenny already has Libby, Moira and Janet in her commune. She doesn't need you, too."

"But I promised. I gave my word."

"Kate, I can't believe that Jenny would hold you to a promise like that. Divorces take a long time. It's tantamount to a separation for us and I don't like separations."

Frank delivered an ultimatum. "I need a wife, Kate. So what's it going to be, Jenny or me...your girlfriends or me? Choose."

"Frank, try to understand how Jenny feels." I really wanted him to understand how I felt. "She needs our support."

I'm the one who really needs the support. I need some time and space to work out this pregnancy. Should I go to term? Would it be wiser to have an abortion? I have to learn to deal with my feelings.

"Frank, at least say that you'll sleep on it."

2

The next morning I was getting ready for my flight home with Frank when the phone rang. I ran to pick it up. There were reverse charges from California. It was Mark. I could barely follow what he was saying, but I got the gist of it. He had eloped with someone named Lucy, and he was hopelessly and happily in love. I could feel his emotions pushing at me through the receiver. They had met as undergraduates in a Berkeley coffee shop. Now they were finishing their MBA's. Lucy was two years younger than Mark and first generation Chinese-American.

"You're going to love her, Mom. She's so pretty, so nice and I think she's smarter than I am."

He was happy and I was happy for him. For me it was a momentary flash of joy coating all of my problems, however brief.

Frank had slept on my Jenny proposal but hadn't as yet addressed it. Maybe the news from Mark would soften his view. I ran back towards the bedroom, "Frank, Frank," I called, "you'll never guess what..."

Chapter Fifteen

"...yesterday is but today's memory
and tomorrow is today's dreams."
        Kahlil Gibran

1

The plane's intercom sputtered. The captain's mid-western voice announced that we were a half-hour out of Kennedy airport. My decision-making time was about to expire. I was sure that I was pregnant. I couldn't tell Frank without revealing the rape, and I couldn't be sure what his reaction might be. I had a hard enough time handling it. I found that it was difficult for me to look into the mirror. I felt contaminated–unclean. I knew that I had to rid myself of these feelings, but it would take some time.

The idea of having an abortion shook my Catholic roots. I found it far easier to have an opinion when it had nothing to do with me. If I knew that Frank was the father, it would have made my decision easier.

I have to use Jenny as a crutch–an excuse. It's my only way out. I need breathing room.

We were about to land. The captain's voice announced, "Attention cabin attendants…" As he braked, I felt the forward thrust of my body. Forward toward the future, I thought, no place else to go. I hoped and prayed that it was a good omen.

Frank took my hand, "What's wrong, Kate? You haven't been yourself for weeks. What aren't you telling me?"

I momentarily froze. "Nothing, nothing," I protested, "I have do this…for…for Jenny." I had to hold my ground with Frank. "I'm going to Jenny's. No matter what, I have to go to Jenny's. She's my friend and she needs me."

As the plane taxied toward the gate, I briefly thought of Aaron and Taf. They may have been buried in my mind, but they were both alive in my old hospital on Long Island. Each had played a part in my past but had no role in my future other than as colleagues. If it hadn't been Aaron, it probably would have been someone else. I remembered Gina's comment that you only regret the things you hadn't done. And yet I had regrets. Denial and repression were not enough.

As for Frank, I wasn't sure what was going on in his life. I chose to ignore the probability that Frank did have someone in London–someone much younger. There were clues, even a photograph in an opened attache case on the desk. Maybe that's the way it was with Peter Rizzo's suicide. No one wanted to see the clues. They were too painful to acknowledge.

Although I was able to brush aside the clues, I couldn't brush aside the competition. I learned a long time ago that there's always a new someone out there who is younger, prettier, smarter, or whatever. I could only hope that "time in" in a relationship really did count for something. As far as I was concerned, my dalliances didn't count, they weren't serious. And if Frank's affairs were dalliances as well–I just didn't want to know about them. The plane was still moving, but the passengers were getting up from their seats anyway, noisily opening overhead luggage racks. Frank and I remained in our seats. I faced him, pleading with my eyes, "But this is not a real separation? It's just until Jenny gets her divorce. Right?" It was half question, half statement.

Frank shook his head.

"If it's a real separation, Mary Ellen and the kids will be devastated. I can keep it from my mother for awhile but Gina can read me like a primer." I ran on, tossing my fears at him. "Mark will be bringing his bride here in a couple of months. Maybe we can bluff it until they go back to California. It seems wrong to tell a new bride and groom, 'Hey kids, you just got married—guess what, we just split up.' Doesn't give them much confidence in the institution of marriage."

We walked through the International arrivals lobby and out into a beautiful New York day. It felt good to be home. It felt good to be with Frank. I slid my arm through his and smiled. He smiled back and squeezed my arm. He slowed down his stride and he looked at me with concern.

"Why are you taking that job at your old hospital? You could have had a job at Manhattan University Medical Center, same title, more responsibility, higher pay, and...you could live in Manhattan...no commuting."

"I don't know. Comfort level? Known commodity? It's a university hospital now. After Jenny is settled, we could open up the house in Oyster Bay and commute to the city."

He shook his head again, "Is there someone there that you want to be with? Is that what this is all about?"

"Oh, my God. No. Not in the least, no way. The attraction is that there's good nursing care there and that makes me happy. "

"How about me? Were you happy with me Kate? Were you ever happy with me?"

"How can you ask?" My life with Frankie deMeo, I smiled. "My life with you on a scale of one to ten...I'd give it a nine point nine."

I didn't ask him to rate me because I wasn't sure that I

wanted to know.

"Look Kate, go to Jenny's for now. I'll call you. We'll make plans. We'll work it out. But don't forget, you're going with me to Washington for the Ad Council. That's a promise you made to me. I need my wife to be there. I need you."

What am I doing? I really want to go to Manhattan with him. I love him now more than I did when I was thirteen, fifteen, and seventeen. I've always loved my life—the good, the bad, the exciting, and the mundane. Mary Ellen always said that once you make your bed you must lie in it. I've had a comfortable bed until now.

Frank kissed me and walked to the taxi line. I never thought it would come to this. He actually left. He left me standing there—on the sidewalk. I was alone for the first time in my life. I was afraid I might lose control. I didn't. As sad as it made me to be left alone by him, I realized that I needed the time without him in order to fully recover. The sins we do, two by two...

I crossed the busy road without waiting for permission from the pedestrian light and headed toward the Long Island Limo.

I needed to talk to Jenny.

2

"You think you're what, and you're not sure who? And who was it that did what to you?" shouted Jenny.

"You can't be. Aren't you physically too old for that?" asked Moira.

Jenny pointed her finger at me, "You must have an abortion...immediately. It's the only solution." She waved her hand, "Forget your promise. You don't have to stay with me. Kate, you actually have more problems than the four of us put together."

"She's right, Kate, you can't have a baby at your age,"

chided Janet.

"And what's more, Frank wouldn't want a baby at his age either," muttered Libby, "even if it was his."

"Okay, here's what you do," ordered Jenny, "First, you must tell Frank you're pregnant."

They all nodded in agreement.

"But not the rape part," whispered Moira.

They all nodded again.

"Take the next train out of here. Go back to Frank. You know that he's always been your true love."

"Don't take a page from my book," offered Libby, "Crawl back if you have to. Wish I had."

"Never mind the train, I'll drive you," said Jenny.

"Me too, me too," they chorused, "We'll all go."

"Listen," I said, "I thank you guys for your loving advice and support, but I'm having problems with an abortion. I'm not sure that I can do it."

Jenny closed her eyes, "What the hell happened to the liberated woman...the right to choose? The age factor alone..."

"Don't you think I know the hazards? Congenital anomalies. I've been over it in my mind a thousand times."

Jenny put up her hand, "Think about your life, your career, your children. I'm calling Bob Jorgenson to see what can be set up." She picked up the phone. "Congenital whatever you call it. That's not your biggest problem. Your biggest problem is that you may give birth to a bi-racial baby."

3

We walked up the marbled staircase while the Marine Band was playing on the landing. It was a thrill to be at the White House. It was a thrill to receive the invitation "In recognition of the Advertising Council, Inc." addressed with perfect penmanship. This group created and prepared over twenty-five "Issue Campaigns" a year and Frank's company's ad campaign for "Urban Renewal" was a great success.

We were on our way to the reception in the East Room. I noticed a painting of JFK on the second floor. He was looking down so his face wasn't all that visible, but everyone recognized him anyway.

Frank and I entered the East Room. People were milling, chatting, and anticipating the entrance of the President. We were talking with a good-looking, soft-spoken man in uniform. It turned out he was the Chairman of the Joint Chiefs of Staff. Frank asked him how he slept at night given all his responsibilities.

His answer came back fast. "I sleep just fine. My staff has been ordered to wake me only if there's a problem I can solve, something I can fix. Otherwise just let me sleep."

The great doors to my right opened and the band struck up "Hail to the Chief." President Emerson, his wife and entourage entered the room and formed a receiving line. On either end were my two Secret Service men, my stone pillars. They blinked at me. I blinked back.

Vice President Emerson became President when the unthinkable happened. The healthy, hardy, sixty-five-year-old President, Robert Norris, had a massive coronary. He was now comatose and on life support in Walter Reed. Now it was evident that Emerson would seek another term. He did what he thought was best for the country and he shrugged off all advice from those who told him that he had to be more political, more traditional. Charles Emerson was clearly the "People's President."

Charles "Chuck" Emerson had been a running back for Ohio State. After graduation, he went into politics. He made a name for himself simply by being fair and honest. People trusted him and, along with his football image, he became popular throughout his state. He was on the ticket as Vice

President because the Republican Party needed Ohio's electoral votes. With New York and California going Democratic, the Republicans needed Florida and most of the Southern States to stay even. Ohio's twenty electoral votes would put them over the top. Emerson's popularity locked in the state and the presidency. Emerson was to be kept under control by giving him multiple, minimal assignments.

But the unthinkable did happen.

As we walked down the receiving line, we were introduced to the Secretary of State, the "in-charge man Fritz" who was indeed his Chief of Staff.

When I finally got to shake hands with the President, he smiled and said, "Dr. Kate deMeo."

"I wasn't sure that you'd remember me, sir. It's been almost two years."

"Did you think I'd forget? Remember, you're my nurse for life." He nodded toward his Chief of Staff. "Fritz let me know that you'd be here today. I've been wanting to speak with you."

He introduced me to his wife and I introduced him to Frank.

Still holding my hand, he said, "You have an appointment with me in the Oval Office. I'll send someone to fetch you." He took a long time before letting go of my hand, much like he did before take-off in Brussels.

"I'm overwhelmed at your offer, Mister President. There's never been a woman in that job, much less a nurse. They've been traditionally held by male physicians." I hesitated, then asked, "Why me, Mister President?

"In general, we need change. Nurses seem to be more in touch with the people, and I know from experience that you are. Kate, I'll never forget what it feels like to be struck down by the hand of God in a foreign country…no English spoken. In those early hours, you were important to me…fighting to stay with me…translating for the doctor. Now we need someone who listens to older Americans and gains their trust."

"There are so many good nurses out there, better qualified, better credentialed…"

Fritz interrupted, "May I, Mister President?"

The President nodded.

Fritz resumed, "The truth is that our pollsters tell us that the older adults are the least likely population to vote for the President. We'd like to move those numbers up," he paused, "and since you're an expert on aging…"

As the President picked up the dossier from his desk and handed it to his Chief of Staff, he said, "This tells me everything about you, Kate. Everything you've written, and every job you've had. I know your GPA in every school you've attended. Your research and articles are on aging. Your book is popular. Why wouldn't it be? Everyone would like to age successfully when you consider the alternative. Here's where it gets rocky. You're a registered Democrat, but you're pretty much apolitical. You marched on Albany for the "Nurse Practice Act," and you were a New York State delegate to the American Nurses Association. Your politics seem to be centered on nursing and health care. Need I go on?" The room was silent. They were both looking at me.

"So what do you say, Kate? Do you want to be my appointee for Deputy Assistant Secretary for Health?" He paused. "You will be working with one of the best medical minds in the business. And he supports your nomination as deputy."

I took a deep breath, "Yes, sir. I would very much like to serve at the pleasure of the President."

"You'll provide advice and counsel to the Secretary on aging and public policy. That's the job. The H.H.S. Secretary will announce the appointment."

Chapter Sixteen

"You are good when you walk to
your goal firmly and with bold steps."
Kahlil Gibran

1

Sagamore Hill University Hospital had changed. It had
grown with the times. They added a new wing and a new
Dialysis Center. In terms of personnel, there were many
familiar faces. They tried to promote Sally to supervisor but
she liked things just as they were. Patti and Mary were still
with her. Sometimes that's best for a unit, to be staffed by
people who've worked together for years and like each
other's company. Aaron and Taf were there. Aaron was still
Chief of the Psychiatric Unit and Taf was Chief of Surgery.
Aaron and Taf didn't get on too well. Aaron still had a grudge
against Taf, telling him that he had unresolved conflicts.
According to Aaron, I had unresolved conflicts, too.

"Me?" I said, "Uh, uh. Maybe you have."

I got along just fine with both of them because, at least in
this case, repression worked. I merely excluded unacceptable
ideas from my memory bank. Now in the white-out of my

mind, their former personal relationships with me didn't exist.

I liked doing rounds. It wasn't usual for the Vice-President of Nursing to do rounds, but I wanted to see the staff and the patients on a regular basis, and more important, I wanted them to see me. "We're all in this together," I'd tell anyone who'd listen.

2

Mondays at the hospital were always busy and this Monday was no exception. Sally called me, patently frustrated. She had a difficult patient in Room 420. Joe Spansky was giving everyone a hard time. He had suffered a shattered right leg the week before when the crane that he operated snapped under its heavy load and crushed his cab. Grant Owens and his team of orthopedic surgeons patiently replaced the bone fragments, fixed them with metallic wires and screws, then sutured the leg and put it in a cast. About three days later they cut a window in the cast in order to observe the suture line and check the healing process.

According to Sally, during the first few days, there were no problems. Mr. Spansky had an IV running, to which they piggybacked antibiotics. They gave him Demerol IM every four hours as needed for pain. While Joe Spansky was in that never-never land between vague pain and Demerol, all went well. Now that the IV had been discontinued, he was given a regular diet and his medications were given by mouth. For the first time he was totally aware of his hospital surroundings. He was a big, brawny construction worker and he refused to allow the nurses to attend his needs.

"I hate to bother you with this, Kate," apologized Sally, "but Mr. Spansky is being very difficult. He refuses a bed bath, medications, the bedpan—you name it. He had Patti Flaherty in tears yesterday. None of the nurses, including Mary, want him as their patient. The aides are scared to death to go in that room."

It was unusual for Sally to complain. She had the two most important attributes for being a nurse. She was knowledgeable (she always knew exactly what she was doing and why she was doing it) and she really cared about her patients.

Sally continued, "I'm afraid he'll do something stupid and hurt himself. He's already threatened to get out of bed. I'm at my wits' end, Kate. Can you help me out here?"

"No problem," I answered confidently. After all, I guess the buck stops with me. I checked through Spansky's chart and then walked into Room 420. Three of the patients were just finishing breakfast. Bed 1 was empty and made up for a post-op patient to facilitate the transferal from stretcher to bed. Mr. Johnson came into the hospital with a traumatic intracranial hematoma, and the neurologists were now drilling appropriately placed burr holes into his skull to relieve the intracranial pressure. He was expected back from the O.R. some time this morning.

"Good morning, gentlemen. How was breakfast?"

"And so where were you this weekend, Dr. deMeo?" inquired Mr. Altman, in Bed 3. "We missed you. We missed seeing your pretty face." His face was yellow from Atabrine, a drug that was once used for Malaria, and was now being pressed into the service of cancer chemotherapy.

"I missed you, too, but I really did need a weekend off."

"You know the guy in bed two? Such a grouch, you wouldn't believe. We liked him better when he was unconscious. Can't you slip him a little something, Dr. deMeo?" chimed Mr. Greenberg from Bed 4. He was recovering from gall bladder surgery.

"Well, maybe he has good reason to be a little grouchy. Maybe you all have." I thought about how horrible it must be to be a patient in a hospital, any hospital, even with something relatively minor. They take away all of your clothes, your personal belongings, your money, they ask if you have false teeth, a glass eye, suffer from allergies, what medications you take, on and on until miles and miles of your private life are laid out before strangers to trod upon. When you're finally stripped of your real identity, they tag you and give you an undignified, however functional, hospital gown. From then on your life is unit regulated and your privacy negligible.

Poor Spansky, I'm sure it's even harder for him. He's thirty-seven years old, a totally physical personality with so much pride in his strength. He can't accept the dependent role so he vents all of his anger on the staff and his fellow patients. I walked over to his bed, pulled the curtain closed and said, "Hello, Mr. Spansky. I'm Kate deMeo. I'm going to be one of your nurses today." He ignored me. I felt his toes for warmth and checked them for normal color. He glared as I ran my finger around the edge of the cast. "Mr. Spansky, I'm just checking for signs of irritation, broken bits of plaster, impairment of circulat..."

"Whatta are you supposed to be, a big-deal supervisor or somethin'?"

"Nope, I'm a nurse, Mr. Spansky."

"Listen good, honey, unless you're gonna gimme a blowjob, you can get your bony ass outa here right now. I don't need no skinny broad givin' me no bath. What's more, I'm gettin' outa here myself today," he threatened.

My, my, such verbal testing, it's no wonder Patti Flaherty was in tears. "Look Mr. Spansky," I said sitting down facing him, "I know what's bothering you, and it has nothing to do with a blowjob." His mouth opened and his jaw began to descend. "You hate being helpless in a hospital. Everyone does. Your male ego is in total revolt against your incapacitation. I understand. I really do. Look, the orthopedic team did a great job on your leg. Now it's up to you. You have to take your medication or run the risk of infection. You have to use the bedpan, or soil the bed." I shrugged. "Take your choice."

His jaw remained open as he stared in disbelief. I stared back blankly. He closed his mouth, swallowed, and thought for a long moment, "Okay, okay, I'll take them pills...nobody tole me what they wuz for. But no bedpan! No way am I gonna use a bedpan."

"As I said, it's entirely up to you. However, if you don't move your bowels in one more day, Dr. Owens will order an enema. I'll attempt to give one, you'll refuse…then you'll become so impacted that we will have to send you to the operating room…" He visibly blanched when I mentioned the O.R. "It's really too bad," I sighed and shook my head for affect, "it could all be avoided."

He looked uncertain.

"Look Spansky, everyone in this room, this unit, this world…" I was groping for something to say. "King Charles the second told his mistress Nell Gywn that 'even Kings used chamber pots.' Kings! You are not in the least unique."

"But I can't use a bedpan. It's…it's embaressin.' I don't know how to use one of them things."

"I'll help you. I'm a whiz with bedpans. I practically majored in the subject. I'll do all that I can to make you comfortable. I'll even talk to Dr. Owens and find out how soon you can use a bedside commode. Come on, Mr. Spansky. Deal?"

He hesitated again, "Okay, okay. But just you, right? I don't want none of them young kids in here lookin' at me."

"I'll take that as a compliment. But and this is a big big but, I'll need help so I'll have a nurse's aide working with me. Her name is Tina and she happens to be the best nurse's aide in the business. I'll bring her in here in a few minutes and introduce her to you. She's not a kid so you should be comfortable with her. Now here's the deal. I'll be here every morning to check your cast, give medications, help you with the bedpan, and supervise your bath. What do you say, Mr. Spansky? Come on. Let's get to it right now."

In a few days, Spansky's disposition improved one hundred percent, along with his bowel habits. Whenever he needed a bedpan, he'd lift his body using the Balkan Frame installed above his bed, I'd slip the flat plastic orthopedic pan under him and hand him a can of aerosol air freshener. He'd eliminate and spray to his hearts content. I'd open the window in spite of the air conditioning to protect the other patients from aerosol asphyxiation. I remembered that feeling. Spansky was so pleasant now–no one cared how much the spray interfered with the simple act of breathing.

Mr. Altman sang under his breath, "Spray, Spansky, spray, if it makes you happy that way..."

By Thursday, Spansky, Tina and I had his care down to a system. Either Tina or I would bathe and lotion his unreachable parts–back, buttocks, and feet. It was easy to accomplish with his upper torso strength and the Balkan Frame. Then while he bathed the rest, shaved and brushed his teeth, I'd get his medications and Tina would make the bed.

I approached the closed curtain calling, "Ready, Mr. Spansky?"

"No, not yet. I haven't finished my private parts."

"Okay, you have five more minutes before I come in."

"I need more time than that, Doll Face, it's such a big area to cover."

"You've got a five minute area, Spansky," I whispered through the curtain, "Never try to kid a nurse. And don't get that cast wet."

Later, when I was finishing up, I casually mentioned that although tomorrow was my day off, I still had to attend a scheduled Deans and Directors meeting. However, I'd be back working the weekend. It took a moment to register.

"Then who's gonna take care of me?"

"Miss Flaherty."

"Flaherty? That BIC kid? I thought you wuz gonna take care of me. You shit. You God damn fuckin' shit! You don't care nothin' bout me. You're a shit, deMeo, just like the rest of them."

"That's neither true nor fair, Spansky. I am not a shit, and neither are the other nurses. They've all tried to help, and you won't let them near you. Do you think for one minute that I'd be in here telling you all this if I didn't care? I'd just leave today at five o'clock and let you find out for yourself tomorrow."

He sat in stony silence with his muscled arms folded across his chest.

"I spoke to Patti Flaherty early this morning. I told her how well we work together. How strong you are with the Balkan Frame. She wants to care for you tomorrow. She's a fine nurse. And by the way, she's not a Brooklyn Irish Catholic, she was raised in Rockville Centre, Long Island."

More silence.

"What do you want from me, Spansky? Do you want me to come in on my day off? Is that it? What kind of a union man are you?"

He hesitated, relaxed his arms a bit and then questioned, "How 'bout my can of aerosol?"

"I'll put a brand-new one on your bed-side table before I leave today."

"Deal," he grinned.

3

I was haunted by my pregnancy and the American version of Paparazzi-like cameramen. Before the Health and Human Services Secretary's announcement, I probably could have posed naked in Bergdorf's window and no one would have noticed, much less cared. It was a strange feeling, and a little frightening to lose one's anonymity. It overwhelmed me. I spoke to Fritz, the Chief of Staff, who assured me that it had to be a mistake. My appointment was not a high enough level to warrant even a single cameraman.

4

I opened the house in Oyster Bay. It was far too large for

me. I closed all the extra rooms and lived in only what I needed. My sole companion was an obedience-trained Doberman pincher named Max. An old friend from Royal Rock Kennel got him for me. He was a bit young, but it was love at first sight. He'd never take the place of Nic, but Max kept the tabloid reporters from banging on my door and peeping in my small-paned windows.

Their presence reminded me that I had impetuously said yes to this appointment. I don't know what I'd been thinking. I had really wanted it. I had thought I could do it and do it well. But I had to tell the President I was pregnant. He needed to know the whole story. An abortion might solve the problem, but if it became public that his appointee had an abortion, it could trouble his Presidency. I had to confess. There had to be a way for me to back out. I kept going over and over it in my mind.

The phone rang. It was Fritz. He asked me to come to the White House the following day.

5

"Sorry about this, Kate," the President passed me a supermarket tabloid with a picture of his Chief of Staff escorting me to the West Wing. The headline read, "Is Fritz procuring for Chuck?"

"It gets worse, Kate." He handed me some eight-by-ten glossy photos.

At first I wasn't sure what I was looking at. Then it hit me. "Oh my God. These photos were taken at Zavantem airport." They showed the President, who was then Vice President, and I near the steps of the plane. We were standing face to face. In every photo we were holding hands or smiling at each other.

"'Intimate moments?' the newspaper headline called it," said the Chief of Staff. "They want to know why it was necessary for a nurse to be there, when the doctor from SHAPE could have handled the situation." He threw the newspaper on the desk. "They seem to think they have a story with legs. That would explain the camera crew."

I was hardly listening. I was focused on the photos. The contrast of our skin color seemed to be highlighted.

He looked very black and I looked very white.

Oh God, I thought, if my baby is bi-racial, no one, not even with paternity testing, would believe that it wasn't his baby.

"Mr. President, I think I should withdraw."

"That's a good idea," Fritz nodded in agreement.

"Listen, Kate, this isn't right. We can't let them get away with this. If you're willing, we can put up a fight and prove we have nothing to hide."

The Chief of Staff lowered his voice grimly, "That's political suicide, sir."

"Mr. President," I blurted out, "I wanted to tell you. I'm so sorry. I'm pregnant and..."

"Pregnant. Wonderful. Perfect. We fight."

I looked at Fritz. His head was down. He was staring at the floor. Suddenly I turned and faced the President, "We have a problem, Mr. President."

"Didn't you file a police report, or a least register a complaint with hospital administration?" asked the Chief of Staff?

"No."

"Why not?"

"I didn't want anyone to know. My husband still doesn't know and I'd like to keep it that way."

The whole media thing was like a fire gone out of control. The President was irate. "I want to fight, but this is too volatile even for me." His face reflected acceptance rather than resignation.

Fritz exhaled audibly.

6

Emergency rooms are almost always hectic and most of our patients come in with a similar list of problems. This day was particularly busy and tempers were beginning to fray. After arranging to post an extra security guard, I went down to the E.R. to see if I could help with some additional staffing.

All of the seats were taken and children were sitting in their parents' laps. A small group of teenagers were smoking just outside the door. A hulking man was pacing the length of the room and mumbling to himself. He stopped and walked over to the triage desk.

"We'll get to you soon, sir," said the nurse. "Please try to bear with us," she added.

"Yeah, but I'm first. I was here before her." He pointed to a woman in a wheelchair disappearing into a cubicle.

The nurse patiently continued, trying to explain triage to the man. He suddenly turned and ran toward the door, but instead of leaving, he tackled the guard and took his gun.

Waving the gun, he looked at the triage nurse, "I guess this makes me first now. Right?"

It took about a second to sink in. Then it seemed that everyone was trying not to breathe. Parents held their children closer to them. Everyone was terrified. A child started to cry. I thought I should do something, but I was afraid. I saw the second guard, who was coming to take his post, enter through the door behind the gunman. Maybe if I can distract him? I took a step forward.

"Excuse me, sir. My name is Kate deMeo. I'm Vice President of Nursing." I watched as the other guard began inching up behind him. "Perhaps I can be of assistance to you?" The guard was now directly behind him. He made a grab for the gun. They struggled for an instant. The gun went off, the bullet striking the man in the leg.

"I guess you really are first after all," said the second guard, pointing at the profuse bleeding of the gunshot wound.

The noise of the shot alerted the stalking tabloid camera crew. The doors were no longer guarded so they came in clicking away. Someone grabbed me and pushed me through the door.

"Take the stairs, Kate." It was Taf. "Bob Jorgenson is upstairs. Private room. Is someone having a D & C?"

We reached the stairwell on the third floor. All at once the door flew open, hitting me full force. I felt Taf's hand trying to grab at me. I lost my balance and tumbled backwards down the stairs. I thought I heard cameras clicking and then there was nothing.

7

At first, all I could see was a soft mist. I seemed to have floated up into the corner of the ceiling. I was looking down on myself in a bed. What was I doing there? I was curious—not frightened in the least. Wait a minute, that's not me. That's Kathleen Mary with a ribbon in her hair. She smiled at me and waved goodbye.

I felt myself coming out of the soft mist an inch at a time. Faces began to close in on me. I thought I was still surrounded by cameramen. But no, I could see the faces of Fiona, Margaret, Simone and my Dad with his briar pipe clutched in his teeth. They began to float away. I wanted to go with them but they said no. I didn't understand. They allowed Kathleen Mary to go with them. Maybe a part of me has to die, so the rest of me can live. As the fuzziness began to clear, I saw Frank, Gina, Mark, Mary Ellen, Jenny, Janet, Moira, Sally, Taf and Aaron. My God, there were so many people. Why were they here? They were looking down at me. I was in my coffin. I was dead.

"Give me some room here." Bob Jorgenson elbowed his way

through the crowd. "Wait outside. I'd like to talk to my patient," he raised his voice, "Alone." He brought his face close to mine. "You gave us quite a fright, Kate." He looked over his shoulder. Aaron and Taf lingered.

"We're physicians, you know," declared Aaron.

"Out," Bob repeated. He walked over and closed the door after them.

I hurt so much that I realized I was alive.

"How are you feeling girl?"

"I'm not sure."

"You had a nasty concussion but you're going to be okay. We had more consultants looking at your brain, which by the way, I always thought was the best part of you. I also had Dr. Wonderful from Plastic Surgery suture up your head. You'll still have a scar," he added.

"What happened, Bob? I remember being in the stairwell, reaching out to open the door..."

"Kate," he interrupted, "there's something you should know. You've had a miscarriage. It wasn't a viable fetus." He paused, "No one will have to know, if that's what you want. Sally took the products of conception down to the lab. There's no physical or written evidence that you were ever pregnant."

"Oh?... Really?... Uhm, uhm...okay Bob. Thanks." I tried to process everything that happened, everything Bob said, despite a massive headache that interfered with my thinking. "Bob, uhm, you know, I had a hard time trying to make a decision."

"The way I look at it, God made the choice for you."

Chapter Seventeen

"If in the twilight of memory we
should meet once more…"
       Kahlil Gibran

1

I lived through the paparazzi, the miscarriage, the loss of a Presidential appointment and a failing marriage. In retrospect, I wondered if I was ever really able to balance my personal and professional lives. It's fair to say that they frequently invaded each of the other's territory. Florence Nightingale had it easier. She wasn't married, and she was rich. Much of nursing is just plain physically hard work. Caring for the sick, the wounded, and the dying is emotionally demanding.

Nurses need to give so much of themselves. They lead complicated lives. As a nurse, I've seen some terrible things. I've listened to pain in the hospital and mourned the dead in both worlds. But I've also seen miracles. I've seen selfless, caring professionals who never give up. I've seen patients with the courage of warriors. I've tried not to bring the hospital home or allow my personal problems to influence my patient care in any way. I'm always amazed at how nurses do what they do, day after day, and keep their heads on straight.

Each day, millions of nurses put their own lives on hold in order to care for the physical and emotional needs of their patients. They also have to deal with their own problems: separations, infidelities, divorces, child-care and on and on. It's difficult to manage both worlds. I guess it has to do with prioritizing and perspective. It's the reality of the hospital world that puts their personal world in order. It has a way of making some personal problems fade.

2

I've discovered that I can live with myself, finally forgive my transgressions and even enjoy my own company. Max and I have a great relationship. He takes me on walks along the shore.

Frank seems to be getting along fine without me. I just can't bring myself to call him and force myself back into his life. I need and want him to need and want me. I sometimes wondered if we both were waiting for the other to make the first move.

Aaron says that I need to see him professionally. When he speaks to me he uses his "couch voice." It's somewhere between a breath and a whisper. He speaks incessantly of unresolved conflicts. Aaron, I think that's called projection. Besides, you're not the only shrink on staff.

I've been really good, though not perfect, at being the Vice President of Nursing at Sagamore Hill University Hospital. The budget is balanced. The staff morale has been high. They've gotten used to seeing me popping in on units and the patients have been pleased with the visits. It means longer hours, but it's worth it.

I think that Taf finally has accepted me as a friend, but he still keeps asking me out for dinner. I keep refusing. I guess I've learned something along the way.

Sometimes one has to eat alone.

3

A month after his discharge, just before three o'clock, Joe Spansky got off the elevator. He was still on crutches. Sally alerted me and I came right up to Four West. His face lit up at the sight of us. The nurses and the aides made a big fuss over him. Sally put her paperwork aside, came out from behind the nurse's station and hugged and kissed him. That has to be the most beautiful sight in the world. A former patient well and happy, functioning on his own. As compared to other units, Four West didn't send out all that many vertical patients.

"How are you, Mr. Spansky?" I said, putting my hand out.

"Hey, what is this, Doll Face? Don't I rate a kiss from you?"

"You sure do." I pecked him on the check. We chatted for a few minutes and I told him how happy I was that he was doing so well. I meant it, but disappointment began to cloud his face. We had spent a great deal of time together and I'm sure he felt that there should have been more of a bond between us. Had he had a life-threatening incident, he would have felt an even stronger bond. He didn't understand that nurses become surrogates to meet the needs of their patients and from the moment they meet, the nurse is working toward the termination of their relationship. That's the whole story of nursing. Give it all you've got to make them well. Then get them out as fast as possible to prevent further complications, and make room for the new patients. Fill up the beds over and over. Of course we can't help but identify with some patients more than others (and they with us), but if we had to actively continue each relationship, we'd rapidly become ineffectual in both our jobs and personal lives.

My pager went off. I had to leave. I met Joe Spansky's eyes, hugged him and ran toward the elevator. I think he finally understood.

4

I took the last sip of my coffee and put the mug on the table in front of me. Max was resting at my feet. I tossed the New York Times aside and patted his head. I sank deeper into my chair and thought about Frank. Bob Jorgenson said he never left my bedside when I was unconscious in the hospital. I hadn't seen him since. I wondered what that meant.

I sighed deeply and began to reflect on my life. Had I learned anything along the way? If we don't grow, then what's the purpose of life? I had grown, but had I grown up? I think there were differences, though not profound, between Kathleen Mary, Kathleen, and Kate. I think I'm smarter, that is, "street smart" smarter. I still have my ideals, but at forty-five I'm realistic. There are far less absolutes in my life now. Maybe life does begin at forty.

I thought about the things that used to scare Kathleen Mary and worry Kathleen. Things like four-letter words, organized religion, male dominance, infidelity, and most of all, not being perfect.

I quickly learned that the fearful four letter words were merely words, part of the vocabulary and the vernacular of the time. Maybe we really had it all together as kids. We knew that "sticks and stones could break our bones…"

In the last nine years, I've managed to toss out the Six Commandments of the Church and violate all but three of the Ten Commandments of God. As liberated as my views are now, I still have a residual problem with abortion. There are always residuals that get in the way from time to time. And yet, I was about to have an abortion when, ironically, it was taken out of my control. Intellectually I believe in choice. It took me a long time to claw my way out of the cocoon of Catholic conscience. The humanistic thinking of the seventies had been burned into my brain. Existentialists believe that attitudes and outlooks are largely learned from experience and can be altered. They claim that each of us has the ability to confront and shape our ever-changing lives. Well, I've confronted and changed, but I'm not sure it's all for the better. Maybe I did whatever helped to make life easier for me, or maybe Bob Jorgenson was right—in some cases God makes some of the choices for us.

While it's true, for the most part, that we all make our own heaven and hell, women learn early on that pain and the inequality of the sexes are part of their lot in life—beginning with menarche. I realized that women originally acquired the dependent role out of physiological and anatomical necessity. Although we have progressed from early tribal cultures to complex civilizations, most women remain in the inferior role economically, socially, and politically. It's hard to believe it's 1978. Equality is the automatic birthright of man—a woman must earn hers. The more highly educated the woman, the more financially independent. The more influential the family, the better chance a women has to develop her potential. We learned that from Florence Nightingale. Only a woman who is truly equal can be sure that her relationship is based on true feelings and not just the need for security.

After twenty-plus years of marriage I had wondered what it would be like to go to bed with another man, and I'm willing to bet that a lot of "one-man women" wondered about the same thing. I suppose it's symptomatic of middle age as well as the tune of the times, a combination of lost youth and the permissive Hippie era. Temptation surrounds us, whether we recognize it or not. I believe in equal rights for women, but do I think that equal rights gives me equal sexual rights? Yes, I do. Damn right! Do I feel that I must have equal time, maybe get even? No, I don't. Absolutely not. What I do want is the same opportunity, to evaluate my own feelings and to answer yes or no, and not be dictated to by the conventional double standard. I am not in the least turned on by the concept of actively seeking, but rather by the freedom of choice.

I didn't know it back then, but Jenny was smarter than I was about one thing. She said that a man, if given the choice, would prefer his wife to have an emotional affair without sex, rather than a sexual affair without emotion. I always believed that it was the other way around. I thought of sex as a biological function; that's why the oldest profession has lasted through the centuries. An emotional relationship, however, touches the heart and soul. It touches the very essence of the person. I guess Jenny thinks more like a man and I think more like a woman. I thought it was better to bare one's body, not one's soul.

What is the definition of an affair? Does anyone know? Do you count the number of times? Is it more than once? Is it three, four, or five times, or do you count the days, weeks, months, or years? And who makes up these rules?

The increase in infidelity is most likely a function of living longer, being healthier and looking younger. When it comes to marriage everyone ought to fasten his or her seat belts. Semper Fi may work for the U.S. Marines, but it doesn't seem to work for many of us. There are good marriages, bad marriages, and indifferent marriages. None that are foolproof and none that are safe. Marriage isn't static; it's a living organism. Marriages are no more or less than what is put into them. I'm convinced, more than ever, that my marriage had worked for me (up until now) because I did grown-up things as a kid, and kid things as a grown-up; and also because Frank and I accepted the realities of life. We could have gone on like that, maybe forever, but the rape had totally derailed me, and Frank got caught up in and reacted to my "I'm not a victim" behavior.

In spite of everything, I've done all that I wanted to do

and I hope that Frank has done the same. Our life together has been all pluses. Frank and I have a lifetime of memories. Selective though they may be, they're ours. Even if it would all end tomorrow, no one could take them away from me. There is nothing on Earth quite so magical as memories.

And as for being perfect, there is no such thing. That's why it was the hardest fear of all to shake. There are no perfect marriages because there are no perfect people. My father used to say, "Aim for the stars, Kathleen Mary, and you'll surely reach the mountain tops." Finally, I understood what he meant.

5

Max was sitting in front of me, with his leash between his teeth. In dog language, that meant, "It's time for our walk." I looked at my watch. It was time for our usual Sunday walk before dusk–my favorite time of day. How did he know? He doesn't wear a watch, or read a newspaper. I clipped his leash to his collar, got up and headed toward the door.

"Let's make this a good one, Max. Tomorrow is going to be another busy Monday at the hospital."

6

A few days later, I waved to Sally as I approached the nurses' station on Four West. She motioned me over.

"Don't you answer your beeper? Someone has been trying to track you down and I've been calling you all morning."

I reached into the pocket of my lab coat and retrieved my pager. I held it up in the air and said, "I haven't heard a peeper from my beeper all morning."

"Very funny, girl. Pick up line 29."

"Who is it?"

"Don't know. Didn't ask. Guy's voice."

I walked behind the desk and I lifted the phone from its cradle, "Hello. Dr. deMeo here."

"Hello, uh…Kate?"

I slowly sank into the chair. I closed my eyes and smiled.

Chapter Eighteen

"… we shall speak again together
and you shall sing to me a deeper song."
Kahlil Gibran

1

It was Frank.
It always would be Frank.

Epilogue

Not so long ago, most people lived and died within three miles of where they were born. Now, it's a movable world. My mother, Mary Ellen, and her sister have become permanent residents of The Cape. "Real Yankees stay the winter," they declared. They could have moved to Florida, been warmer, but they believed that Florida was for old folks.

I'm careful not to repeat that sentiment, since Jenny, Janet, Libby and Moira have, one by one, relocated to Florida. They've scattered themselves in different areas of both coasts, and three of them with new husbands.

Lucy and Mark are now Californians. Lucy's getting her start in the Public Defender's Office in Los Angeles. Mark, always the entrepreneur, has opened his own communications production company. Gina and Alex have settled in Boston. He's teaching at Harvard and she's in practice as a Doctor of Veterinarian Medicine.

I've kept in touch with Chantal, who is happily married to Guy Peeters and expecting their first child. Martine and

Willie Goosens are expecting their second child. Martine walks to work each morning, pushing a stroller as she heads for the hospital crèche where her child will be cared for while she works. They tell me that *Monsieur* Anton is no longer *Chef de Service*—Willie is. Anton isn't working anywhere as a physician. It appears that he had made too many medical-surgical errors. According to Willie, Anton's problem was diagnosed as substance abuse. I guess Lepage had it right all along.

After Marie Louise was promoted to *Chef des Infirmieres, Mademoiselle* Follet moved south to Charleroi where she believed there were no Americans or Flemish to contend with.

The news that was the real shocker was that Marie Louise pressed charges of attempted rape against Karambuku. But he quickly fled the country and disappeared into the African tapestry. Sometimes there is no justice and we all have to live with it. The best news though, was that lawsuits concerning medical malpractice had finally come to Brussels.

Although I'd like everyone to be living within a one-mile radius of me, I'm content to know that they're all well and happy. Between my children and my friends, I do have some nice places to visit.

It was with mixed emotions that I gave notice at Sagamore Hill. I would miss Sally and Patti, but we all must move on—fulfill our potentials. Sally is now supervisor, Patti is the head nurse on Four West and Mary is—still Mary.

Frank's telephone call was my birthday and Christmas present all wrapped into one. It was our second chance. We talked for weeks and realized that we had both made our share of mistakes. We found that we have an appreciation for the past but we choose not to dwell on it.

Without trepidation, Max and I moved into Frank's Manhattan apartment. Max endeared himself immediately to Frank by rushing to him, sitting in an alert position, and waiting for a command. Now Max takes Frank and me for walks along the East River. Frank is President and CEO of his company. Luckily for me, Manhattan University Medical Center still had a search on. MUMC is a huge complex with a great reputation. When they offered me a dual appointment, Vice President of Nursing and Professor of Nursing, I accepted on the spot. I think I've finally found the balance I've been looking for. I've given up repressing—with the help of a colleague. And although it's only been six months, I no longer stand naked in the wind.

References

Gibran, K. (1966). *The prophet*. New York: Knoph.

Kubler-Ross, E. (1979, Nov.). *Life and transition*.
Garden City, NY: Nassau Community College.